THE TEASHOP TERROR

A WEAL & WOE BOOKSHOP WITCH MYSTERY

CATE MARTIN

Cover design by Shezaad Sudar.

Ratatoskr Press logo by Aidan Vincent.

ISBN 978-1-958606-36-0

❀ Created with Vellum

CHAPTER
ONE

The thing about the Weal & Woe Bookshop was that, from the very first minute I stepped over the threshold, I instantly felt completely at home.

And given how intense that first minute was, that's really saying something.

It was the smell that did it, that made me feel warm, safe, and protected even as everything going on around me was the opposite of that. Well, with the growing flames and all, I *was* warm. But never mind that for now. Let me explain about the smell first.

You know how some people can take a sniff and then a sip from a glass of wine and tell you all kinds of things about it? Not just that it's a full-bodied red or a bone dry white, or that it has hints of cherry or a floral bouquet or whatever. I'm talking about people who can take a sip of wine and tell you what kind of soil the grapes grew in, maybe even guess where in the world it was bottled.

I can't do that. To me, it's all just fermented grape juice.

But with the smells of libraries? I can tell so much just from sniffing the air. I am a real connoisseur of printed materials. From modern digital books all the way back to sigils marked out on leaves the size of dinner plates, I have read it all, or at least tried to.

In every school I had ever attended—and there had been literally dozens of them—the library was always my safe haven. I would study there, take my lunch or dinner to eat there, sometimes even sleep there. Part of this was because it was always safer to be away from other people. But mostly it was the books. Just the smell of them was like a hug. And growing up, I had often felt the need for hugs.

You see, I've lived on six of the seven continents at some point or another, attending magical schools tucked away in every imaginable climate or environment from a school hidden behind an apartment bathroom mirror in the middle of Manhattan to the last university I'd attended deep in the hills of what was once called Transylvania. The schools were all different, the students were all different, the grounds were all different.

But the libraries always felt the same. Safe. Home. Where I belonged, in the way I never belonged in the school itself. Even if I hadn't kept moving around, that would've always been true. Libraries are my home. Books and scrolls are my family and friends.

Dry paper or musty paper, freshly supple leather covers or moldy leather covers, cracking vellum or crisp rice paper. I swear I can distinguish it all.

So back to that slice of time, me walking into the bookshop for the first time. I'll explain about the fire and the general chaos of it all in a minute, I swear.

Okay, so, the minute I stepped inside the Weal & Woe Bookshop, leaving a bright June afternoon in Minneapolis behind, I could smell thousands of books. And I was sure I could identify each, even track them down individually by smell like a bloodhound on the trail. I only needed to introduce myself to each first.

And not accidentally set them on fire. That was rapidly becoming a key point.

To say I'm accident-prone would be a colossal understatement.

Kids learning to use magic blow things up, a lot. Or turn their hair green or their lab partner into a rat. It all happens every day, and it's not a big deal.

My accidents, on the other hand? Tend to become big deals.

In this particular moment, I had managed to open the door to the bookshop without incident and plunged into the murky semi-darkness beyond. After walking in the sun for the better part of an hour, I was more or less blind, at least temporarily. But the smells enveloped me, like I said, so thick I could taste the dust of a thousand books at the back of my throat, old wood pulp and just a hint of ink.

Newer books with fresh, modern paper and ink were closer to me, I could tell. But other, older things were lurking just beyond. From the point behind the new books back to beyond the limits of my perception. The space around me felt close, but the smells were telling me the books went on forever.

As I came inside, the bell over the door chimed brightly to announce me. It was a cheery sound, and if the smells hadn't been enough to make me feel welcome, that bell would've filled that gap. In truth, I suspected a bit of a charm had been placed on that bell.

Happy little magic. My favorite kind.

Then it chimed again, and I realized I was somehow blocking that door from closing. The suitcase I was pulling behind me was stuck on something. I tried pulling it again, then harder, blinking rapidly as if I could somehow make my eyes adjust to the lower light faster.

I admit, I had the stupids. But who could blame me? I had taken a train from my last school in Transylvania to Amsterdam, then taken an airplane from there to Minneapolis. The light rail line had ended a dozen or so blocks short of my destination, so I had walked the rest of the way. It had been a nice little walk, the air still with a little spring chill to it so I didn't get sweaty even dragging the suitcase with all my worldly possessions behind me.

The road I had been following even went over the Mississippi

River, the bridge offering a lovely view of the banks that once had been home to the clusters of mills that had birthed the city.

As usual, I had researched my new home before I got there. I knew more about the local history than most of the locals, I would wager.

But I hadn't slept on the plane at all, and I wasn't even sure what hour of the journey I was on. Maybe thirty? It felt like a hundred. Too long in the same clothes without a shower. Too long in the same shoes, even if they were my most comfy pair of Converse sneakers.

I was exhausted. And, like I said, I had the stupids.

But worse, I could feel my old bad luck starting to spark up. Literally.

And now I really have to explain. As much as I hate to admit this bit.

You see, I live in the world of witches. If you're what we witches call a prosaic—ugh, as if we magic types are by nature more poetical —this might be news to you. Basically, there is another world inside of your world, tucked away in little pockets, unseen and unknown to most people. That's where witches dwell. It's like a book where some of the pages are elaborate pop-ups, but only a few people can get those pages to open.

My parents were witches. I went to witch schools. But I've never been able to do magic. At least, not deliberately. The only time I have any power at all is when I'm tired and stressed and at the end of my rope. Which makes it really hard to learn to master it in a school environment. Not that being magic-less in a magic school isn't incredibly stressful. Believe me, it is. But even if it were possible for me to learn to control my randomly occurring magic, it only appears in moments where that kind of effort is just beyond me. By the time I calm down enough to focus, it's gone again.

At least until I get stressed out again.

Like at that moment, at the end of my long journey, with the stupids. It took me far too long to work out why my suitcase was caught. Even as the door kept trying to close and that cheery bell just kept chiming. But finally I realized that the suitcase had dragged against the worn carpet just inside the door, not rolling over it like it was supposed to. It had pulled up folds of faded woven fabric that promptly got caught in the wheels.

I tried to free the wheels by putting my foot down on the carpet, but that just seemed to get some sort of fraying situation started. It was a really old carpet. But I was clearly actively destroying it even as I still tried to get it free.

And yes, the door kept trying to shut on me and the suitcase both, swinging just enough each time to chime that bell again. I tried moving the carpet and the suitcase together out of the way of the door, but the carpet was caught on something else, or was tacked down somewhere. My eyes still hadn't adjusted enough to the book-store interior for me to really tell.

But I could smell that bookstore. And even as I struggled, that smell comforted me.

Maybe this wouldn't be so bad after all. I had been so nervous. An uncle I barely knew, another uncle I had never even met, and a place I had never even heard of before my mother's brother Carlo had written to me and invited me to stay. I don't really like change, like even more than normal people don't like change, and this was a lot of change. More than just trading one magical school for another. I couldn't remember life before boarding at my first magical school. I didn't even know how living outside of the halls of academia was even going to work. But the smell of books was giving me a much-needed hug.

Meanwhile, I was still struggling with the carpet in my suitcase wheels. It was well and truly frayed now, big holes torn in the weave and loose threads dangling everywhere. I was really tempted to just pull it apart, to viciously rip it and get my suitcase free. But what a terrible first impression that would make. What if my uncle really liked this carpet?

The door kept swinging and chiming, over and over again. That cheerful sound had morphed into something sort of passive-aggressively chiding me, I swear. And my hair kept swinging into my eyes as I worked at the carpet. Now, even though I was adjusting to the light, I was still blind half the time by billows of staticky hair that hadn't seen a brush since one very long flight, one medium-length light-rail ride and one short walk ago.

Somewhere between Transylvania and Amsterdam. Sometime on that train. That was the last time I had brushed my hair. But the stress was what was causing all the static.

The hug from the books was no longer enough to calm me. I could feel my nerves frazzling.

Then something banged like a firecracker and there was a charred, smoky smell all around me.

That was the point where the carpet caught on fire.

And all I could think was, not again. Not that old bad luck again. It was too soon after my last conflagration. Usually they spaced out more.

I stomped at the carpet, grateful that my suitcase was a hard-sided model and would probably be okay. Except my stomping only seemed to be aggravating the situation. Like the flames I was attempting to blot out were opting instead to lurk on the underside of the carpet and smolder with a thicker, moldier-smelling smoke.

"Step back, Tabitha," a man's voice said. I stumbled a few steps away from the door, just in time to avoid a stream of white foam that coated the carpet, the door, my suitcase, and a good chunk of the sidewalk outside.

The man blasted a few more bursts of foam at the more tenaciously burning bits of the carpet, then stepped back to look at me, adjusting the rectangular glasses that perched on the end of his nose as if to bring me into better focus.

I only had one memory of my uncle. A fragment of a memory, really, from before I started school. A general feeling of kindness, a sharp sense of contrast from my mother, his sister, who had also been there. Still, I recognized him at once. He hadn't changed a bit. Even the tattered forest green cardigan with the patches at the elbow and the missing button just at his thickening waistline were familiar.

"Uncle Carlo," I said. I held out a hand to shake, but somehow, even though I was sure I had stepped back in time, I had foam all over my palm. I wiped it on the leg of my jeans and offered it again, but he stepped past it to pull me into a hug.

Then he took a step back to smile at me. "I don't suppose anyone ever tells you that you look just like your mother," he said.

"No, not really," I said, pushing back the tangle of curls that had fallen into my face. My brown hair, green eyes, and round cheeks were nothing at all like my mother's sleek black hair, icy blue eyes, and thin face. I mean, her cheekbones are to die for. Anyone looks at her, they think supermodel. Anyone looks at me, they think chipmunk or squirrel.

"And yet you make just as splashy of an entrance," he told me, clasping what looked like an antique perfume atomizer made from cut blue glass in his hands. He had made the foam come out of that, I realized. More happy little magic.

"I'm so sorry," I said. "This is a lovely shop you have here, and I almost burned it down."

I said those words before I even took my first proper look around. But now I did, drinking in the sight of the bookshelves all around me. They ran from floor to ceiling, and that ceiling was at least twelve feet up. They were in rows set so close together it would be impossible for two people to pass between them without turning sideways and brushing against each other. And every shelf was jammed with books.

And like my nose had told me, the books around me were new editions, the shiny spines unbroken, the crisp pages as yet untouched. But a dozen or shelves in, I could see older books. Tattered paperbacks and well-preserved old hardbacks both.

But there weren't *just* books. The back walls were covered in racks something like the racks used to store bottles of wine, but these held scrolls. So many scrolls.

And a lot of the bookshelves had other items on them. Objects made of crystal or bronze or wood. I longed to see it all, to set off into the labyrinth of shelves and lose myself entirely.

But there would be time enough for that later. Now that the fire was out, my exhaustion was back.

"It's our life's work, Frank and I," Carlo said to me as he stepped up and behind the desk that faced the door. It was elevated on a platform like the counter in an old-fashioned pharmacy. The dark wood that ran from the surface of the desk down to the top of the platform was old, a few mysterious scratches gouged near its corners, the finish worn away in spots by countless hands over the years. He put the perfume atomizer away in some cubby out of my sight, then shuffled a few other things away. "I was surprised that you wanted to travel so far in the prosaic world. Did everything go all right?"

Better than they would have if I had tried just stepping through a portal on my own, but I didn't say that. At some point he and his husband would know that the sparks I had emitted that had nearly burned down their lives' work weren't an infrequent phenomenon, but this didn't need to be the time. I was too tired to explain it properly, and I really didn't want to explain it wrong.

"It was an interesting experience," I hedged.

"It is definitely interesting, their world," Carlo said as he came back down from behind the desk. "And it's always there, just outside this door. You know, most of our customers are prosaics. You'll be interacting with them every day while you're working here." There was just a hint of a question in his voice. Whether I could handle that.

"I'm looking forward to it," I assured him.

Which was true. Even if it scared me a little. But I had to get used to it, didn't I? With no magical skills, it might just be the only world left for me.

My uncle was looking at me closely, like he could hear my thoughts and wanted to respond to them. But he could also see I was tired. In the end, he just gave me a smile, smoothing back my hair, then running his hands down my arms, over the sleeves of my button-up shirt.

Then he motioned for me to come away from the door. I took a few steps further into the bookshop, so I was out of his way, but my attention was really on my shirt. He had barely touched me, and yet somehow every one of the millions of wrinkles I had picked up during my travels—no-iron, that shirt had promised me—had been smoothed away. And my hair was no longer hanging in a cloud in front of my eyes.

"Frank is waiting in the apartment upstairs. I just need to lock this door and then we can go up. He can't wait to meet you," he explained, knocking me out of my reverie.

"Oh, I'm sorry about the carpet, Uncle Carlo," I said as he picked it up to carry it outside.

Whatever it had been caught on before was gone now. Somehow, I didn't think it had been freed by the fire. I was starting to see that, whatever branch of magic he had studied in school, he definitely had an all-around handy magic touch.

Carlo shook the carpet, snapping it in the air three times with a loud crack each time. Then he came back in and spread it back on the floor.

The foam was gone. I suppose *maybe* that might have been shaken off outside.

Except there was no sign of fire damage. And no sign of loose threads or holes in the weave. It wasn't like new by any means, but it was certainly *newer*.

I mean, it looked exactly like I supposed it had before I had come into its life.

"There, that's just fine," Carlo said as he smoothed down the corners. Then he shut the door with one last chime of the bell and turned a simple lock built into the door just under the doorknob. The kind where it locks on the inside with a key, a key he just left in there.

But it was a magical bookshop. Keys and locks were not its only means of keeping intruders out, I knew.

"Shall we?" Carlo said to me.

"Lead on," I said.

But this time I collapsed the handle of my suitcase and picked it up to carry it.

I might be feeling less sparky now, but I still didn't trust those wheels.

CHAPTER
TWO

From the outside, the Weal & Woe Bookshop sat in the middle of a building that covered an entire block. Not a bunch of buildings close together, but one solid building containing businesses all around the first floor, but unknown things lurked behind the darkened windows above. All the walls were thick blocks of a pinkish sort of granite, so old they were still stained from wood smoke that hadn't wafted through Minneapolis in nearly a century. It was a solid building, another thing that made me feel safe.

Most magical schools were old keeps, castles or towers, built from enormous blocks of stone. That meant they were cold in the winter and hot in the summer, but safe from invading armies, apparently. Just another thing that made this bookshop feel like home to me, those oh-so-solid walls.

But as I followed my uncle Carlo through the shelves—passing long tables with green-shaded lamps and comfy chairs, smaller reading nooks that were just a single desk tucked between the tall shelves or racks of scrolls, and even an open carpeted area with big, flat pillows all over the floor just waiting for a gaggle of children to come and peruse the picture books—I realized that as big as the bookshop had appeared from out on the street in Minneapolis, it was even bigger on the inside. That feeling of it all going on forever around me, in all directions, only intensified as I tried looking for the far walls.

And that sense of immense size was even before we started going up flight after flight of stairs. Seven levels in all of narrow stairs between stuffed bookshelves with brief glimpses of more and more books—and study tables and nooks and comfy chairs—before we reached a final staircase with more conventional walls of paneled wood to either side. That final staircase ended on a tiny landing before a single door which stood open, spilling warm light down onto the stairs.

The smell of cooking garlic spilled out, too. Garlic in olive oil. Then I heard a hiss followed by the unmistakable smell of lamb starting to brown.

"I hope you like Greek food," Carlo said to me as he waited for me to navigate my suitcase through that doorway before closing the door behind us.

"I love it," I said. "Is Frank Greek?" I had no idea. I had never met Frank, or even heard his name until I had gotten my uncle Carlo's letter.

The hallway on the other side of the door was even narrower than the stairs, and I was having trouble getting my suitcase down that hall without bashing it against every possible surface. I still didn't trust those wheels, but I was really feeling all those hours of travel without sleep weighing me down. And the stupids were coming back. I was about to break something. I didn't know what, but some rare object in my vicinity was about to meet with an accident, I could just tell.

Then a large hand closed over the handle, taking it from me with ridiculous ease.

"Not Greek, just currently on a Greek food kick," the large man in front of me said with a wink. Then he added, "And hello, Tabitha. I'm your uncle Frank. Pleased to meet you."

"Likewise," I said.

He smiled down at me. He looked a lot like my uncle Carlo. Both tall, round men with neatly trimmed but thinning hair that was fading from brown to gray. Both wore faded wool cardigans and shapeless but comfortable-looking trousers.

I have heard that old married couples start to resemble each other, but I never quite believed it until that moment. Frank lacked only the glasses to look just like Carlo.

A sudden memory caught me, that fragment from before with my uncle Carlo and my mother had gained a little shred of context.

The glasses I wore, the glasses I had always worn since I had started school, had been a gift to me from him. I reached up and touched the frame, stainless steel just like his, only where his lenses were small rectangles, mine were large circles. Not only had those frames grown with me as I aged, but the lenses had adjusted over time to my changing eyesight. But they had always been big and round. I remember loving them at once when he had given them to me, because I thought they made me look like an owl.

I had been four, maybe?

I was vaguely aware of Frank watching me as I reacted to these fragments of memory, but he said not a word. He just hefted my suitcase up into the air and then carried it the rest of the way down the half-lit hallway and out of sight around a corner to the left.

Then Carlo touched my shoulder to direct me through the doorway to my right. "Tabitha, I know you're exhausted and probably feeling what the prosaics call 'jet lag', but I think you should eat something before you go to bed. That way, you won't wake up hungry before you've caught up on your rest."

"Sounds good to me," I said. Although the grumbling of my tummy might have drowned me out. Now that I was in the kitchen, the lamb smell was beyond tantalizing.

The rest of the apartment was dark, but this was where the light and smells had been coming from: a cozy little kitchen. I think the galley in the jet I had flown from Amsterdam to Minneapolis in had been roomier. A butcher-block table dominated the center of the room, and Carlo slipped between that and the front of a stove made all of cast-iron but with modern knobs and a gas flame, not wood-burning heat. I don't think I'd ever seen a manlier stove. Not a bit of it was remotely delicate, like it had been built to take a beating from whatever cook used it. Like you were meant to clean it by spraying it down with a fire hose and leaving it to drip-dry when you were done.

Carlo adjusted the flame under the pan then picked up the wooden spoon to start breaking apart the browning chunks of ground lamb, mixing it in with the garlic before reaching up to grab a spice jar without looking and sprinkling some of the contents over the pan. It was hypnotic, watching him cook, but my legs were complaining about standing, or even leaning in the doorframe.

On the opposite side of the butcher-block table from the stove was a little nook that contained a built-in table and two built-in benches. This kitchen was feeling more and more like something on board a ship somewhere, no wasted space. I slid into the nook, telling myself I just wanted to make sure I was not in the way, but really, I just wanted to sit down.

I looked around some more while Carlo whistled to himself as he cooked. The stove was indeed modern, but the refrigerator standing beside it looked more like it had been called an icebox when it had been new to the world. It was made from cast-iron painted robin's-egg blue and had three separate compartments, each with one of those long handles that actually latched when it closed. The bottom compartment was just the right size for a block of ice. I wondered if they had it delivered, and how they got it up all those stairs if they did.

The shelf over the stove held various unlabeled jars of herbs and spices. And tucked in the far corner was a pantry cupboard with no doors that ran from floor to ceiling. Its shelves were crammed with plates and cups, an extra pan and a few pots, and a few shelf-stable items like canned goods and sacks of flour or sugar.

As I watched, Carlo reached among the canned goods for a tube of tomato paste. He popped the seal open, then squeezed a measure of it into the pan before recapping it and putting it inside the icebox.

I know that doesn't sound thrilling, but it really was hypnotic. And not because I was tired, although that probably helped. It was because, although I could never quite see it happen, everywhere my uncle reached, things became just a little bit tidier after he'd passed over them.

Grab a jar of spices, shake some out, set it back, and now all the jars were lined up in a row.

Reach for a tube of tomato paste, and suddenly all the cans were standing with their labels out. Even a little spill of flour that had been dusting the shelf just... disappeared.

It was like the way the wrinkles on my shirt had just smoothed out at his faintest touch.

"I was doing that," Frank said as he came back into the kitchen.

"Just keeping an eye on it for you," Carlo said, stepping back then shooting a conspiratorial grin over to me in the nook.

"If you want to be helpful, you can get the feta cheese for me," Frank said, not quite grumpily. "I know I bought some this morning at the Abergavennys' shop, but of course I can't find it now."

"I'll get it," Carlo said, and reached past Frank to poke inside the icebox. He emerged with a tub of feta cheese just as Frank was taking the pan off the heat. Then Frank opened a warming cabinet under the stovetop and took out a covered casserole dish that was filled with roasted cabbage.

Soon, the two of them joined me in the little nook, each of us with a bowl of steaming food in front of us. The cabbage made a nest for the spiced ground lamb, and everything was generously covered with crumbles of feta cheese.

I had had nothing but train or airport food for the last couple of days, so take that into account, but I honestly think that bowl of food —whatever name the dish might have, I never asked—was the best thing I had ever eaten.

Only when the bowls were empty and Frank had gotten up to put the kettle on for tea did Carlo start the serious talk.

"Tabitha, I'm sorry your last job application process ended so disastrously," he said.

I mumbled something incoherent, even to me. I had warm food in my belly and felt a bit more alert than I had at any point since arriving, but not so much that I was ready to tell them the truth about my magic.

I needed them to let me stay, at least for a little while. Until I could figure out what else could possibly come next. I had no other options. I was prepared to work hard and earn my keep, but I was afraid I was about to blow my only chance to show my worth.

"What happened?" Frank asked as he set three mugs down on the butcher-block table, then dug into the pantry cupboard for the tea canister which had been sitting right in front. He had to move everything around first, but he found it after a bit of rummaging.

I had to say something. As much as Frank had asked the question, it was Carlo's eyes I felt on me. Curious to hear what I had to say.

"Well, it started out really well, actually," I said. "I mean, compared to the other apprenticeships I had applied for."

"Tabitha graduated with honors a semester early, but has remained a boarder at her last school while she applied for various graduate problems and internships," Carlo told Frank. Then he said, "this last one was for a position studying under the head librarian at our world's version of the Library of Congress."

And just like that, I realized that my uncle's husband was a prosaic. I suppose someone had told me at some point, probably Carlo in the letter inviting me to stay with them, but I hadn't remembered.

I really should've remembered. A witch marrying a prosaic? That was almost never done.

"And it was going well?" Frank asked me, prompting me to finish the story.

"It started out well, yes," I said. "Not even just compared to my other application processes. Those had all been disastrous from the start. But for this one, I had to stand in front of the hiring board. That was the head librarian, the wizard who oversaw acquisitions, and the wizard who was the building administrator. But mainly I had to impress the head librarian, who would've been my teacher. If I had passed."

"So they were all men you were interviewing with?" Frank asked.

"No, two of them were women," I said.

"Remember, Frank, a wizard is like a Ph.D. in your world, someone who has higher learning than the average witch in a specific field of study. It's not a gendered thing," Carlo said to Frank, who nodded. "Tabitha's application to apprentice with this particular wizard was a twelve-day process."

"Wow. Sounds grueling," Frank said. The kettle started to whistle, and he turned to take it off the flame.

"It was, but the first eleven days went really, really well," I said. But no amount of stressing those words were going to make them any more true. And Carlo was clearly waiting for more details. "Every topic they grilled me on, I had it down cold. I was prepared. I could answer every question. Even the trick ones."

I wasn't really boasting. I mean, I know my limitations. Book learning is not one of them.

But more than that, while most witches figure out what they're particularly good at from a young age and focus on it, it was different for me. Not being good at anything meant I never focused down on any one thing. I studied every kind of magic, always hopeful I would find something I could do. I never found the thing, but I just kept studying the books. I knew more about the theories behind all the branches than most of the actual practitioners did.

It was just that I couldn't actually *do* any of it.

"What happened on the last day?" Frank asked me as he poured steaming water into the waiting mugs.

"Yes, what *did* happen?" Carlo asked me, leaning forward over his folded hands on the table between us. "I understood that your situation had been explained, and that they were willing to consider you anyway?"

I didn't know he had known that. I mean, he knew I couldn't do magic, because that had been true since I was a little kid. No, it was the bit about things being explained and accounted for. I didn't know he had known that. I didn't know *how* he had known that. I didn't think he had any more contact with my mother than I did. Which was minimal. Perhaps he had inquired of my professors before offering me the job in his bookshop. Like checking my references or something.

"That's true," I admitted, but the way those words drawled out had them both raising their eyebrows at me. "It was explained. They knew. And I think they were prepared to offer me the position anyway. They were that impressed. Or, at least, the head librarian was. And I think he was ready to argue for me against the other two wizards if he had to."

And it would have been amazing, working in the world's largest magical library. Studying under a wizard, being his apprentice. Maybe one day, somehow, being a wizard myself. It was a reach for someone with book learning but no skills, but on the morning of the last day of my application process, it had felt so doable.

"Then what?" Frank prompted as he set mugs of tea in front of Carlo and me.

"It was the last day of the interview. That was when the acquisitions wizard asked me if I could do any magic at all. Like, even a little bit. She just wanted to see."

What I didn't tell them, was that even at the time, it had felt like a trick. She had been the one asking all the trick questions. Now she had thrown down the guaranteed interview-stopper. But how could I have said no?

"And then what happened?" Frank asked.

"Then, I tried a little magic," I admitted. I rushed to add before my uncle Carlo could say anything, "I know it was a dumb idea. She just... provoked me."

"Provoked you," Carlo repeated, but tonelessly, no hint to what he was thinking about that. He took a sip of his tea.

"It was dumb," I said miserably.

"Nothing happened?" Frank guessed.

"No, something happened," I said. "The acquisition wizard's pants caught on fire."

"And they didn't give you the job?" Frank asked in mock surprise.

"They didn't give me the job," I said. "And there was nowhere else for me to apply. And the school wouldn't let me stay on in the dorms any longer. Not after the semester ended."

Which had been surprising. I had always stayed over during the summer breaks before. Those were some of my favorite times, being left all alone in the buildings to explore or spend all day in the library if I wanted. But with nothing waiting there for me in the fall, they wouldn't let me stay through the summer. Not anymore.

"Which is how you ended up here," Frank said, and reached across the table to give my hand a squeeze. "I hope this ends up being a good thing for you."

"Me too," I said, trying not to sound as glum as I felt.

"Your mother didn't come to see you?" Carlo asked, not looking at me. His gaze was fixed on the surface of his tea.

"I haven't seen my mother since..." I trailed off, then frowned. "You know, I can't really say? I think it was just before graduation, maybe."

"You don't know?" Frank asked. He was squeezed into the bench on the other side of the table beside Carlo, and I saw the two of them move ever so slightly. I was pretty sure that Carlo had just elbowed him under the table. But I answered the question anyway.

"My mother tends to drop in on me in the middle of the night and disappear again just as quickly," I said, more brightly than I felt. "Sometimes I think I only dreamed she was there. I have dreams of long conversations, but I don't remember them very clearly in the morning."

"Well, you're here with us now," Carlo said. I sensed his tone was just as artificially upbeat as mine. We were both anxious to get off the topic of Serena Greene, my mother and his sister.

"Yes, and we're so happy to have you," Frank said. He shifted in the bench so he could look more directly at Carlo beside him, a warm fondness in his eyes. "We haven't had a trip together, ever. Not even a honeymoon. And now we get to spend two whole months together, traveling all over the world, collecting books and artifacts. It's like a dream come true."

"It is," Carlo said, but he was looking at me. "I'm sorry your academic career ended so abruptly and so disastrously, I truly am. But I'm also delighted you could come and watch our shop for us so we can get away."

"I appreciate room and board and time to figure out my next step," I said.

"But you also love books," Frank said with a knowing smile. "I can tell."

And he hadn't even seen me walking through the bookshop. I must just have a look about me.

I reached up to touch my hair, as if my fingertips could sense whatever he was seeing. But my curls which had lain down at my uncle Carlo's touch were more tangled than ever now, and a jolt of static electricity zapped me.

It felt like a warning, that little zap.

"Finish your tea," Carlo told me, and I drained the last of my cup. It tasted like chamomile and lavender, not usually my sort of thing, but once it was gone I felt different. Calmer doesn't seem like the right word. It was more like... stiller. Like all the loose electrons that had filled my hair with static charge were gone now, and my body was electrically neutral, if only for a while.

But mostly I was just so very tired.

I think I started to nod off, there at the table. I heard the two of them talking then a gentle laugh when they realized I wasn't listening. I think my eyes were closed. But Frank pulled me to my feet to give me one last hug before sending me out of the kitchen.

Then Carlo led me around the dark apartment, through a darkened sitting room and past a set of French doors that led out onto a shadowed veranda. The blinking of my eyes were more like long periods with my eyelids closed, and my impressions were like little slices of the world. Like still-life paintings, all in shades of blue, gray and black.

I thought I saw a cast-iron table and chairs out on that veranda, with shadowy shapes all around it like plants just coming into the full leaf of spring. But my eyes closed again, and when they opened once more I was in another wood-paneled hallway.

Then it was up another steep staircase to an attic room. I vaguely saw my suitcase waiting for me on a little padded bench, but I didn't have the energy for any of it anymore. Not unpacking. Not even brushing my teeth.

I was going to regret *that* in the morning.

But the minute Carlo went back down the stairs, I collapsed face-first on that bed and started to drift off into a deep sleep.

I still had all my clothes on, even my Converse sneakers. But it didn't matter.

Nothing mattered but that perfect combination of being just that tired, but also feeling so much at home.

I sleepily reminded myself that it was only for a few months, while they were away. Then I'd have to find a new place. And it probably wouldn't be a bookshop or the world's largest magical library or anything remotely like that. It might be something awful, out in the world of the prosaics. But for a few months, I was here.

I had never had a home before. That was my penultimate

thought before sleep took me. I had never had a home before, and yet somehow I knew exactly what it was supposed to feel like. It was supposed to feel like this place.

And my very last thought: isn't that strange? And yet it was true. I was finally home.

CHAPTER

THREE

I t's always disorienting, the first time I wake up in a new place. But this time it was even more so, because I wasn't waking up in another dorm room. There was no hubbub of student activity all around me, no sound of classmates heading for the showers before breakfast.

No smell of breakfast.

My eyelids were gummed shut, so I stayed where I was for a bit longer, smelling the air and listening to the world around me. I could just discern the aroma of books, but no part of that scent was strong enough for me to distinguish old books from new like usual.

And I could hear people, but distantly, and not in large groups. Also, I heard two dogs barking at each other before two adult humans intervened. I had never been to a school that allowed dogs.

I frowned and started to sit up, rubbing at my eyes.

I was still wearing my shoes.

And just like that, I remembered where I was. At my uncles' home on top of their bookshop, inside the magical community known—rather unimaginatively—as the Square.

I was still wearing all my clothes. All the clothes I had already been wearing for too long before I had collapsed onto the bed.

I looked around the attic room I had barely glanced at the night before. Sunlight was streaming in the window now, and I could tell by the angle I had slept until noon or past it. The bed was far enough away from the light that it had never touched me.

It was a north-facing window, but mostly that lack of reach was because the room was so long. Narrow, but long. There was barely room to pass between the foot of the bed and the wall, but lots of room between the bed and the space in front of the doorway for a large night table already stacked with books that nearly crowded out the lamp resting there, a tall dresser with smaller drawers built along the back of its top surface, and a padded bench that was the current home of my still-packed suitcase.

I blinked towards the source of the sunlight to my right. The window was a French window, the sill only half a foot off the floor, the window itself large enough for someone to open up and step through. A pair of comfy-looking over-stuffed, wing-back chairs sat to either side of that window, perfect for curling up with a book and soaking up the sunbeams. One was situated for the morning sun, and the other for the afternoon, although currently they were both equally illuminated. The faded upholstery had probably once been a deep royal blue before decades of sunlight had leached it all away.

And outside the window was a tiny cast-iron porch, the railings twisting around in fleur-de-lis motifs. The porch wasn't even large enough to hold a chair. It was really just a place to stand and look down at the Square below.

As curious as I was to get a glimpse of my new home, the bathroom was calling me far more urgently. I looked to the left. There was another pair of chairs as well as a low coffee table between them, also stacked high with various books, but beyond that was a pair of closed doors. I took off my shoes, finally, and headed to those doors.

The first one I tried was the closet, of course. It was empty, save for a large number of wooden hangers waiting for my clothes.

The other was the bathroom. It was about as old-fashioned as you could get and still be indoor plumbing, with a clawfoot-tub encircled by a cloth shower curtain hanging from the largest metal rings I had ever seen, a pedestal sink with separate faucets for hot and cold water under an all-metal medicine cabinet, and the kind of toilet where the tank is built into the wall overhead. I would have to reach up to pull the chain to flush it.

But I didn't mind. Perhaps it was the overwhelming aroma of lavender, such a calming smell. Not fake chemical lavender, but the real flower smell. I didn't like it in tea, but in the air it was quite lovely. Mostly it was just a joy to get out of my travel clothes and take the world's most indulgently long, hot shower.

The soap smelled of lavender, too.

After I had finally had enough, I wrapped up in the fluffy towels waiting for me on a warming bar I hadn't noticed before, or I would've turned it on. It was plenty warm in the steamy bathroom already, so I didn't mind. But I could just imagine how nice that feature would be in the cold of winter.

I had spent a few winters in schools located in places that got colder than Minnesota. But not many.

I got dressed but still didn't bother unpacking the rest of my suitcase. I was in no hurry for that, even if all my clothes were a mess of wrinkles and could really use a good airing out. I did dig down to the bottom of the bag to get my other pair of sneakers, though. The ones I had been wearing since Europe and then slept in for more than twelve hours were definitely not ready for my feet again just yet.

I picked them up and carried them to that French window. I opened the window and ducked outside, leaning on the railing to get a look at the Square.

I couldn't see the bookshop or anything else beneath me, and straight across was a large, modern building. It looked hazy, like I was seeing it through a fog. But that was no city smog or anything like that. It had a shimmer to it, and I knew I was looking through a magical bubble, looking out from the magical world and into the prosaic world. It was a good-sized building, maybe fourteen or so stories.

The Square was called the Square for a pretty good reason, I decided. It was all one building, more or less square in shape, just like I'd seen from the outside, but with an open courtyard in the middle. There were paved walkways connecting the doors on the first floor. Those all looked like businesses, with windows I couldn't quite see through, and signs I couldn't quite read. I had gone up at least nine flights of stairs the night before, after all. But I could see that people were moving in and out with packages in their arms, waving and nodding to each other as they passed.

The two floors above that bottom level were joined by a continuous walkway with cast-iron railings just like my little porch. I didn't see anyone moving around on those walkways at the moment. But the patterns of doors and windows brought to mind rows of apartments. Some of the top floor apartments had second levels, making the roofline jagged in a way it hadn't looked from the street in the prosaic world. From there, everything had been granite walls, few windows, and ended in a flat roof after a mere three levels.

Actually, despite all the stairs I had climbed the night before, I only looked to be about five stories up from the ground below me. So that bigger-on-the-inside-thing the bookshop possessed worked in all three dimensions.

I was used to magical spaces, of course. But what the bookshop had going on was pretty epic. Most places like that I had been to had been in very old parts of Europe, where witches had been living for centuries if not millennia. Generations of magic went into crafting such places. I hadn't expected to see anything like that in Minneapolis.

Then I saw something even more unusual, just as I was about to step back inside. It was in the far corner, and the glimmer of magic around it had been blending with the glimmer of the bubble that separated the Square from the building beyond. But out of the corner of my eye, I could see it clearly.

It was a stone tower, like something from the Neolithic age, all dark gray stone covered in green moss and white and gray lichen. I turned to look at directly, and it was gone again. But I knew I had seen it.

I headed down the stairs into my uncles' apartment. Everything was quiet in a way that I knew I was alone. I went into the kitchen and saw a note left out on the butcher-block table in the middle of the room.

They were both in the bookshop, and I was welcome to join them, but my training wouldn't start for at least another day. I was told to help myself to anything in the kitchen. And I was starving. But I really didn't want to eat alone. I thought of finding them in the bookshop and seeing when they were having lunch, but then I thought better of it.

I really wanted to see what was going on down in the Square.

I went out onto the veranda I had seen the night before. The plants were all perked up now, basking in the sun, and there were a lot of them, all crowded together, so much so that I almost missed seeing what I was looking for: a way down to the Square.

But there was one. Tucked close against the granite wall, and so narrow it was easy to overlook it, was a staircase of the same patterned cast-iron as the railings. I had to open a little gate to get through it. As much as the plants were close all around it, the gate opened easily with no hint of rust. The staircase creaked loudly under my weight, but didn't rock or pull away from its anchoring in the wall as I descended it.

It ended at the beginning of the higher of the two walkways that circled the Square. I followed it past a few doors, all the windows either with curtains closed or shimmering spells keeping me from spying anything inside. Definitely private homes, then.

I reached the corner where I had seen the Neolithic tower, but before I could make out any of the mossy-stones beyond the rosy granite walls that I was still walking past, the walkway ended in another flight of stairs. It was enclosed in cast-iron, with vines growing thickly around the bars of metal, so thick I couldn't see out of it. It was like walking through a secret passageway in a magic garden, something I've actually done before.

When I reached the lower walkway, I left those plants behind for the opener air overlooking the Square once more. Now I was walking parallel to the bookshop the entire length of the back of the Square until I came upon a final staircase that brought me down to ground level.

I looked around again, seeing the world from this new ground-level angle. The center of the Square was all trees, shrubs and plants. It wasn't jungle-thick by any means, and I could see paths winding through it all. But they were very winding paths, not straight lines at all, and I could see the shimmer of more magic. I wasn't up for traipsing through a bigger-on-the-inside wood, so I stayed on the wide tiles of the patio, circling back the way I'd come, back towards where I had seen the Neolithic tower.

Which I still couldn't see.

I looked up at the signs as I passed under them. The Violenta Court Boutique. Was that the name of a person or a place? I wasn't sure. The clothes in the windows were an interesting mix of witchy and prosaic styles, and if I hadn't been so hungry, I would've ducked inside. I could use some new clothes, now that my days of wearing school uniforms were done. But there would be time later.

The next sign read "Bartholomew Bullen's Potions & Magical Sundries". This shop had no windows, but the sharp smells of potion ingredients permeated the air outside of it even with the door closed. Pepper of some sort, something like gunpowder, and was that... durian?

Ew.

The next business was called the Square Pub. An unfortunate, if appropriate, name. But it wasn't open for the day yet. I could just catch glimpses through the mullioned windows of two women arranging tables and chairs while a man fussed behind the bar.

Then I was distracted by a strong urge to move away from the direction I was walking. A very strong urge.

Exactly where I had indirectly seen that tower. Not a coincidence, just powerful warding.

I didn't try to fight it. My steps followed a line that angled away from that corner of the Square, then left the tiled patio completely, cutting that corner across the sparse early spring grass to catch the patio again further on. There was a long stretch of wall with no doors or windows on the ground floor, although there was a short flight of stone steps that led down to a basement door. Those steps looked nearly as old as the tower, but the moss covering them was lusher. The whole staircase looked slickly wet, the steps themselves worn and uneven, almost certain to trip up anyone trying to go down it.

Then I was passing by doors and windows again, but these were all soaped up. A really low-tech and low-magic way to keep me from peeking inside.

I realized I was almost back at the bookshop again and was regretting not just finding something to eat in my uncles' kitchen when I finally saw something that looked promising.

A teashop. The Loose Leaves Teashop, by name. The tiled patio was wider here, and a couple of cast-iron tables and chairs were gathered on it. The white paint on the furniture looked shiny and new, but no one was sitting on them, as inviting as they were on such a warm day.

Still, I was sure I could smell bread. And I was pretty sure that bread was croissants. The teashop must have a bakery selection. My stomach demanded I investigate at once.

I went inside.

CHAPTER

FOUR

The interior of the Loose Leaves Teashop was as newly painted as the outdoor furniture, everything white and gleaming. All those white surfaces really made the most of the sunlight, making everything warm and inviting.

But no one was there.

"Hello?" I called as I came further inside. I could see a bakery case, but it was empty. My heart sank, but at least I could get a cup of strong black tea in me before I resumed my search for food. And whoever worked here would surely know where the croissant smell was coming from, right?

I approached the counter, but heard a low, growling sound. A warning not to come closer, I knew that, but I couldn't see just where it was coming from.

"Houdini, stop that," a woman said, and I followed the sound of her voice to see a little office just off to the left behind the counter. A woman with steel gray hair was sitting there, bent over some sort of accounting book, a pen in her hand.

The growling kicked up into a higher gear before I finally found its source: a little black dog was curled up in a pillowy dog bed just beside the woman's desk. He was curled up tight, his nose tucked almost all the way under his own little thigh, but those eyes were open and watching me.

He was tiny. I mean, I had seen bigger cats. I had seen bigger *rats* back when I had ducked in and out of the witchy places that hide in the depths of the New York City subway system. He couldn't have been more than ten pounds.

But that growl was surprisingly fierce. He was very good at pretending to be a much larger dog.

He didn't seem to like me looking at him, and he lifted his head, the growl building to some crescendo. There would be barking soon. Maybe howling.

But before he could really get started, the woman bent over and picked him up. He didn't seem to know what to do about this. It's hard to sound tough when someone else is carrying you, I'm sure. The growl stuttered out with something like a whine of complaint.

And finally, the woman noticed me.

"Oh. Pardon me!" she said, stepping out of her office to stand behind the counter. The dog in her arms still kept his eyes locked on me. Like he wasn't going to let me get away with anything.

"I'm sorry to disturb you. Aren't you open?" I asked.

"As much as I can be," the woman said with a sigh. But then some thought seemed to strike her, and she looked me up and down very deliberately. I resisted the urge to touch my hair. I was sure it was all in a staticky cloud again, floating around my head in a tangled mass, but actually touching it was just risking setting off another spark. I adjusted the frames of my glasses instead.

But that little motion seemed to click something into place in her mind, because she stopped examining me and gave me a warm smile. "You must be Tabitha, right? Tabitha Greene? Carlo's niece?"

"That's right," I said. I hadn't realized my uncles had told anyone I was coming. But then I had no idea who their friends were. Maybe everyone in the Square.

"I'm Agatha Mirken," she said, thrusting out a hand for me to shake. I took it gingerly. She had a frail look to her, thin and pale, and I was afraid this was going to be like shaking hands with a bird. All delicate bones, too easily broken. But to my surprise, she was stronger than she looked. She grasped my hand firmly, with a squeeze that instantly made me feel welcome.

But then she gave me a wavering frown. "Did you want some tea?"

"I was hoping to get some," I said. "Ceylon, if you have it? Maybe with a little cardamom?"

"I have it," she said, but slowly. Evasively.

"I can pay," I said, not sure what the problem was. I had American money in my wallet, crisp new bills from the currency exchange at the airport.

"It's not that," she said. But then she took a deep breath and summoned up a smile. "Well, let's just see how it goes, shall we? I mean, maybe you're just what I need to break this pattern."

"What pattern?" I asked.

"You'll see," she said, that desperate smile still on her face. She put the dog down on the floor, then turned to get to work.

I watched as she set a kettle to boil, then opened up one of the array of cabinet doors behind her. She took down a series of tea canisters and measured a couple fractions of a spoonful from each of their contents and put into the basket of a little teapot. Then she moved down to the end of the cabinets to a smaller door and took down a little spice shaker. She added some of its light brown powdery contents to the basket. By the time she'd put the shaker away, the kettle was already whistling. She added the water to the pot, put the lid on, then wrapped the whole thing snugly in a tea towel.

Then she turned back to me.

"Milk? Sugar? Honey?" she offered.

"Just black for me," I said.

The dog made a noise that sounded just like a scoff.

"Ignore him," Agatha said.

"Is he your familiar?" I asked.

She barked out a sudden laugh. "No, he's just a little pup. Found him in the alley and sort of got stuck with him. I'm not really a familiar kind of witch at all. I prefer not to be responsible for the care of other living things if I can help it."

Which sounded harsh, but the look she directed at the dog, who was once more curling up in that pillow dog bed, was pure love. What she said had likely been true her entire life, until she had met this dog.

"And his name is Houdini?" I said.

But before she could answer, the door behind me opened, and I turned to see a man of about thirty come inside with a Siamese cat in his arms. He was dressed like a prosaic in what I guess you would call business casual: slacks and leather shoes with a lightweight cream-colored sweater over his button-up shirt. But that shade of cream, almost ivory, was a bad choice, given the excessive amount of fine black cat hair that clung to it.

Houdini started growling again, but the tone was different this time. It was less of a warning for Agatha and more of a rote demonstration of annoyance.

The cat was making a similar sort of sound, a low and growly mew. Houdini's growl had that feeling to it again, like it was about to become a bark or a howl. But again Agatha picked him up and carried him back to his bed, and his growling sputtered out in embarrassment.

The man seemed unbothered by any of this, only stroking the cat in his arms until its upraised hair relaxed down again. The cat's deep green eyes regarded me for all of a fraction of a second, then swept disdainfully past me.

"Hello, Barnardo," Agatha said as she set a cup and saucer in front of me and poured out the steaming tea. The cardamom smell hit me first, then the smell of the tea itself.

"Is that wise?" the man named Barnardo asked, looking at my

teacup. I didn't understand that question at all. I looked up at Agatha, but she only gave me a drink-up gesture.

I picked up the cup, blew the steam from the surface, and took the tiniest of sips, all too aware of both of them watching me far too closely.

I tried not to grimace, but the tea was not just bitter, it was undrinkable. There were sour undertones that lingered on my tongue even as I very impolitely let the little bit I had sipped dribble back into the cup.

"Sorry," I said, wiping my mouth on my sleeve and just resisting the urge to wipe my tongue as well. The sour aftertaste was something more cheesy now. Like I had accidentally washed down a big mouthful of curdled milk.

"I don't get it," Agatha said, but Barnardo shifted the cat to perch on one arm so he could use the other hand to pat Agatha encouragingly on the arm.

"I told you, you should see my witch doctor. He's very good," Barnardo said, but Agatha was already shaking her head.

"I've not needed my magic doctored once in all my many years, and I'm not starting now," she declared. But then she saw me still struggling with the taste in my mouth which had morphed again. It was like I had washed down the remains of a beer that had been filled with cigarette butts.

"You have to help her, Agatha. Miss Snooty Cat and I can wait," Barnardo said.

"Can you help?" I asked desperately.

"It's not so much me helping you as you helping yourself," Agatha said miserably.

But there was no way she was more miserable than I was. Now my tongue was insisting there was moldy bread in my mouth, but that wasn't the main thing.

The main thing was, I had no magic. I literally couldn't help myself with whatever she had in mind.

"Come around the counter, dear," Agatha said, opening the little panel in the counter to let me through.

"No, that's okay. I can just..." But I had no idea what I could just do. Not even a clue where to start.

"It's all right, dear," she insisted. "I'm so sorry. I was hoping since you were new and I've never made tea for you before, that you would break my cycle of bad luck."

"Or break the spell," Barnardo said pointedly.

"It's not a spell!" Agatha said, brandishing a single finger at him.

"Because never in your many years has someone ever been able to put the whammy on you without you knowing it," Barnardo finished for her, then started strolling around the shop, stroking his cat until whatever Agatha wanted me to do was done.

"I'm not very good at... whatever kind of magic this is," I said.

Rancid meat. I was tasting rancid meat.

I was tasting so many things I had never tasted before.

"It's not really magic, dear," Agatha said as she filled the electric kettle and switched it on again. "I just need you to mix your own tea. Then it will be right as rain."

"I just wanted Ceylon and cardamom," I said, looking at row after row of far too many kinds of tea.

"I know, dear. I'm afraid I'm incapable of doing something so simple," she said regretfully.

"Don't let her fool you," Barnardo said, loudly from across the room. "She could mix you a blend of tea that was just the thing you never knew you always loved best in the world. Back in her day."

He buried his face into his cat's fur, but not before I saw his mischievous smile.

For her part, Agatha was ignoring him. She just pointed at all that tea again, and the lonely little teapot waiting for me to fill it.

I picked a single canister labeled Dimbula Ceylon Black and opened the lid. I took a deep sniff of the contents, which to my delight went a long way towards ending the flavor rollercoaster my tongue was still on. I spooned some into the teapot, then headed for her spice cabinet to find the shaker of cardamom. I added a generous sprinkling of that. Then the kettle whistled before shutting itself off, and Agatha gestured for me to pour the water into the pot myself. Once that was done, she handed me a fresh tea towel. I had never done this step before, but I tried to replicate what she had done, swaddling the whole pot up like a baby.

"That should do it. Let's just give it a minute," Agatha said. I went back to the customer side of the counter and Agatha went into her office. I could hear the opening and closing of more cabinet doors and drawers before she emerged again, a plain brown cloth bag in her hands. It looked like the sort of featureless bags that flour and sugar used to come in, in pioneer times, but was barely large enough to be a pillow for Houdini.

"Thanks, love," Barnardo said as he took the bag from her and slipped it into his sweater pocket.

"You're taking your life into your own hands, you know," Agatha said, a stab at humor I was sure she didn't feel.

"Nonsense. Whatever is going on with your beverage skills, your medicinal teas are still reliable. You and I know this is true," he said.

Agatha just shrugged. But when she turned to fetch a new cup and saucer for me, I could see a slight twitch up to the corner of her mouth. Almost a smile. "It's old stock," she confided to me in a whisper. I just nodded.

Barnardo started to head outside, then spun on his heel and rushed back to the counter. The cat in his arms objected, but he shushed her.

"Is something wrong?" I asked.

"Depends on what you consider *wrong*," he said, stroking his cat to calm her. "Many, many people enjoy the company of the Trio. But Miss Snooty Cat and I are not among that number."

"Nor I," Agatha said, as she set the still-wrapped teapot in front of me.

"Who are the Trio?" I asked, leaning away from the counter to look out the window towards the Square. I just had a glimpse of three women walking past. I didn't see their faces, but they all had long waves of golden blonde hair and were wearing summer dresses a little too skimpy for the still-brisk spring air outside.

"Cleopatra, Delilah and Cressida. They all work at the Inanna Salon & Spa just past the Weal & Woe Bookshop. I'm sure you'll have the pleasure of meeting them yourself soon enough," Barnardo said with a tight smile. Then he gave Agatha one last nod before exiting the shop.

"It's best if you pour it out yourself, dear," Agatha said. I picked up the wrapped pot and filled the cup. Then I inhaled another lungful of cardamom and black tea. It smelled just as good as it had before.

It took a lot to build up the nerve to take a sip. But when I did, the last remnants of foul tastes on my tongue were well and truly gone.

"Wow," I said, taking another sip. "I know I'm jet lagged and really needed this caffeine, but I would still say this is the finest tea I've ever tasted."

"It ought to be," Agatha said, almost defensively. "I get the tea imported fresh from all over the world. That's from the Dimbula region of Sri Lanka. European royalty has been drinking that since they discovered the wonders of tea."

"It's very good," I said. "But what went wrong before?"

"I'm dying to know the answer to that myself," Agatha said. She was leaning on the counter across from me, head on her hand as she watched me take sips of the hot tea. She almost seemed half-asleep, or caught in a reverie.

But then she was scowling, and Houdini was growling that warning growl again. Only this time, he ran through all the gears of that growl in a matter of seconds before charging out of the office, shooting like a flash under the door in the counter to plant himself in front of the door to the Square.

I couldn't make out more than a silhouette in the morning light, of someone drawing closer. The door opened and a tall, middle-aged man came in. He had olive skin, warm brown eyes, and hair that was still jet black where it grew on the back and sides of his head, but not a single wisp of it traversed his scalp. He smiled at Agatha despite her deepening scowl, but the minute he opened his mouth to speak, Houdini started to bark.

And what a bark it was. How did a sound that loud and that deep come out of that teeny, tiny body? And it just kept coming, a constant torrent that the man was incapable of getting an audible word over. Then the bark morphed into what I can only describe as a crow. Like this little dog thought he was a rooster, and was he ever determined to greet the sunrise as no other rooster had done before him.

The man made pleading gestures at Agatha, which she ignored, before finally giving up with a shrug and stepping back out of the store. He looked around, straightened his jacket, then headed to the left, the same direction the Trio had gone.

"Not a customer?" I guessed.

"Not a customer," Agatha confirmed. "Titus Bloom. He and his wife own the coffeeshop on the other side of the Square. We don't like him, do we, Houdini?"

Houdini barked one more time in shrill assent, then headed quietly back to curl up in his bed.

I guess it was some kind of coffee versus tea thing. Lots of people consider that to be a dividing line, never to be crossed.

Myself, I often enjoy a nice French roast with steamed milk. Especially if I had any of those croissants I had smelled before.

But in that moment, nothing existed for me but that cup of tea. I savored the rest of that pot, but once it was gone, I knew it was time to find my uncles in the bookshop.

At the very least, I wanted to pull some books. If Barnardo was right and what had happened with the first cup of tea had been some sort of spell or curse, perhaps I could help. I was no good at casting or dispelling anything, but I was very good at research. With all of those taste sensations plaguing me after that one little sip that didn't linger on my tongue for more than an instant, magic just *had* to be involved.

And whenever I, a witch without magic, could be of any help, I was always eager to try.

Especially because it felt like Agatha and I could be friends in time, and I hadn't felt that way in many, many years.

CHAPTER

FIVE

The next week went by in a blur. I hadn't expected there to be so much to learn about running a bookshop, even a magical one, but there was always one more thing to learn, one more thing my uncle Carlo had to be sure to show me before he and Frank left on their trip.

It certainly didn't help that I was still going through one of my bad luck phases. I had stopped shooting sparks, thankfully. But I was still prone to random accidents, and it was really hard to explain how it wasn't my fault.

Sure, that old scroll rack had been on its last legs, and I had only walked by it before it crashed to splinters and sent antique scrolls rolling everywhere. My sweater hadn't caught on it or anything.

And the leak in the corner of the ceiling on the top floor had surely been there for some time, given the size of the water stain. It had gone unnoticed until I found it while exploring in the stacks, and I had gotten a basin under it right away. Only a few books had been damaged, and they had only been old paperbacks, nothing magical or valuable.

·I was used to this sort of thing. It had happened at some point or another at every school I had attended. These random events were usually what prompted the next move, or at least I suspected as much. Someone in the administration would call my mother, and she would come in the dead of night to talk with me, and then I'd wake up somewhere new and have to start the work of fitting in all over again.

Or, rather, starting failing to fit in all over from square one.

But it was different this time. Because no matter what happened, my uncle Carlo always sincerely believed it was not my fault. Even when his trusty old computer suddenly flashed the Blue Screen of Death the moment I touched its mouse for the first time, he insisted I shouldn't feel bad about it. He couldn't get it working again, but he had been diligent with his backups and was due to buy a new one, anyway.

It was weird. This complete acceptance, this kind sympathy. The time I had set the carpet on fire was the only time I had even managed to get an apology out. After that, Uncle Carlo was forgiving me faster than I could even grasp what had happened.

Was that what family meant?

Even just living in the Square was different from being in school, though. Every day of my life that I could remember, I had woken up knowing I wasn't the same as everybody else, and that was always followed by hour after hour of having that demonstrated clearly over and over again.

So it was a little ironic how hard I had worked to never leave that environment. But it was the only world I knew. I knew how to handle classes, and I knew so long as I could spend all the time I wanted in a well-stocked library, I would be happy enough in my existence. I had been afraid what the wider world held for me. I assumed it would be the same, but worse.

Only it wasn't. I knew a dozen people well enough to nod hello to around the Square. I got my daily black tea from Agatha's shop every morning. And after I had mentioned the tantalizing smell of croissants, she had started picking up two fresh ones from the French bakery on the far side of the square. She brought the croissants, and I made tea for the both of us, and we had breakfast together with Houdini every morning. Sometimes Barnardo joined us, with Miss Snooty Cat.

And I went into the corner shop to pick up groceries for Carlo and Frank, and hence knew the couple who owned that establishment, the Abergavennys. And we had dinner in the pub one night, and I met the family who ran it, the Wolseys, as well as some of the other neighbors.

But not once, not one single time, did anyone ask me to do anything magical. I saw them all use their own magic all the time. Only they never seemed to want to talk about it. I respected that.

But I had watched Cato and Octavia Abergavenny in the corner shop casting charms over their dairy delivery to keep it fresher longer. Robert Wolsey, who owned the pub, was doing something magical when he brewed his signature ale. I couldn't hear his words or see clearly what he was doing with his hands over the kegs, but it was something.

And while I had yet to meet the Trio properly, I had seen them strolling by often enough to be certain there was a lot of glamor going on there.

But if anyone even noticed that I wasn't doing anything special, they never said so. Maybe they assumed that I was a prosaic, like Frank. Or maybe they thought I was struggling with something like whatever was keeping Agatha from brewing her own tea.

Not that anyone knew what that was all about either. I kept researching things and bringing new possibilities to Agatha, but she didn't want to hear any of it. It was her problem to solve, and she gently invited me to butt out. So I did.

But in regards to the Square and my lack of use of magic, I didn't know *what* they were thinking. I just really appreciated that I was accepted without question. It was a nice feeling.

Still, I was nervous for the day when my uncles left and I would be alone in the bookshop. And it was coming soon. They had their entire trip mapped out, a process that filled our dinners with lively debates that were gradually becoming a settled itinerary.

Then the packing began.

Frank did the bulk of the packing, which didn't seem like a good idea to me, but I held my tongue. I had seen ample examples since arriving of how Frank operated. To call him absent-minded would be an understatement. Scatter-brained might be closer to it.

All I'm saying is, the enormous piles of things they absolutely had to take with them started to dominate the living room, and the two suitcases that were all they were planning to take were never going to hold it all.

When I pointed this out to Uncle Carlo, he just smiled, then adjusted his glasses. "It will all work out," was all he said.

I hoped the same was true with me and the bookshop, but when the last day before their departure finally rolled around, I still felt very far from ready.

Especially as I sat on the edge of the counter and watched my uncle Carlo unbox his new computer and set it up on the battered old desk behind the counter.

"Maybe it's better if I don't try to use that again," I said nervously.

"You'll be fine," he assured me as he double-checked all the cords plugging into the back of the tower one last time before pushing the power button on.

"I don't think technology likes me," I said.

"You just need to come at it with a little caution," he said as the operating system's logo appeared on the monitor. "Like with a wild animal."

"Except I think *I'm* the problem, not the computer," I said.

"Let me see your glasses," he said, to my surprise. I slipped them off and handed them to him. He turned them over in his hands, testing the hinges and inspecting the wings. Then he handed them back to me. "Those are indestructible," he said.

"I know," I said. "I've had some pretty spectacular accidents in my day. Things falling on me, me falling off of things. But those glasses have never gotten so much as a scratch."

"They do more than that, though," he said. "Haven't you ever noticed?"

"No," I said as I put them back on. "I mean, they correct my vision. And if I focus on something far away, they adjust like binoculars. That's pretty handy."

"They also help with other things," he said. He was talking slowly now, deliberately, like each word was being selected from a drop-down menu of options he had to think about. But he was also busy answering all the computer's setup questions at the same time.

"Like what?" I asked.

But he was just frowning at the computer as he inputted the enormous, very random selection of characters that was the password for the bookshop Wi-Fi.

He got it right on the first try. I never did that. Too many punctuation marks and things that could be the numeral one or a lower case l.

"Like what?" I asked again when he had connected and started re-importing all the store's data from the cloud.

"Hmm?" he said distractedly.

"My glasses. What do they do?" I pressed.

He looked at me in complete confusion. I started to wonder if I had only been imagining the whole conversation. Was I going crazy?

But then he said, "Oh!" in such a way I half expected him to slap his own forehead. "Well, I just find them so comforting, don't you? When things start to feel a little... disordered or unsettling, I guess. I just touch my glasses, and adjusting them sort of adjusts the whole world. Don't you find?"

I just gaped at him. I had never felt anything remotely like that.

And yet I totally believed that he did. Because I was remembering now a hundred little times when the tornado of disarray that was Frank passed through a room, I had seen Carlo do just that. He would adjust his glasses, and then set about righting everything that was threatening to fall off of a shelf or was simply in the wrong place in Frank's wake.

Did my glasses do that too?

I pushed the bridge up a little higher on my nose. But everything still felt the same.

"This is going to take a bit," Carlo said, frowning at the computer. "I'll be back to check on it, but I need to go upstairs and see Frank for a minute first. Are you all right on your own?"

"I better be. You're leaving tomorrow," I said, and truly wished I was joking as much as I was trying to sound like I was.

"You'll be fine," he said once more, then headed up the many staircases to the apartment.

I hopped down from the counter and looked at the computer. It still felt like a ticking time bomb to me. I adjusted my glasses at it, but it was still as menacing as ever.

Then the bell over the door chimed, and I turned to see a young man about my own age coming in from the prosaic world. Magical world visitors tended to just appear among the books, but the prosaics always had their arrival announced by the bell.

This guy was on his own. He was dressed just a little too grubby to be someone from the office tower next door out on a lunch break, his thick blond hair a little too long to be properly corporate. But as faded as his jeans and T-shirt were, they didn't look like he did any manual labor either. Too clean. I decided he probably worked in the service industry, a server or barista maybe. Someone like that might have a bit of book-shopping time in the middle of a workday, between shifts.

And indeed he had a bag under his arm already, flat but reasonably thick, with the logo for the comic bookstore that was the only storefront on the Square that was not in the magical world. It opened up in the middle of the alley, what would normally be a very bad location for a retail enterprise. And yet Agatha told me they did really good business.

It took everyone off the street a minute for their eyes to adjust to the bookshop interior, especially on sunny days like the one we were having that day. And most prosaics didn't even realize they were never seeing all the way through the bookshop. The shelves at the front were all that most of them could perceive.

I watched him blink until his eyes finally focused on the shelves of books around him. Then he saw me looking at him, and his cheeks flushed. "Hi," he said.

"Hi," I said. "I'm new."

"Oh?" he said and flushed a deeper shade of crimson.

"I'm sorry. Aren't you a regular?" I asked. I hadn't seen him before, but most of the prosaic crowd who came in were regular shoppers. Carlo and Frank knew almost all of their customers by name, and I had endured far more introductions to people than I had ever expected.

"No," he said. "I'm new too, I guess. I mean, I just moved into the neighborhood."

"Me, too," I said. "Welcome."

"Thanks!" he said, then blinked as he looked around the shop.

"Can I help you find anything, or do you just want to browse?" I asked.

"Just browse," he said, and flushed again. "I just like the smell of books, you know?"

"I *do*," I said.

"Yeah, I spent all my cash already," he said, adjusting the bag under his arm.

"No worries," I assured him. "Browse as much as you like. You can even sit down and read in one of the nooks if you want. My uncles own the shop, and I know they don't mind."

"Is that good for business?" he asked with a little hint of a grin.

"Encouraging the love of books is *very* good for business," I said, and felt myself grinning back at him, ridiculously huge. But it was nice, meeting a fellow book lover. "I'm Tabitha, by the way. In case you need anything."

"Liam," he said, and wiped his palm down the front of his jeans before offering it to me. If he had been sweaty at all, that little gesture had taken care of it. It was a warm, dry handshake.

"If you're browsing for smells, I would recommend the back of the shop. The older books are back there, and they just smell better than modern books, don't you think?"

I pointed straight back, to the false wall that was as far as the prosaics could go. But the books there were still a delight, old and obscure titles that genuinely smelled wonderful. Like they sparked memories of days that never were.

"I suppose," he said slowly.

Clearly, he needed more guidance. Which was my job now. "If you're browsing for something to read, I would need to know more about what you're interested in to direct you," I said.

He started to answer, but then stopped with a little laugh. Then he said, "sorry, it's just, that's the story of my life."

"Sorry?" I said.

"I have no direction and too many interests," he said. "I just graduated from college with a major in philosophy. Do you know how I picked that as a major?"

"How?" I gamely asked.

"I just took every class that seemed interesting to me, no real plan. And when they told me I absolutely had to declare a major, philosophy was the one I had the most credits in. So I became a philosophy major."

"And what do you do with a degree in philosophy?" I asked. That was a tricky question to get out. There were a lot of tones that would imply a lot of things, all far judgier than I wanted to come across as. It was hard to stick down the middle of *I'm just asking*. And not feeding him the prompt for the classic punchline about thinking deep thoughts about unemployment.

But I guess I hit it, because he didn't look offended or like he was bracing himself for all the usual jokes. He just laughed again and said, "I'm not currently employed. I just moved into a two-bedroom apartment I'll be sharing with five roommates."

"Ouch," I said.

"It's okay," he said. "The rooms are... small."

I wasn't sure how that was any kind of plus. Cost, maybe.

"Well, if you get along with your roommates, maybe it's not so bad?" I offered.

"Yeah, we'll see," he said. "Two of them I went to college with, but we weren't super close. The other three..? Well, it could be interesting. But it beats the alternative."

"Homeless shelter?" I said.

He laughed. "Okay, it beats two alternatives. Mainly, I was thinking that as long as I can stay in Minneapolis, no matter how bad the living situation here is, at least I don't have to go back to the tiny, tiny town I'm from. Back in my childhood bedroom. Which is now my mother's sewing room. A hobby I had no idea she had."

I heard footsteps approaching, my uncle Carlo returning from his trip up to the apartment. Liam heard him too and started to step away from me, gesturing towards the far end of the shop. "Old books are in the back? I think I'll check that out. See you."

"See you," I said.

He disappeared just before my uncle Carlo came down the staircase to the upper levels. He bent to catch a glimpse of Liam's sneakered feet, but didn't recognize the shoes.

"Was that a regular?" he asked me.

"Not yet," I said. "But maybe in the future."

"Drawing in new customers already," he said as he settled back into the chair before the computer. "I knew bringing you in was a good idea."

I liked the sound of that. It sounded more long-term than just watching the shop while they were away. And now that I had gotten a taste of life outside of school, I really wanted to stay where I was.

Five roommates in two bedrooms? Ugh. And I didn't see any way around it being five prosaic roommates. And a prosaic job. A whole prosaic life, something I wasn't remotely prepared for.

In that moment, nothing in the world felt safer than life in the Square.

But little did I know how quickly that feeling would be gone.

CHAPTER
SIX

In the end, Uncle Carlo got all the stuff Uncle Frank had set out inside those two suitcases.

I'm pretty sure that took a major expenditure of magic.

I walked with them down to the Square, through the maze of footpaths that ran through the gardens to the very heart of a hedge maze. Because the Square, like the bookshop, was very much bigger on the inside.

But the heart of the hedge maze was the home to the portal. It, like any other magical portal I had ever seen, spent most of its time just looking like an ordinary stone arch. In the magical schools, they were usually doorways that led to seldom-used rooms. But here, in the center of the Square, it looked like a decorative piece of garden arch, part of a folly that had gotten isolated on its own. It was sculpted to resemble two trees, one taller than the other, their branches drawn towards each other to tangle together in the middle.

Very powerful witches can take any portal to any other portal at any time, but most witches go with the scheduled flow of magic. In this case, the break of dawn was when this particular portal synced with another portal in a certain small town in Italy that was my uncles' first planned stop.

"Remember, you can call us whenever you need us," Uncle Carlo said.

"Some of the towns might not have good cell reception," Uncle Frank reminded him.

"You can call," Uncle Carlo assured me.

"Hopefully, I won't need to. You guys should enjoy every minute of your trip!" I said, hugging them both.

The stone arch that housed the portal started to glow. At first it only seemed to be reflecting the pale colors of the rising sun, but then the shimmer grew and filled the arched space. Carlo and Frank paused to give me one last wave. Then they stepped into the light and disappeared in a flash.

And I was left standing in the middle of the hedge maze, all alone.

I went back to the apartment, but it felt weird being there alone. I sat on their breakfast veranda and watched the sun finish rising over the eastern buildings of the Square. Then, when it was finally late enough, I went down to join Agatha for our tea and croissant breakfast.

Houdini was watching for me through the glass door. He was standing on his hind legs, one front paw bent across the white star of his chest. It was a weird posture for a dog, but he did it all the time. I could almost imagine him as a southern lady, clutching a lace hand-kerchief to his heaving bosom. It had that kind of air to it. Like, if he could talk, he'd be saying, "ah do declare!"

He hopped back as I opened the door, balancing briefly on his hind legs until he could brace himself against my shins, still with that one paw to his chest. I bent over and picked him up. Not only did he let me do this these days, he even squatted into a hovering sit so I could more easily scoop him up from the bottom of his spine rather than dangling him uncomfortably by his armpits.

He *hated* that.

But so long as I picked him up correctly and didn't attempt to touch the ears that stood straight up off his head like two radar dishes, he would allow me to carry him around.

I think he was starting to warm up to me.

"Good morning, Miss Tabitha," Agatha said. Her voice was warm and welcoming as always, but today that energy was slightly forced. And when she emerged from her office, her gait was slower and more shuffling than I had ever seen it before.

"Are you doing all right, Agatha?" I asked.

"Fine, fine," she said, waving her hand at me dismissively. "Just slept funny. I'll be fine enough once I get some tea in me."

I took the hint, and set Houdini down to wash my hands before touching anything behind the teashop counter. She might have lost her touch with brewing tea, but Agatha still kept a very clean kitchen.

Houdini started that low growl as I was spooning tea into the teapot, and I looked back over my shoulder to see Titus Bloom passing by the door again. He glanced into the teashop, then saw Agatha standing just inside the door, glaring at him. He looked taken aback, his steps stumbling ever so slightly. He raised a hand to wave at her, but she just scowled fiercely at him until he hurried away.

Only then did Houdini stop growling, all at once like someone lifting a needle off a record.

"Houdini really doesn't like that man," I noted as casually as I could.

"Houdini is a very smart dog," Agatha said, then shuffled back into the office to retrieve the bag of warm croissants she had left on her desk.

"Houdini doesn't like Miss Snooty Cat either," I said. "But you don't chase her away when she comes."

"Of course not," Agatha said, and just for a second, she treated me to the death glare she usually directed at Titus Bloom. I don't know how he could stand it. I felt like my whole body was about to burst into flames, and like if it did, it was no more than I deserved.

53

"I wasn't trying to be rude," I said quickly. "Barnardo seems like a lovely man."

"Miss Snooty Cat is all he has in the world," Agatha snapped at me. "Especially now that his father is gone. If he can't bear to part with her, who am I to say otherwise? This little troublemaker never leaves my side day or night, does he?"

Houdini gazed up at her adoringly. And he wasn't even begging for a piece of her croissant.

After breakfast, I went into the bookshop and unlocked the front door. My uncle Carlo had left everything in perfect order, so there wasn't a single thing for me to do. Not until a customer needed something.

Then I'd probably have to confront that computer. The one waiting for me on the corner of the desk, the bouncing ball of its screensaver taunting me.

No one came into the shop all morning. It was like all the regulars knew that Carlo and Frank were out, and would prefer to wait for their return for all their book buying needs. Of course, it was still only Monday. The weekend would surely be different.

I hoped. Otherwise, this was going to be a very long and dull two months.

I was just pondering my lunch options when I became aware of someone else inside the shop with me. The bell over the door had never chimed, so that meant someone had come in through the Square. There was a door that opened up onto the patio that circled the Square, but I had never noticed anyone use it. The witch shoppers just preferred to enter by their own means, teleporting or walking through walls or becoming a bright green mist that oozed through the gaps in the window panes. Whatever.

But they usually came straight to the front desk when they entered, and whoever was there now had yet to do so.

I hung the "Out to Lunch, back in 30" sign on the door to the prosaic world and locked it, then started up the central staircase. I could hear footsteps and books moving, but they were several floors above me, in the more magical sections of the shop.

For some reason, I didn't want to call out. I kept telling myself it was just another customer, nothing to be afraid of.

And yet every strand of my hair was standing on end, floating around my head in a staticky cloud.

Wait, that wasn't usually a warning of danger around me. Usually, that was a warning *I* was about to be the danger.

I touched my glasses, adjusting them needlessly. But for the first time, I found that gesture *did* bring with it a sense of calm. I could feel my hair laying back down again.

Nice.

"Is someone up here?" I finally called. I had reached the floor where I thought I had heard the noises, the second to the top. The top was mostly storage of old prosaic books, anyway; this level had to be where my magical shopper was lurking.

"Yeah, sorry. Didn't mean to frighten you," someone said. Young? No one I knew.

"Can I help you find something?" I asked as I passed row after row of bookshelves. Whoever he was, he sounded close. And yet every step I took, I still couldn't see him anywhere.

Then suddenly he spoke from directly behind me. "You don't seem to have what I'm looking for in the front. Did your uncles show you how to get to the back?"

The question was almost nonsense to me. The shop had no func-tional front or back above the first level. It barely had any sense of direction at all.

But whatever answer I had for him faded from my mind when I turned around to see a startlingly tall and thin young man with pale skin and a truly epic tangle of thick, dark hair. He was dressed all in black, perfectly conventional pants tucked into tall black boots and a tunic-y sort of shirt that was belted tightly at his waist. But over that ordinary outfit was a cloak that floated around him, like there was a wind machine somewhere that was holding it aloft. It shimmered, its pattern of jewel-toned colors swimming around in a way that just screamed magic.

It was a good thing no prosaics were in the store at the moment. I don't know how I would even explain him to them.

"No one's here," he said with a wry grin.

Great. A mind reader.

"No, just a good guesser," he said. "Anyway, I'm here at your lunchtime on purpose. And I know Carlo and Frank are out, but I'm sure you planned to eat at the same time because the customers know to expect it."

"You're pretty knowledgeable about the shop," I said.

"Thank you, Tabitha," he said. "I try to be *pretty knowledgeable* about lots of things."

"Right," I said. But then I couldn't put off asking any longer. "So, who are you?"

"Stephanos Underwood," he said.

I blinked at him.

"I work for the Wizard," he said. "I'm his apprentice."

I blinked again. Trust me, I had heard that capital letter on Wizard. I just didn't know what it meant.

"Your uncles didn't mention me?" He finally sounded a little less sure of himself, which was a relief.

"No. Sorry."

"My master sent me to retrieve a text," he said. "But you don't seem to have it here. As I mentioned previously. But perhaps it's in the back?"

"I really wouldn't know," I said.

"You don't know if it's there, or you don't know about the back of the store at all?" he asked. He wasn't quite taunting me, but the question was still rubbing me the wrong way.

"Well, obviously, it's the latter. If it was the former, I would just go check," I said.

He looked startled for a second, but then he laughed. "Fair enough. I can show you what I'm talking about, if it that helps."

"Carlo knows you and would approve of this?" I asked.

"Of course," he said. He reached into that robe and pulled out a wand of polished wood. Some very dark sort of wood, almost like ebony. Then he led me down a long row of books until it ended in a brick wall.

This was unusual for the bookshop. Everywhere else, the walls were lined with bookshelves or scroll racks or tables with maps or illustrations hanging over them. This was the first bare wall I'd seen in the entire shop.

Of course, I hadn't been everywhere yet. It was a very large shop.

"May I?" he asked, freezing in place with his wand at the ready.

"Feel free, Stephanos," I said.

"Just Steph is fine," he said, then aimed his wand at the wall.

It shimmered, then disappeared, and I could see another space on the other side. It was like a mirror image of the bookshop, the same arrangement of bookshelves behind me now appearing in front of me as well.

"It would be just inside, in the necromancy section," Steph said, as he put his wand away.

"Necromancy," I repeated suspiciously.

"It's just for research purposes," he said. "The Wizard just wants to check a footnote, really. A single note on a single page. He's read the book before, but he doesn't own copies of such texts. It would be dangerous to keep such things inside the Tower."

Again with that clearly heard capitalization.

"I suppose if my uncle keeps this book inside his shop, it can't be anything too evil," I said slowly. But I wasn't at all sure that was true. In fact, probably the opposite. My uncles were acquirers of things, all sorts of things. I wasn't sure if they drew lines anywhere, let alone where they would draw those lines. "Wait, why would it be dangerous to keep it in the Tower?" I asked.

"Because of the other things that dwell within the Tower," he said. Then he waved a hand as if to dismiss that entire thread of the conversation. "I mean, he does keep it in the back, where the casual customer would never come across it. But I hope the fact I knew how to get here demonstrates the level of trust your uncle puts in me. Even if he didn't tell you about me."

He sounded a little hurt when he uttered that last sentence, and he wouldn't quite meet my eyes.

"Do you shop here often?" I asked.

"I do," he said. "For my own studies as well as picking up things for my master."

"Must've just been an oversight, then," I said. "We only had a few days to go over everything."

"Of course," he said, but I could see he was getting impatient. He gestured towards a shelf nearby. "Do you mind if I look?"

"Go ahead," I said.

He swept over to the shelf of books, the cloak gliding along with him. That sounds weird, and it's hard to explain how it looked. But it was less something he was wearing and more something that was a textile companion to him. It went with him, but only because it *chose* to.

He scanned the spines of the books on the shelves from top to bottom, then circled around to do the same thing on the opposite side. He glanced at the other shelves nearby, but quickly dismissed them.

"It doesn't seem like you have it," he said.

"I can put an order in," I said. That, at least, had been covered in my training. "There's a nexus of magical bookshops that my uncles are part of. Anyone that has a copy, they'll let us know."

"Perfect," Steph said, and the two of us went back down to the front desk. Luckily, being a magical tome we were looking for, I didn't have to touch the computer. I didn't need to try to use my nonexistent magic, either. The spells were built into the enormous book that was used for this purpose. I had to use a quill and a bottle of ink, which was messy, but once I had written out the request on the page, it would appear in similar books in shops all over the world.

"If anyone has it, I'll know by tomorrow lunchtime," I told him.

He had gone behind the counter with me and was leaning over my shoulder, watching me scrawl and dribble ink all over the page. As a customer, he shouldn't really be back there, but I had no desire to chase him away.

That cloak of his kept fluttering around me, like it wanted to pull me inside the same protective bubble that Steph was in. It felt warm, being inside the folds of that cloak. The smell was intoxicating, kind of spicy. Or maybe that was coming from Steph?

But the taste in my mouth like butterscotch on my tongue? No way was that coming from Steph.

Then he was touching my hair, which was totally unacceptable. I slapped his hand away by reflex, then stepped back out of his reach. I could feel my hair reacting, rising up in a super-charged cloud.

I touched my glasses, but that only brought the charge down halfway.

"Sorry," he said. "Just curious. But you're not the problem."

I was still annoyed, but now I was also confused. "What is *that* supposed to mean?" I asked.

"Nothing," he said with another dismissive wave. "Wizard business. Forget it." Then he took a deep breath and summoned up a little smile. "So, tomorrow at lunchtime, got it. Thanks. But I've taken up your whole lunchtime today, I fear. I'm sorry about that. I'll bring you something tomorrow to make up for it?"

"No need," I assured him, but I could see his mind was made up.

"Picnic lunch. Tomorrow. Book or no book. It's a plan."

Then he was gone. Before I could even object to plans being made without really ever asking me. But I didn't mind. It was a small overstep, and after half a day of just waiting for something to do, having plans for the next day sounded really nice.

Provided he didn't try to touch my hair again. Aside from mere personal boundaries, that kind of thing could be downright dangerous.

But he had smelled so good.

I was still thinking about it that night as I crawled into bed. My sleepy brain was trying to figure out what had been Steph and what had been his magical cloak, and if there was a polite way to ask him to leave the cloak behind when he came for lunch, just so I could tell.

But it felt like I had just fallen asleep when I was jerked rudely awake, heart pounding at the sound of a dog barking.

I knew that bark. I had heard it many times, even at its shrillest.

But I had never heard it so distraught before.

I threw back the covers and ran outside to see what was going on.

CHAPTER

SEVEN

I could see nothing from the little porch outside my window, so I ran down the stairs and out onto my uncles' breakfast veranda. But then I headed for the railing to the left first rather than the down the staircase on the right. That was the direction I had heard the barking coming from.

I knew Agatha's apartment was on that side of the Square, on the third floor. I had never been inside, but she had mentioned once that hers was one of the apartments with a higher level. That higher level had a veranda more the size of the one off my bedroom than the one I was currently standing on, but apparently Houdini loved to sun himself out there when the weather was warm. At least, according to Agatha, he did.

I was pretty sure that was where the barking was coming from now, that veranda. And it was continuing, on and on, but gaining more of a howling quality to it as it went unanswered.

"Houdini! I'm coming!" I called down to him. There were street-lights all around the Square, old-fashioned gaslights that did nothing to illuminate anything as high up as we were. I thought I saw a gleam, like the moonlight reflecting off the moisture in his eyes as he looked up at me. But I couldn't make out exactly where Agatha's little porch was, let alone the outline of a miniature black-haired dog in all that darkness.

I wished there was a faster way, but the best I could do was to pick my way down that narrow staircase, then run around the other three sides of the Square before I reached Agatha's front door.

Some of the other neighbors were also outside in pajamas or robes, murmuring sleepily together. Houdini's barking above us was sporadic now, but no less distraught.

"Did you knock?" I asked the people gathered there. Even on the third floor, we were too far up for the lights to reach us through the fleur-de-lis patterns of the cast-iron railings.

"Yes, but—" someone started to say, but then another voice below us cried out in surprise and alarm. I rushed to the railing, grasping it tightly as I looked down.

There, below us, right in the middle of the glow from the nearest streetlight, was the sprawled form of a body. It was lying face-down, but I recognized Agatha's gray hair.

It was quickly darkening, that hair, as the puddle of blood below it spread.

There were two people standing over her on the patio now, the woman who had cried out and a man who was holding her tightly as she sobbed.

"Is she—" I tried to call down, but the words failed me.

"She's dead," a man said. Then he looked up, his face full in the light, and I recognized Titus Bloom. "How did she fall? And at this hour?"

But no one had answers to his questions.

I left Agatha's doorway, my sneakered feet pounding along the veranda, then clanging down a cast-iron staircase. Then the same thing again until I was on the ground level and could finally reach Agatha's side.

More neighbors were gathered now, but they huddled close to each other, not getting close enough to the body to even be in the light. I fell on my knees beside her and was just reaching out to try turning her over, when a voice behind me said firmly, "No. That is my duty."

The others around me were murmuring again, but they were also pulling away. I looked back over my shoulder to see a positively ancient woman in a long flowing nightgown coming towards me. She held a lantern in her hand, the kind that hangs from a chain. The kind made of such solid metal with such pointy decorative touches it looked like it could easily double as a weapon.

But the light within that lantern wasn't firelight or gaslight. It was greenish, but a warm, comforting shade of green I had never seen before in my life. It felt like a living thing, that light.

Yet its glow on this woman's face did nothing to make her look any less skeletal. Her long white hair didn't look very firmly attached to her skull, like a stiff breeze would be enough to render her totally bald. And her eyes were too blue to be real. Not that I suspected colored contacts or anything. It was clearly a result of some very old magic. But that shade of blue was the opposite of the green light from her lantern.

It was not comforting at all, especially when those eyes focused on me.

I scrambled back from the body, stumbling in my attempt to get up. I ended up sprawled on my butt on the grass at the edge of the garden. But at least I was out of that strange woman's way.

"Let me help you," a man said. It was only when he had me back on my feet again that I realized it was Titus Bloom. In fact, we were standing right outside his coffeeshop, the Bitter Brew. "Volumnia can take it from here. You can rest your mind."

I guessed Volumnia was the old woman. She was standing straight-legged but bending deeply at the waist until her face was a hair's breadth away from the back of Agatha's head. Her lantern swung close by, but she didn't look like she was trying to see anything.

I was pretty sure she was smelling Agatha. Smelling that coppery pool of blood.

I felt like I was going to be sick.

"Titus, love, she needs to sit down. Open up the shop for her," said the woman standing beside him. They were wearing matching bathrobes and slippers of a khaki color, belted close around them. She looked to be on the heavy side, but no one looks good in a bathrobe, really. Her hair was blonde, but had the coarse look of chemically-treated hair and was standing up in the back in a crusty sort of bedhead.

"Right, right," Titus said quickly, as if he had forgotten himself. They both took me by the arms and guided me into the dark interior of the coffee shop, then helped me into a surprisingly comfortable padded chair. It was close enough to the window that I could still see Volumnia examining Agatha.

"Do you want a glass of water? Or something stronger?" the woman asked me.

"No, I'm okay," I said, although I was pretty sure that wasn't true.

"They were close," Titus whispered to her, not particularly softly.

"I'm so sorry, dear," the woman said, giving my shoulder a comforting squeeze. "We haven't met yet, although I know who you are, of course. Tabitha Greene. I'm Nell Bloom. Titus and I run this establishment. Well, you know Titus."

"We've never actually met," I said, looking up at Titus, who flushed in apparent embarrassment.

"No, although we've nearly done so more than once," he said. Then he gave his wife a hurried glance. "The dog."

"Oh, yes," she said, as if that answered all her questions.

But I had questions too.

"Who would do this?" I asked, gesturing out the window to where Volumnia was speaking to two of the younger men lingering outside, directing them in moving the body, I assumed.

"Do what? This was an accident, wasn't it?" Nell asked, looking to her husband for confirmation.

"It must have been, although at this hour, I can't imagine what Agatha would've been up to," he said, glancing up at the ceiling as if he could see through everything to the veranda above. Her personal veranda, as tiny as mine. How easy would it be for someone to accidentally fall off of one of those?

Not very, I decided. The railings on mine were sturdy and high. I couldn't imagine even tripping on the windowsill stepping outside would be enough for me to fall over it. And I was far clumsier than most.

But Titus wasn't wrong. I couldn't think of a single good reason why she would be out there at this hour.

"If there is any sign of foul play, Volumnia should find it out handily enough," Titus said.

"Do you think so?" Nell asked nervously.

"She's very good at what she does," he told her.

"What does she do? Specifically?" I asked.

"She performs our death rites," Nell said. "Whatever anyone wants done with their remains, be it burial or cremation or more esoteric preferences, she is ordained to do them all. And she's been here in the Square longer than any of us."

"Well," Titus said, but trailed off, as if he didn't want to contradict his wife in front of me.

"Maybe not the Wizard," Nell allowed, and Titus nodded. Apparently, that was what he had been thinking. But something in his eyes told me it wasn't all he had been thinking.

"But she also autopsies the body? You said she'd look for foul play," I said.

"If the authorities request her to," Titus said. "They would need reason to do so, but I'm sure they'll be here soon enough to examine her apartment and veranda for clues."

"What about Houdini?" I asked, suddenly realizing that at some point, the barking had stopped. I could still hear people speaking lowly together outside through the glass doors of the coffeeshop, but no hint of the dog.

"You think the dog did it?" Titus asked. I couldn't tell if he was joking or not. Then he gave me a puzzled look, like *he* couldn't tell if *I* was being serious or not.

"Is Houdini okay?" I clarified.

"Oh, I'm sure he's fine," Titus said. "He's quiet now, for once. He must be fine."

"But what will happen to him?"

"That will be up to Agatha's niece, I suppose," he said.

"Someone should call her," Nell said.

"I will do it," Titus said. Then he yawned. "In the morning."

"Agatha never mentioned having a niece to me," I said. "She mentioned her sister once or twice, but I gather she died some years ago."

"Audrey is technically her grandniece," Nell told me. "We met her once, years ago. Titus, do you remember?"

"Hm. I believe so," he said. But something in his tone was heavily implying the opposite.

"She was just ten at the time. Shy little blonde girl, always sniffling from something, didn't speak to anybody," Nell said.

"Oh. Yes," Titus said, nodding.

I was pretty sure he had no memory of this girl at all. But Nell seemed satisfied by his answer.

"Will this grandniece inherit the teashop as well?" I asked.

I only meant it as a casual question. Honestly, I'm not even sure why I asked it. It was almost inappropriate, to wonder about that when Agatha was still lying on the patio tiles not ten feet away.

But the minute the words were out of my mouth, both of the Blooms took several steps away from each other. He stayed close to me but seemed to be preoccupied with something in the pocket of his robe. She went over to the counter to fidget with something close to the register.

They were very carefully not looking at each other.

But one of them had to answer me. It was getting too awkward for them, that question hanging in the air over all of us.

"I'm sure that must be the case," Titus finally said, then cleared his throat nervously. "Yes, I'm sure that's what will happen. But we'll know more in the morning."

I watched as the two young men Volumnia had been speaking to finally lifted Agatha's body up on a stretcher. A long sheet was draped over her, bits of it clinging in dark patches where the blood was thickest. I wanted to look away, but the green glow from that lantern caught my eye again, and the comfort it leant me was rather overwhelming.

I mean, my only friend had just died. I didn't want to be okay with it yet. Not this soon.

But that lantern's light was like all the hugs I had missed out on as a lonely kid, all at once. I could feel tears building in the back of my throat. Not exactly happy tears, but tears of relief all the same.

Then Volumnia turned her head and locked her gaze on mine. And those cold blue eyes brought all the bad feelings back in an instant.

She turned away from me again and led the men with the stretcher into the gardens, and the light from her lantern was soon gone amongst the dense foliage.

"I'm going to check on Houdini," I said, and got up from the chair. "Thank you for everything. And let me know when you hear anything."

"Of course, my dear," Nell said, and gave me a quick hug.

"Take care, Tabitha," Titus said, showing me out the door. I heard the lock turn behind me. Then he and his wife were speaking together, but too low for me to catch any words.

I headed up the stairs, back to Agatha's front door. There was no one there now, but the door was standing open, so I guessed someone had gotten inside.

The interior was dark, and there was no sound of anyone inside at the moment.

"Houdini?" I called, but there was no response. I called twice more, then decided whoever had opened the door must've taken the dog home until Agatha's grandniece could pick him up.

I closed the door behind me then headed back to my own room, but it took me a very long time to find sleep again.

CHAPTER
EIGHT

The next morning was pretty awful. No tea and croissants with Agatha. No uncles in the bookshop to talk with. That bigger on the inside space really felt too big for just me that morning. It made me feel absolutely tiny inside all of it.

It was nearly ten when the bell over the front door chimed and I saw Liam coming in. He had been in a few times over the last few weeks, although he had yet to make an actual purchase. But we would chat about books as long as I had time around the bookshop's sparse customers. So far as I knew, he was still unemployed. Every time I brought it up, he would shake his head then bring up a book-related topic again.

Today he was dressed much the same as every other time I'd seen him, not quite nice enough to be coming from a successful job inter-view. He smiled when he saw me, but something must have shown on my face because that smile froze, then fell away almost at once.

"What's happened?" he asked.

My initial impulse was to insist nothing was wrong, but when I opened my mouth, the words that came out were, "Someone died. A friend."

"Oh. I'm so sorry," he said. "How did they die?"

"I don't know yet," I said. "She might have fallen from her veranda. That's what it looks like."

"That's terrible!" he gasped. Then he studied the expression on my face. "But you don't think she fell?" he guessed.

"My gut says that's not right," I said.

"And you always trust your gut?" he asked. He sounded like he assumed the answer was yes, that he was already prepared to agree that my gut was probably right.

But the thing was, I had never trusted my gut before. Not even once.

"Usually, when everyone says one thing, and I'm feeling something else, I'm the one who's wrong," I admitted.

"Like what? Give me a 'for instance'," he said.

And I realized I couldn't. Not without explaining about magic, and how I couldn't do it even though I was, technically, a witch.

"I don't know," I said with a shrug, and really hoped he would drop it.

"Well, I'm sorry to hear about your friend. Are you doing okay? Do you need anything?" he asked.

"Like what?" I asked, honestly confused. What would I need? For that matter, what could he give me?

"Like food, maybe?" he said. "It's traditional. Well, I mean, it is where I come from," he amended, that peaches and cream flush back to his cheeks. "Back home, when someone is sick or grieving, my mom sends them a casserole."

"You're offering me a casserole?" I asked.

"Or maybe just lunch?" he said with a nervous grin.

I was *this close* to saying yes.

Then I remembered someone was already bringing me a lunch.

"Oh," I said. "Well, I'm here all day. I'm the only one working."

"I could bring you something," he said. Then he quickly added, "nothing fancy. But you like ramen, right?"

"I *do*," I admitted, but I couldn't help the fact that my face was actually wincing. That was how badly I didn't want to tell him the truth. I wasn't even sure how I would explain what lunch with Steph actually *was*. It didn't feel like a date.

Wait, was it a *date*?

Liam was still waiting for an answer. "Just not today?" I finished lamely.

"Oh, right," he said in a rush. He waved his hands around like he could dispel the awkwardness between us so easily.

"I appreciate the offer, though," I said. "It's sort of a customer thing, but I did promise."

"Sure. No problem," he said. But he was backing away from me, heading for the door.

"Wait! Didn't you come in for something?" I asked.

"No. Well, I did, but I just remembered... something," he said. "I've got to go. But I'll see you soon."

"Definitely!" I said, but he was already gone.

I dropped my head down on the counter and just moaned. I could've handled that better, I was sure.

"Um? Excuse me?" a voice called out to me. Female. Young. Not familiar.

I hadn't heard the bell chime again, but it was possible someone had slipped in while Liam was running away. I lifted my head to see a young woman standing in front of the counter, looking up at me on my elevated platform.

Her skirt and sweater and sensible flats looked more librarian-like than the jeans and hoodie I was wearing. She was even wearing thick knit tights, like she was already prepared for the cold air that always lingered in the back of the stacks. Her long blonde hair hung loose to her waist, almost perfectly straight, but she lacked the head-band that would conjure the total Alice in Wonderland image. Instead, she had blunt cut bangs that ended just above her eyebrows.

She had a bag over one shoulder. It looked like a stuffed-full overnight bag. But I was clearly making her nervous, staring at her for so long without saying a word, because the two hands that were grasping the straps of that bag at her shoulder were twisting and twisting.

She was dressed like a prosaic, if not a typical one. And yet something about her was telling me she wasn't. I studied her again, but could find no clues to back up that feeling.

But just staring at her was making her more nervous by the minute, to judge from the way she was twisting those straps.

"Sorry," I said. "Can I help you with something? I didn't hear you come in. Are you from the Square? I'm new, so I don't recognize everyone yet. But you have a bag, maybe you just got here. Sorry," I said again, aware that I was just barraging her with words, not putting her at ease at all. "Are you looking for a book?"

"I'm Audrey," she said, as if that should mean something to me.

"Tabitha," I told her.

"Audrey *Mirken*," she said with anxious emphasis.

Then I finally got it. "Agatha's grandniece?"

"Yes!" she said, relieved. Although she was still twisting those bag straps in her hands. "Agatha told me if anything happened to her, I should speak to you first."

"Agatha said what?" I gasped. I felt like I needed to sit down, but when I grasped the edge of the counter to grope beneath it, I realized I was already perched on the high stool.

"She trusted you," Audrey said.

I didn't know how to answer that. If I had so much of Agatha's trust, why hadn't she trusted me to tell *me* so?

"Am I the executor of her will or something?" I asked, still confused.

"No. Well, maybe. I don't know," Audrey said, all in a rush.

"Who does know?" I asked.

"The authorities, I'm sure. But I really wanted to see her apartment first. Will you come with me? I don't want to go in there alone. Not the first time," she said.

She sounded perfectly miserable. Which made total sense. I had lost a friend I had only had for a few days. But Audrey had lost a grandaunt she had known her whole life. One who had apparently been in close contact with her if she already knew about me.

"Of course," I said, sliding down off the stool. "I just have to lock up."

"Oh! I'm sorry! Of course you should stay open," Audrey said. "I didn't mean to interrupt."

"Don't be silly," I said, walking past her to turn the key in the lock of the front door. "I didn't have any customers at all yesterday, so I'm sure it will be fine."

"There was someone just leaving when I came in," Audrey said with a frown.

"He wasn't really a customer. At least, I don't think so," I said. "Look, this is important. People will understand and come back later. Don't worry about it. Although I have to warn you, I don't know who has Houdini."

"Houdini?" Audrey repeated, as if the name meant nothing to her.

"Agatha's dog?" I prompted.

But her frown just deepened. "Agatha had a dog?" She sounded deeply skeptical. But also anxious.

"Agatha told you about me, but not about Houdini?" I asked. That made no sense to me at all. She only pretended she didn't care for the little guy, I was sure of that.

"I guess so," Audrey said. But she was looking more stressed than ever now.

"What is it?" I asked.

"It's just, I can't take care of a dog. I really can't," she said.

"Let's just deal with one thing at a time," I said, putting a hand on her arm to guide her out the back door. "The apartment first, right?"

"Right," she said. She didn't sound confident at first, but then she hoisted that over-stuffed bag higher on her shoulder and gripped it tight in both hands. Both nontwisting hands.

She didn't seem to know the way, so I took the lead up to the third floor, to where Agatha's door stood open once more. Why did that keep happening? But it was nearly midday now, and the interior was not the murky darkness of the night before.

I let Audrey step in first. She stopped in the middle of the sitting room, looking around at the neat bookshelves, the array of framed photographs on the mantlepiece over the fireplace, and at the old but well-maintained mid-century style furniture. Then she put her bag on one of the chairs and headed to the far side of the room, towards the kitchen.

"Did Agatha tell you about the troubles she was having with the tea?" I asked as Audrey looked at all the kitchenware arranged on the cabinets without touching anything.

"No," Audrey said. "You mean business has been bad?"

"There weren't many customers," I said. I was pretty sure that total number was two: Barnardo and I. No one could maintain a business at that level. Not in a big city for sure, and probably not in a small town either.

"She didn't mention it," Audrey said. Then she headed towards the stairs. I followed her up a steep, narrow staircase much like the one that led to my own attic room. Then we were in a bedroom. The bed was in disarray, as if someone had thrown back the covers in a great hurry then never returned.

A pair of slippers were neatly arranged in the perfect spot to be slipped into when getting out of bed, and a loose robe that had been draped over the foot of the bed was now tangled up in the bedding. There was even a glass of water still waiting on the nightstand, untouched. The whole scene just made the absence of Agatha, who should be in the center of everything, feel that much more acute.

Audrey sneezed three times in succession, powerful sneezes that seemed to hit her out of nowhere. I looked around and saw a box of tissues on the dresser across from the foot of the bed. I held them out for her, and she grabbed several with a muffled word of thanks.

She blew her nose, then nodded her head towards the window at the far corner of the room. "Is that the veranda?" she asked.

"I think so," I said, and we walked over to it. The windows were standing wide open, the curtains blowing ever so slightly in the breeze.

Everything outside that window was a total mess. Apparently, Agatha had used the sunny location to grow a variety of herbs and flowers. From the stems, leaves and blooms I could see, they looked like they had thrived improbably well. It was only June, after all, and in a fairly northern climate.

But the stems, leaves and blooms were all smashed now, mixed in with shards of pottery and piles of drying soil.

"Why would she have gone out there?" I wondered. "Look at all these pots. There wouldn't have been any room for her to stand out there, or even step out the window."

"How—" Audrey started to ask, but then another succession of sneezes seized her, more powerful than before. She staggered back from the window, holding the tissues at the ready for whenever the fit left her.

But it just kept going.

"Are you allergic to anything?" I asked, looking out the window at the remains of the plants. I had done really well in botany. I mean, my potions had never done a thing they were supposed to, but I could identify hundreds of plants by sight. I didn't see anything particularly toxic, but allergies were another matter.

But Audrey was shaking her head. She clearly wanted to say something, but the sneezes wouldn't stop long enough for her to take a breath, let alone get a word out.

"Maybe we should get you back downstairs," I said. I closed the windows in case that helped, but her sneezes only seemed to get stronger.

"There must be—" she tried to get out between sneezes. Then she tried again. "There must be—"

But whatever she was thinking, she couldn't tell me.

Then I heard something, something like the skitter of dog nails on a hardwood floor.

I looked at Audrey, and I saw she had heard it too. But the sound seemed to strike terror in her heart. She backed up quickly towards the top of the stairs even as I dropped to the floor and lifted the skirt to peer under the bed.

"Houdini!" I said. I couldn't see him clearly, a black dog in the shadows. But I could see a smear of white, the star on his chest. Then, nonsensically, I found myself telling him, "I'm sorry, little guy. I thought you were at the neighbors."

"As if I could trust the neighbors. You and I both know this was a murder," said a churlish voice in my head.

Then he came out from under the bed. While I was still struggling with the fact that I—who had no magic—had just heard a dog speak, he marched purposefully out of the room. Audrey yelped and pressed herself back against the wall as he passed her then headed down the stairs.

Audrey gaped at me. "I just heard that dog talk. No, no, no, no, no. I just heard that dog talk."

Then she was sneezing again, over and over. But some of the tears in her eyes had nothing to do with her allergies.

Generally speaking, the only animals that witches can talk to are their own familiars. And as much as she couldn't stop sneezing long enough to explain it to me, I knew why Audrey was upset.

Firstly, because clearly it was Houdini—or rather Houdini's dander—that was making her sneeze so violently.

And secondly, she assumed that she had heard Houdini speak because she had just inherited the familiar she had never even known her grandaunt had ever had.

Only, I had heard him, too. Which didn't track at all.

Witches didn't share familiars. Not even if Agatha had somehow tried to specify such a thing in her will. It was just impossible.

And in all the reading I had ever done, there was no other case where witches spoke with animals. Not prosaic animals, anyway. Magical creatures are a whole other thing.

But Houdini was just a normal rat terrier-chihuahua mix. A runty little mutt, perfectly ordinary.

Wasn't he?

"Something weird is going on here," I said.

Audrey wanted to agree. But she couldn't. Not at the moment.

I handed her the rest of the box of tissues, then headed downstairs to see where the dog had gone.

It was a good thing he could talk, because he had a lot of explaining to do.

CHAPTER
NINE

I expected to find Houdini downstairs in Agatha's sitting room or otherwise her kitchen, but there was no sign of him in either place. I poked my head out the open front door and just caught a glimpse of the tail that corkscrewed in an arch over his hindquarters before he disappeared around the corner of the exterior corridor, towards the stairs down to the lower level.

"Where's he going?" Audrey asked as she appeared at my elbow. She looked miserable, her nose red and swollen and even her cheeks flushed to a rosy pink.

I stepped closer to the iron railing and looked down. I could see him as he appeared at the bottom of the stairs. He wasn't coming towards us or towards the stain on the patio tiles below where Agatha had lain the night before. But he was certainly heading somewhere with deliberation, his pace never faltering.

"I think he's heading to the teashop," I said. "But listen, Agatha was very clear that he wasn't her familiar. And I can hear him too. So whatever is going on, it's happening to both of us."

"I guess that's a relief. But also a mystery. Like, why would he be going to the teashop?" Audrey asked.

"I'm not sure what he's thinking, but I think we should go there too," I said. "Agatha had a lot of ingredients for medicinal teas. There might be something in her cupboards that will help you."

"Getting out of this apartment will certainly help," she said, pulling the door shut behind her. "There's dog hair everywhere in there."

"The teashop might not be much better," I said even as I led her in that direction.

"No, you're right. But she'll have the ingredients for the tea she sends me when my hay fever gets really bad," she said. "The recipe will even be in her big book."

"You've been here before?" I said. "I mean, some of the neighbors remember you from when you were young."

"I was here just one time, and not for very long," she admitted. "But my grandaunt and I were close all the same. She sent me more care packages when I was at school than even my own mother. And we still chat through our matching scrying glasses almost every night. Or, we *did*, I mean."

"And she never mentioned that her dog could talk?" I asked.

"Not even once," Audrey said. She was starting to breathe more clearly now that we were outside, and the nasal quality of her voice was shifting back to her normal, clear tones. But then she gave me a sharp look. "Wait, you can hear him too?"

"Yeah," I said. "So he's not bonded to you as a familiar. Although what's going on with him really, I can't even guess."

I itched to research it, but that would have to wait.

"Thank goodness," Audrey said with palpable relief. "I don't know why Agatha would bond a familiar with me when she knows I'm allergic to dogs, especially one she never bothered to tell me about. But in the last few months, she seemed like she was dodging all sorts of topics. She always wanted just to talk about me. I didn't think it was weird at the time. I just graduated from school and didn't really have a plan for what was going to come next, so we talked about that a lot."

"I'm in the same boat myself," I admitted. "I'm here for the summer to watch the bookshop while my uncles are traveling, but after that I'll be adrift again. No real skills. What branch of magic were you studying?"

"Oh," Audrey said, then gave an uncomfortable laugh. "Well, I never tested very well with any branch of magic. When the stakes are down, I just can't do it. Any of it."

"Really?" I said. She shot me a nervous look, and I was quick to add, "I thought I was the only one."

"You were in the same boat with me? What school were you at? I was in the Hidden Hills Academy in Mankato."

"That's in Minnesota?" I guessed, and she nodded. "I went to lots of schools, actually. Never that one, though. Technically, I graduated from the Sectum Apulum in Transylvania. Well, it's Romania now, but the faculty still considers the university to be in Transylvania. Witch communities in Europe are different than they are here."

"I know. Well, a little. I spent a semester in Paris when I was fifteen," she said. "The school I was at had been founded shortly before the French Revolution. I think the teachers had been around since then. The uniforms certainly had been."

"Exactly!" I said with a laugh.

"But what branch of magic did you spend your last two years studying? Everyone has to pick something," she said knowledgeably.

"I got a special dispensation," I admitted.

"To not study?" she asked with a frown.

I felt my cheeks heating even before I got the words out. "I got special dispensation to audit classes from all the branches. Only the history and theory classes, though. I didn't take any practical labs."

Audrey gaped at me, then shook her head in amazement. "Well, I'm glad I didn't know that was an option. It sounds like the exact opposite of what I would've wanted to do."

"I like research," I admitted. "In a real, practical sense, though, I have no magic at all."

"None?"

"Not a bit," I said. To my surprise, it no longer hurt to say so out loud. It simply no longer mattered. And Audrey fell right into the pattern of everyone else I had met in the Square. My lack of magic in no way changed how she was looking at me. "But what about you?" I pressed. "You had to study something."

She chuckled that nervous laugh again, but in the minute that had passed since the last time I had asked this question, she had gotten far more comfortable with me. Still, there was a flush of embarrassment to her cheeks when she confessed, "I majored in ritual magic."

"Ritual magic?" I repeated. "You just said you hated research."

"I know!" she laughed. "I just thought, if I was memorizing every motion and every word and all that, there would be no room for me to mess anything up."

"And how did that work out for you?" I asked, suspecting the answer.

"I graduated," she said with a shrug. "And I'll never do it again."

"It's possible you have a talent that you just haven't discovered yet," I said.

"Anything's possible," she said, but not in a way that sounded like she believed it.

The door to the teashop was unlocked, but of course that did Houdini little good. He was waiting for us, not very patiently.

"Why are we here?" I asked him as I pulled the door open.

"There must be clues here," he said just before slipping his body between the door and the doorframe the instant it was opened to the narrowest of cracks.

"Why would there be clues here?" I asked him.

"Because there weren't any in the apartment. Believe me, I looked," he said. Then he disappeared behind the counter.

I glanced over at Audrey, who was sniffling a little. Then I swung both the doors open wide, sliding down the stops that would hold them open. Hopefully, a breeze would help with the dander.

"The book is in her office," Audrey told me as she dug into her pocket for tissues. "I think I should start with that."

"Right," I said, and lifted the door in the counter open.

Houdini was already in the office, sniffing around the corners of the room.

"So you didn't see anything when it happened? Because you sure were barking a lot," I said as I looked around for the recipe book.

It wasn't hard to find. It was sitting on a wood fixture that held it up and open at an angle that made for easy reading. It was also, unquestionably, a big book. The bookshop had an unabridged dictionary that might be larger, but I'd have to put them side by side to be sure.

I picked up the book and holder both and carried them back out to the teashop. Audrey was already opening all the tea cupboards and scanning the contents. She was also sniffling more violently than before.

"Here's the book," I told her, and set it on the counter. Then I went back to the office doorway to look at Houdini again. "Maybe you should stay in here until we have this allergy situation under control."

"If you insist," he said even as he sniffed around the baseboards. But then all of a sudden he threw himself down on his little dog bed and gave me a deeply pathetic look.

"What's up?" I asked him.

"I can't smell anything useful," he said.

It was at this point I realized he never used his mouth when he spoke. I just heard this deep, sonorous voice that sounded like it was coming from his direction. But lying there like he was, with his head buried in the tattered pillow that was jammed in one corner of his bed, it was clear he wasn't moving his jaw or anything like that.

"Did you expect to?" I asked him.

"Well, yes," he said.

"*Did* you see anything?" I asked him again.

He sighed. That made his head move a little, but the eyes were as sorrowful as before. That, and the ears that usually stood straight up were just hanging behind his head. It was a deeply pathetic look. "I didn't see what happened. I only heard her fall. The sound that woke me... I'll never forget it."

"I'm sorry, Houdini," I said, sitting on the floor beside the bed so I could put a gentle hand on his back. I knew he didn't want me trying to touch his ears, but he tolerated me stroking down the length of his spine.

His tail, too, was dangling limply. Gone was the tight coil of perpetual excitement I was used to seeing.

"I failed my human," he mourned.

"I very much doubt that Agatha would see it that way," I said, still petting him in long, slow strokes. "Are you sure it wasn't an accident? I mean, if you were sleeping when it happened, how can you be sure?"

"She was out on the veranda when she fell. Without her robe, and without her slippers. None of those things makes sense," he grumbled. "She was always cold. Always. She would never get up without covering up first. She just wouldn't. And going out on the veranda? She never did such a thing. Ever."

I tried to think of a diplomatic way to point out he had only known her a little while, only five months or so longer than I had, but decided to just drop it.

I heard the whistle of the kettle, and then the gurgle of hot water being poured into a teapot. Soon a sharp, minty smell assaulted my nose. Just the smell was clearing my sinuses, and I hadn't even realized I had been even the tiniest bit congested.

"That's done it, I think," Audrey said as she came to stand in the doorway. She had a steaming mug in her hands and a bright smile on her face. Her face, which was no longer pink or red or swollen.

"Ooh, you've done very well," Houdini lifted his head to tell her. "Agatha tried, but she could never get it so... right-smelling as this."

"Agatha was having trouble with her magical teas lately, wasn't she?" Audrey asked him.

"Only recently, from what I've gathered," I said.

"For as long as I've known her," Houdini insisted.

"About six months," I said to Audrey.

"She was cursed!" Houdini said dramatically. "But she never knew by who."

"Did she suspect anyone?" Audrey asked.

"She always had excuses, why anyone I said was behind it had to be perfectly innocent," he said huffily. "She trusted everyone in the Square. She didn't like a lot of them, but she trusted them. She even trusted the people who came in the other door, and they *all* smelled wrong. She never trusted my instincts."

"What did your instincts tell you?" I asked. But I knew before he spoke which name he was bound to say.

"Titus Bloom," he said, his voice even lower than before. Low and dark.

"Who's Titus Bloom?" Audrey asked. She had already drunk half her tea and was now inside the office itself, sneeze-free as she looked at the papers on her grandaunt's desk.

"He owns the coffeeshop on the other end of the Square," I said. "He was the one who said he was going to call you."

"Oh, yes. That's why that sounded familiar," she said, but her tone wandered as she grew distracted by something she was looking at. A slender book, but not a magical one, by my guess. It looked like a standard accounting book with all the columns preprinted on the pages to be filled in by the business owner. The sort of thing that was quite a bit more common before the advent of computers.

"What is it?" I asked, getting up from the floor. Houdini made a complaining sound that the pets had stopped, but the puzzled look on Audrey's face drew me closer so I could see what she was looking at.

"I think it's a list of some kind, but nothing makes sense," she said, showing me the page near the back of the book. "I don't recognize the language, but maybe you do, Research Girl?"

"It looks like a code," I said. The blocky letters were in all caps, but also sized so that even a capital I took up as much space as a capital M. "Some kind of cypher?" I guessed. "There might be a key somewhere else in this office."

"Do you know anything about it, Houdini?" Audrey asked the dog.

He only made a low, growly sound that we both took to be negatory.

"The rest of this book just looks like a normal, run-of-the-mill accounting ledger," Audrey said as she flipped through the pages. Then she looked up at me with sadness in her eyes. "The business wasn't going at all well."

"I'm sure you could turn it around," I told her. "I mean, if you wanted to. It's all yours now."

"A teashop," Audrey said. "Not what I was thinking for my future, but then it wasn't *not* what I was thinking." She sighed.

"I'm sure you don't have to make any decisions right away," I said.

"What *do* I have to do right away?" she wondered aloud.

I wasn't sure if she was talking to me, Houdini, or herself. But no one else was answering, so I said, "I suppose you should see the authorities, in case they have any information for you."

"What if I wanted to see Agatha?" she asked almost shyly.

"I think I know where she is," I said, although the thought sent a shiver down my spine so intense I was sure it was visible. The goose-flesh on my arms certainly was.

Not that I was squeamish about dead bodies. But that woman, Volumnia, who had taken the body away, didn't look like someone who came out in daylight. And I really wasn't sure I wanted to see what her home was like. At all.

"Then let's do that first. If you don't mind?" Audrey said.

"No, I don't mind," I lied.

She smiled at me, then turned to rinse her mug in the sink in the teashop's backroom. I was just putting the book back in its spot in the office when it was like a bomb of barking went off.

I would've thought, with human speech something he could easily do, Houdini would have no need for that torrent of noise. But he indulged in it with relish, his toenails skittering over the floor as he charged to the open doorway that led out onto the Square, barking furiously the entire time.

Clearly, we had a visitor.

CHAPTER
TEN

After all that noise, it was scarcely surprising to see that the man standing in the doorway without coming into the teashop was Titus Bloom.

Houdini redoubled his barking efforts, but this time Titus didn't slink away. He just glared down at the dog, hands in the pockets of his slacks as he waited for the noise to stop. Then he gave me a pleading sort of look.

"Houdini! Bad boy!" I said—I'll admit—performatively. Then I bent to pick up the little dog.

"Hey!" Houdini objected. He was squirming in my grasp, trying to break free. Even so, I managed a quick glance at Titus's face.

If he had heard the dog speaking English inside his own head at all, his expression showed not a hint of it.

"Like I want him to hear me," Houdini chastised me. But he was still squirming, so violently I almost lost hold of him. I changed the position of my hands so that I was hugging him close to my chest.

"I'll just put him in the office," I murmured.

"You will do no such thing!" Houdini said in his biggest voice. But

I ignored him. I leaned into the office far enough to toss him onto his little bed, then quickly shut the door before he could charge out into the teashop again.

"Are you taking him with you when you go?" Titus was asking Audrey.

"Am I what?" Audrey asked, blinking in surprise.

"She's allergic," I said as I joined them at the counter.

"I see," Titus said. "Well, I'm sure we can find someone to take him in when you go."

"I'm not sure why you think I'm going at all," Audrey said. "I just got here."

"Oh, I assumed..." he broke off, his eyes moving from her face to mine, then back again. "Well, we don't get many young people in the Square. Most choose not to stay. So many more exciting places to live. The hidden floors of the Foshay Tower are quite popular among your age group."

I bit my tongue before I could make any cracks about *his* age and the assumptions I could draw from it. Audrey seemed to be going through a similar conundrum, and an awkward silence settled over the three of us.

Well, silent save for Houdini, who was both barking and scratching at the office door like a dog and also calling out to us both in his human voice inside our heads.

"Not that you aren't both welcome to the neighborhood, of course," Titus said, far too late.

"So far, I've been made to feel very welcome," I said.

"Good, good," he said, nodding as if to himself. "Have you been to the authorities yet?"

"Not yet," Audrey said.

"We were going to see the body now, if that's possible," I said.

"Very possible," he said. He was trying to be helpful, but almost too forcefully so. "In fact, the sheriff is with Volumnia now, so you can do both things at once if you're quick."

"Great," I said, and nodded to Audrey. But before we could move away from the counter, Titus grabbed a hold of her arm.

"Just a moment, Miss Mirken," he said. "I was wondering if I could have a word?"

"About?" she asked. But rather than answering, his eyes shifted to me then back again.

"I can wait outside," I offered, but Audrey shook her head.

"No. Anything anyone can say to me, they can say in front of you," she said. Then she lifted her chin at Titus.

"Only, I was wondering," he stammered.

"What were you wondering?" she asked him.

"Your grandaunt must have given you some indication of her wishes with regards to this shop?" he said, all in a rush.

"Well, I would imagine that's all in her will," Audrey said. "Which I haven't read yet. Doesn't that usually come after seeing to her remains?"

"Traditionally," I put in for her.

"I know, I know," Titus assured us both. "I was only curious. Only curious."

"You'll know when I know," Audrey told him. But then added, "if it turns out to be relevant to you, that is."

"Of course. Quite right," Titus said. Then he gave us both a nod and swept back out the open doors.

"What was *that* all about?" Audrey asked me.

"I have no idea," I said. "All I know is that Houdini hates that man. But then, I think that's pretty clear at the moment."

Titus's departure had not soothed Houdini's mood at all. He was still barking and demanding to be released.

"What did my grandaunt think of Titus Bloom? Do you know?" Audrey asked.

I pondered that. "I don't think she was fond of him, either. But that might not mean anything."

"Why not?"

"Well," I drawled. "He wasn't the only person she didn't seem too fond of. If you know what I mean."

"Oh, yes," Audrey laughed. "My grandaunt Agatha was not very shy about sharing her opinions. It's going to be very strange, meeting people here and matching them up to her stories. I almost hate to prejudge people that way, but how do I forget everything I've ever heard?"

"I'm just glad she seemed to like me," I said.

"Oh, yes. She was very fond of you," Audrey assured me. "Shall we go?"

"Yeah, but let me let Houdini out first," I said with a sigh. I opened the door. The barking and scratching stopped at once. Houdini just sat there, glaring up at me. I could kind of hear his human voice seething, just a little.

"We're going to see the body," Audrey told him. "Did you want to come along?"

"No," Houdini said. "I was with her before, until that old hag chased me away."

"Volumnia?" I asked, but he just simmered. "Where do we find her?"

"She lives at the bottom of the old stone steps," he said with great reluctance.

"I think I know the spot," I told Audrey.

"Do you want us to meet you here afterward? Or up in the apartment?" Audrey asked Houdini.

"I'll be around. I'll find you," he said. But he was clearly still cross.

"All right. Suit yourself," I said, and Audrey and I left him there alone in the teashop.

I noticed she had taken the accounting book with her, clutching it to her chest as tightly as any awkward schoolgirl with her textbooks.

"She probably did leave the business to you," I said. "You'll have to decide if you want to keep it or sell it."

"From the looks of this book, it's not worth much," she said.

"Not currently, but she was having trouble with her tea-making," I said. "If you could make her recipes without the same problems she had, you could do better."

"I suppose," she said, but she didn't sound like she was really weighing her options. Since we were on our way to look at her grandaunt's body, I wasn't surprised she was distracted.

I found the old stone steps just where I remembered them, tucked away on the far side of the back wall of the comic book store, near the Wizard's tower. Even though the weather had been dry, the steps still looked slickly wet, covered in delicate strands of moss. But that was at least partly an illusion, I found, as I walked down the steps without slipping on the wet rock, and the moss survived my footfalls without being disturbed in the slightest.

But the air at the bottom was decidedly colder than the air at the top. It was like the sun never penetrated this far down, even though the stairwell was open to the sky above us.

The door at the bottom of the stairs was heavy oak, weather-beaten and faded, but still as solid as ever. The hinges and handle were iron, and there was an iron ring in the center of the door I took to be a door-knocker.

I knocked twice. I was afraid I wouldn't be able to knock hard enough to be heard through the thickness of that oak door, but I could hear my knocks echoing through a cavernous space on the far side.

The door swung open almost at once and I saw a young man who was totally unfamiliar to me blinking out at me. He had very pale blond hair but intensely dark brown eyes, an unnerving pairing of features, and was so slender and slight of frame I was sure he was mistaken for a teenager a lot. But even standing as he was partially in shadows, I could see the trace of age lines just beginning to form around his eyes and mouth. Past thirty years, I guessed, but probably not much more than that.

He wasn't dressed in the wizardly robes of an academic, but he wasn't dressed in modern prosaic clothing, either. It was more like a uniform, designed purely for functionality, almost like what a security guard might wear in the prosaic world. And the belt around his waist that sagged low under the weight of a variety of tools and pouches definitely looked like something a guard might wear. The tunic he wore over it had a drapey look to it, almost cloak-like, and yet tighter around his forearms and wrists to keep from interfering with any work he'd have to do.

He was a magical authority, I had no doubt of that. I hadn't seen quite this sort of uniform before, but most of my run-ins with actual authorities had been in Europe, Asia and Africa. Never once in North or South America. And fashions vary widely, even in uniforms.

"Yes?" he said. He sounded bewildered, like this was his first time answering a knock at a door after only reading about it before.

"I'm Tabitha Greene. This is Audrey Mirken. We're here to see Agatha," I said.

"Oh, yes. Of course," he said, stepping back into the darkness. I took a breath and followed after him. Audrey stayed closed by my side.

I think we both flinched when the door shut with a boom behind us.

"I'm Deputy Fluellen," the young man said with something like a bow. "I work with Sheriff Jane MacMorris. She's in the Mummy Room with Volumnia right now."

"The Mummy Room?" I repeated. It was clear from how he'd said it that the words were capitalized.

"Was that what she wanted done with her remains? Mummification?" Audrey asked.

"Oh, no, no!" Fluellen said quickly, waving his hands wildly as if he desperately wanted to clear our minds of any misconceptions. "I guess you're both newer to the Square than I am. I thought everyone knew it was called that. It has a... dry smell."

Drying flesh smell, I guessed. Fun.

"I've been here a few weeks, but I've never seen you before," I said. I could hear the distrust in my own voice, but decided not to apologize for that.

"I just arrived this morning," Audrey said.

"Of course," he said to her. "I understand." Then he looked at me. "I'm sure you've not seen me around because I don't live in the Square. It's just part of my jurisdiction. Well, it's part of the sheriff's jurisdiction, but I go where she goes."

"How large is her jurisdiction?" I asked.

"Just Minneapolis," he said with a wave of his hand. As if that were a little thing.

"The boroughs of New York have more than a hundred jurisdictions," I said, a little factoid I remembered from my very brief time as a student there.

"And they need that level of coverage, believe me," Fluellen said. "There are far fewer magical communities hiding within the city limits of Minneapolis, and of course, we only deal with magical crimes. But it keeps us busy enough, I can tell you."

"Can we see my grandaunt now?" Audrey asked.

"Oh, of course," he said, then gestured for us to follow him deeper into the darkness. But already I could see what he was aiming for: the mouth of a tunnel was just visible on the far side of the squared-off stone room. It was like we were standing inside a sort of mudroom, complete with hooks for coats on the wall over a long wooden bench.

I was very glad we weren't asked to slip off our shoes, as the tunnel at the far end of the room had more in common with the staircase we had come down to get to the door than the dry flagstones of the mudroom. It was wet, for real wet, and slippery enough to keep me paying attention to my own steps. But it wasn't a staircase, just a long winding surface like a down ramp in a parking garage only scaled for pedestrians. The moss was thicker close to the walls, which were rounder here, less squared off than the walls in the mudroom.

And there were also toadstools growing in the corners, and on the walls, and long, flatter patches stretching across the ceiling overhead from time to time. It was some sort of bioluminescent fungus, but despite my semester of magical mycology, I couldn't quite identify the species. It was far brighter than any I remembered from my studies. And it was the exact same shade of green as the lantern Volumnia had carried the night before.

Fluellen led the way, but was constantly turning back to look at us as if worried that we wouldn't be following him. From what I'd seen, there was nowhere else to go, no way to get lost. Still, he looked worried.

I could hear voices ahead of us a full two turns of the tunnel before we emerged into another squared-off room with dry flagstone floors and more traditional gas lamps affixed to the walls. One was louder and distinctly Irish. The other, older and raspier one had to be Volumnia.

Then we were in the room itself, and I could see a red-headed woman built like a powerlifter standing with her arms crossed and her feet widely planted with her back to me. She had the same uniform and over-loaded belt as Fluellen, although she wore her belt a little higher and snugger than Fluellen.

She was still talking, but I couldn't quite tune in to her actual words just at the moment, because I was once more in the presence of Volumnia. It may be daytime, but we were deep underground, and the flickering lights from the gas lamps were almost worse than the green glow of the fungus in the tunnel because it made the shadows around her jump and dance.

All I could think was, at least she wasn't looking at me. Volumnia was once more bending over Agatha's body. Only this time Agatha was up on a stone table, so Volumnia only had to incline her head a little and not bend from the waist. Her hair stayed flat against her back.

I swallowed hard, clenching my hands into fists, but only briefly. She was an unsettling woman, but surely I had nothing to fear. Not with two authorities in the room with us.

Then she did look up at me, and those eerie blue eyes fixed on me, and I was instantly glad that I had nothing to do with Agatha's death.

Because I was sure if I had, this woman would know. Just by looking at me, she would know.

CHAPTER

ELEVEN

Volumnia only glanced up at me for a second, really. Then her eyes moved on. I felt like I had been momentarily trapped in a bright searchlight, suddenly the center of everything but unable to see anything but the light myself. But then that light had moved on and I was once more safely hidden in the background.

Volumnia said something else to Sheriff MacMorris, too low for me to hear. I was too focused on getting my breath back after being pinned down by those unearthly eyes. That, and really drinking in the details of the space around me.

We had left the wet, fungus-lit tunnel behind, a mere crack in the stone block wall behind us that glowed that oddly cheery shade of green. But only the crack glowed; none of that light reached into the room we were standing in. Perhaps because that light was so faint even compared to the gaslights flickering along the walls of the room and down the three long corridors that started at the bottom of short flights of stairs on my left and right and directly across the room from the crack in the wall.

The room we were in was dominated by the stone table where

Agatha's body laid half-covered by a gleamingly white sheet. There were two heavy wooden cabinets to either side of the crack in the wall, the kind that I was used to seeing behind the counter at an apothecary, where the proprietor kept the dangerous or expensive items. The doors were all shut, though. I could only imagine what was kept within.

But the room didn't smell like death. I realized I had expected it to pretty much in the same moment that my nose informed me that it definitely didn't. There was no formaldehyde smell, no coppery blood smell, no smell of rot or even the begins of decay. I didn't know when bodies started to smell, and Agatha had been dead less than a day and had been moved into this chill room almost at once, but still. I was pretty sure I should be smelling something.

Like Fluellen had said, it was a dry smell. But not an unpleasant one.

I took a step back towards the tunnel behind me, and the wet fungus smell was just perceptible coming from the crack in the wall. But that was it. That, and a dusty smell that managed to somehow be a *clean* dusty smell, if that makes any sense.

And yet I was sure that Agatha's wasn't the only body down here with us. I was pretty sure the gaslights I could see dimly down the long corridors were marking out the locations of specific tombs contained within the walls. I moved closer to the corridor to the left and even took a step or two down the staircase. As far as I could see, that corridor ran straight and true beyond the reaches of my sight. Maybe it ran on forever.

"You're Tabitha Greene?" Sheriff MacMorris asked me in her Irish brogue, and I hurried back into the room. The sheriff had either a large cellphone or a small tablet computer in her hand and held a stylus over the screen expectantly as she waited for me to answer.

"That's right," I said, and she made a little tick mark on the screen I couldn't see. She either had one of those privacy screen protectors on it that they sell at airports so your fellow passengers can't see your screen, or there was some magic involved. I couldn't quite decide which.

"You are minding the Weal & Woe Bookshop for your uncles?" she asked, that stylus poised again.

"That's right," I said.

"Well, not at the moment, surely," Fluellen said.

"No, I put up the Closed sign so I could help Audrey get a handle on things," I said.

"You two are friends?" the sheriff asked, her hazel eyes shifting from me to Audrey, then back again.

I said, "Yes" in the same moment that Audrey said, "We just met, actually." Then we both fell silent at once. My cheeks were burning, but hers were just flushing pink even in the dim light from the gas lamps.

Then Audrey said, "Tabitha showed me my grandaunt's apartment and her teashop, and she's helping me take care of her dog Houdini since I'm terribly allergic."

"I would've thought Titus Bloom would take charge of you," MacMorris said, scrolling the screen of her tablet with one thick finger. "Isn't he the one who called you?"

"Yes, but I took prosaic transport to get here, and I came in through the bookshop and not his coffeeshop," Audrey said.

"Why?" MacMorris asked.

Audrey flushed a rosier shade of pink, but she lifted her chin before speaking in a steady voice. "My grandaunt told me if anything happened to her, I should speak to Tabitha Greene first. She said I could trust her."

"If anything happened to her?" MacMorris said with a frown. "What do you think happened to her?"

"Well," Audrey said, looking significantly over at her grandaunt's body.

"Volumnia says she fell," MacMorris said.

"I said her injuries were consistent with falling from that height,"

Volumnia said, and the whispery echo of her voice sent shivers up my spine. "I did not rule out someone causing that fall."

MacMorris scrolled through her tablet again, stopping at some specific place only she could see. "You said there was no sign of a struggle before the fall. No sign of impact against the railing, such as from being pushed by another person, and no sign of defensive wounds on the body."

"I know what I said," Volumnia said. It sounded like it took a lot of effort for her to force the air out of her lungs to form words. She took several raspy breaths to recover each time she spoke. "I also told you I don't understand the precise nature of the material smudged on the back of her hand."

"But you said it was probably just dirt," the sheriff said.

Volumnia said nothing. She certainly seemed to be out of breath. MacMorris just frowned at her tablet.

"We ran all the standard spell checks at the scene, both on the veranda and on the patio where she..." Fluellen broke off, then cleared his throat, too loudly in that echoing space. We all flinched, then he went on. "There was no sign of magic being used. Agatha made no attempt to save herself with magic, which usually means she didn't see danger coming. Like with a sudden slip and fall."

"It also means there is no sign of her being attacked by magic," MacMorris added. "All our findings point to an accidental death here. Unless you know something we don't?"

"Not really," Audrey said. But she was clutching that accounting book awfully tightly in her arms.

It might contain evidence. Or it might contain needlessly encrypted accounting information. We had no way of knowing. But I could see that Audrey didn't want to hand it over to the authorities. Not that I blamed her. MacMorris's scrolling half the time looked like she was checking notes to be sure she had her information correct, but the other half of the time she looked like she was checking unrelated messages. And everything Fluellen was doing on his own phone definitely fell into the second category.

I suspected the number of messages the two of them were glancing at and snoozing to respond to later was a big part of the reason that MacMorris had to keep checking her notes to remember things that were just said minutes before. She was stretched too thin.

And this looked too much like a case she could close without taking up any of the time she had too little of.

I was pretty sure I'd agree with her, if not for Houdini.

"How about you?" MacMorris asked, turning her attention on to me. Her narrowed hazel eyes were nothing like Volumnia's eerie gaze, but they were capable of fixing on me until I wanted to squirm away all the same.

"I don't think it was an accident," I said, completely truthfully. "But I don't have any evidence to back that up."

"Just a feeling?" MacMorris asked. But not dismissively. She was watching me as steadily as ever, that stylus at the ready, prepared to take seriously anything I had to say.

"Just a strong feeling," I said.

MacMorris studied her tablet and chewed her lip. I could hear the soft chimes of Fluellen's phone as he stood behind me in the corner of the room, snoozing messages one by one. But MacMorris was in no hurry. She scrolled slowly through what I guessed to be all her notes on the case, tapping her stylus against the side of the tablet as she mulled over what she was reading.

"Fluellen," she said suddenly, making her deputy jump. He shoved his phone into its compartment on his belt before stepping forward. "What do we have on Agatha Mirken's finances?"

"All of her accessible accounts show her getting by, but not doing well," he said, then gave Audrey an apologetically flinching look.

"So money wasn't a motive," MacMorris said.

"Not unless it's money she was keeping hidden somewhere," he said. But his tone said clearly he didn't think that was very likely.

"No known enemies," MacMorris said, tapping her tablet again. "Aside from the two of you, she doesn't seem to have had any close, friendly relationships either."

"Just Houdini," I said without thinking.

"Houdini," MacMorris said, frowning at her tablet. "That's the dog?"

"A mutt she found in the alley just a few months ago," Fluellen put in. "It's not registered at all. Not a familiar. Just a pet." Now it was me on the receiving end of his flinching look of apology.

"Just a dog," MacMorris nodded. Then she tapped her tablet into sleep mode and tucked it away at the back of her belt. "Unless something else turns up, I'm going to file this as an accidental death. I'm very sorry for your loss, both of you, but I don't see anything else here that needs my attention?"

"No," I agreed, and Audrey murmured the same.

"If that should change, you know how to reach me," she said, then motioned for Fluellen to follow her back through the crack in the wall.

That left Audrey and I alone with Volumnia. Volumnia's attention seemed fixed on Agatha, but in a distracted sort of way. She was just rubbing a lock of Agatha's silver hair between her bony fingertips. I think she might've been singing something to herself, but very, very softly.

Audrey gave me a pointed look, but I just shrugged, not knowing what she was trying to tell me. She mouthed the words "the dog," then rolled her eyes towards Volumnia.

Perhaps it was just because she wasn't looking at me in that moment, but I thought it was probably more that we were here, in her most personal space. But either way, I was finding myself a lot more comfortable around Volumnia. When she wasn't gazing into my very soul with her unearthly eyes, she was almost a comforting presence. She certainly felt like she was comforting the dead now. She might be fussing over the mortal remains of Agatha Mirken, but something inside me felt sure that the song she was singing was so quiet to my ears because its intended audience—Agatha's soul—was somewhere very, very else.

She tended to the dead. That was her office. And from the looks of her, she had held that office for a long, long time. And she didn't just tend to the recently dead like Agatha. No, I had the strong visual image of her moving down those long corridors, singing her songs to the long dead as well, those whose remains sat just beyond the walls of those corridors.

And anyone who tended the dead like that was definitely a keeper of secrets. It went with the job, right?

So I thought it over, but in the end shook my head. I didn't think we should tell anyone about Houdini the talking dog, not even Volumnia.

Not without Houdini's permission, anyway.

Audrey chewed her lip for a moment, but then nodded. She agreed with me. We would keep Houdini's secret, for now.

"Miss Volumnia?" she said as she stepped closer to the stone table.

"Yes?" Volumnia said in the sudden silence that crashed down when she stopped singing. Weird how such a soft sound had completely filled that enormous space like that.

"You know what my grandaunt wanted? To be done with her body, I mean," she said.

"Yes," Volumnia said. I held my breath, waiting for the rest of the words to follow, but had to let it go again when dizziness washed over me. That was it? That was her final answer?

"Okay," Audrey said uncertainly. "We'll leave you to it, then?"

"She wished," Volumnia said in her wheezing, labored voice, "to be held here for seven days. I have woven spells of stasis around her, and here she shall remain until that time is up."

Then she was looking at me again, and it was just as terrible as the two times before. "You are not alone in thinking there is more to this. But seven days is all I can give you."

"Seven days," I said. "Got it."

Then I turned and fled back up that wet tunnel, back through the pitch-black mudroom, and up those old stone steps into the bright light of midafternoon on a sunny summer day. Then I just collapsed.

Like all the strength went out of me. And I fell into a heap on the grass just off the edge of the patio tiles. I clutched at the green, growing living grass around me and smelled the sappy smell that rose up as my fingers crushed the blades. And I threw my head back to stare up into the blue sky dotted with white puffs of cloud as the gentle breeze stirred through my hair.

There was a whoosh of noise as Audrey collapsed beside me, her breath ragged from the run up the stairs and from a tangle of emotions both.

"I don't want to go back down there," she said at last. "Ever."

"Me neither," I agreed.

We sat in companionable silence for some time, drinking in the living smells and the warmth from the sun both.

Then Audrey asked me in the softest of whispers, "What do you think would happen? If we told anyone about Houdini?"

"I don't know," I admitted. "I don't even know why I keep feeling so strongly that I *should* keep it a secret. But it's like every time I'm about to say something about him, I just clam up."

"I feel it too," she said. "His magic? Or Agatha's?"

"I don't know," I said. "We should probably find out, at some point."

"I wouldn't even know where to start," Audrey said. "Like with this accounting book. I didn't want to give it to the sheriff, because I'm sure it would just get set aside and forgotten about. To be honest, I know it doesn't look like much of a clue. Only maybe it is. Why else is there a page clearly in code?"

"We could decode the page, and if it looks important, we can call MacMorris," I said. "If it looks like a clue, she'll have to take it seriously. We just need to do the work first. I mean, we kind of have the time and they don't."

"I know," Audrey said, opening the book to look at the coded page. "Only, like I said, I don't know where to even start."

"Oh," I said airily. "Well, I might have a few thoughts about that. Let's go up to the bookshop. We can start there."

CHAPTER
TWELVE

The Weal & Woe Bookshop had seven levels, but not all the levels were created equal. The top, for instance, is largely used for storage. There are so many boxes of prosaic paperbacks waiting to be shelved, crates of magical texts and objects yet to be assessed by my uncle Carlo's careful eye, as well as even less exciting items like broken furniture and cleaning supplies.

And the first level, the one that opened out on the prosaic world, was almost entirely prosaic books. A few shelves near the wall furthest from the prosaic door had low-level magic texts, but those were all the kind that wouldn't do any harm if they got out into the real world. Largely charms that had only minor effects or divination methods that only gave hazy, murky glimpses at the future. And even then, only a prosaic with some innate amount of magical ability could get any use out of them. Those sorts of prosaics were few and far between, and I was pretty sure my uncle Carlo could spot them on sight if they came into his bookshop.

In fact, I think that's why those books were there. Like a lure. Although I think he just wanted to find and keep an eye on whatever he attracted with those books.

Anyway, the main floor is where the front desk is, so that was where I spent most of my time. Sitting behind the counter, waiting for the customers who never quite showed up.

But there was a little nook on the fourth level that kept calling to me. The fourth level placed it at the shop's halfway point vertically, and this nook was centered over the prosaic door, making it at the halfway point horizontally as well. There was a window seat there that overlooked the Minneapolis street outside. It was a lovely view. It was also an impossible one, or at least a magical one. Because the building only appeared to have three levels if you were standing on that street looking up. Three levels, and no windows.

I don't know if that's why it called to me. The feeling of being able to watch the world without being seen by it was intriguing, to be sure. But, as much as my uncle Carlo had never specifically shown me this place, I think he had arranged it for me. The window seat had new pillows arranged over its sun-faded, stained wood surface, their colors a variety of jewel tones. I don't have a favorite color, but I do have a favorite color palette, and these pillows were a nice example of that run of amber, garnet, sapphire and emerald that I loved best. It felt deliberate.

It felt more like my own space than the attic bedroom. And I loved that attic bedroom.

Maybe that was why I felt a little shy when I brought Audrey there. Like I was showing her a little bit of my soul. Which was silly. I had only been there for a matter of days, and no one had ever said that space was mine.

But when we had climbed the stairs to the fourth floor, then ducked around the oddly-shaped shelves that housed the books that my uncle called the "rare materials books" (by which he wasn't referring to the topics covered inside the books, but what the books were made out of, like stone or dinosaur scales or magically-fixed clouds of glitter), I couldn't help watching Audrey's face as I brought her into my nook.

The window seat looked cozy even when the fireplaces to either side weren't lit. The back sides of the last row of shelves for the rare materials books were covered in scrolls of art that had no magic to them whatsoever; they just featured finely rendered landscapes and scenes from epic stories. The other two sides were more open, with shelves of old grade-school level spell books running past on one side and magical cookery on the other.

And in the center of the space was a heavy wooden table, thick like a butcher block and scarred in the past but recently refinished with a wood polish that glowed like honey under the green-shaded lamps that hung from above. Six chairs were gathered around it. They looked old, the cloth coverings faded, like the stuffing would be lumpy and probably not cover one hard wooden joint here or a nasty metal spring there, to be discovered too late by whoever sat on them.

But they were perfectly comfortable. I knew that from experience.

"Oh, hello," Audrey said as she set the accounting book in front of one of the chairs. I looked around, not sure who she was talking to, but then I heard Houdini in my head.

"I was wondering when you'd get here," he said. Then he sat up, and I realized he had been curled up on the chair at the head of the table.

"How'd you even know to meet us here?" I asked.

"You smell like this place," he said with a sniff, as if that were perfectly obvious.

"I do?" I asked.

Audrey just shrugged. She slid into her chair, then flipped the book open to the coded page. "Okay, Research Girl. You said you knew how to do this?"

"I said I knew how to start," I said, slapping my hands then rubbing them together as I looked around the bookshop. "I know we have some prosaic books on code breaking on the first level, but I doubt that's what Agatha was up to. But it's not out of the question, either. So we'll keep that in mind for later."

"Why keep it in mind when you can write it on the board?"

Houdini asked in a bored voice. His head disappeared as he curled back up to resume his nap. Which left only Audrey for me to shoot confused glances at.

"Doesn't he mean that?" she asked, gesturing behind me.

I turned to see some of the scrolls were gone from a section of bookshelf backs, replaced by a sheet of slate. Not a chalkboard, just an entire sheet of slate with all of its jagged, layered edges bare. I ran my fingers over the stone. It was cool and almost oily, but it was definitely real.

I turned back to Audrey at the table and saw a bowl of chalk sitting there that I was sure hadn't been there before. I picked one up and rose up on tiptoe to write "check prosaic code-breaking books" in the top lefthand corner of the slate sheet.

I settled back down on my heels, eyeing the rest of the space. There was a lot of room to write a list of suspects, if we had any. We could list possible motives, if we had any. We could even write down every detail of what we knew about the evidence from the crime scene.

If we had any.

"I think this is really going to come in handy," I said optimistically as I returned to the table to put the chalk back.

Audrey almost grinned at me. Almost.

"Do you know anything about magical codes?" she asked me.

"I took a semester in magical espionage tactics," I said. Her eyes grew wide, and I was compelled to add, "Historical tactics. It wasn't a... practical course."

"But you know where to start?" she said, sliding the book towards me. I looked at the coded page again. Block letters, written by hand, but if they had been typeset, I would've described them as mono spaced. A fixed font, every letter taking up the exact same space, no matter how much space it actually needed. Kind of irritating on the eyes to read, quite aside from it being a completely nonsense string of letters.

"Should we write it all out on that board?" Audrey asked. "Or maybe on paper so we can make a bunch of tries. Isn't it usually a thing where, when you break part of it, the rest gets easier?"

"No, this definitely isn't a prosaic sort of code," I said, fumbling my way into the seat next to Audrey. I put the book between us and touched some of the letters. "It's not just a swapping out of one letter for another, right? Because the fixed spacing means something."

"If you say so," Audrey said. Needless to say, she didn't sound convinced.

I rubbed at the ink of one of the letters. It didn't look like it was hiding anything. No other letter lurked beneath, covered by its ink. But something wasn't right about the look of that page.

"I know a spell," I said, trying to summon up the memory from that long ago class. I had been forced to drop it before the midterm and had never attempted to find another version of it at another school. But I *had* enjoyed it. It had almost felt like something I could do.

Although, even before midterm, it had been clear that wasn't going to shake out.

"I have to find a book," I said, shooting back up out of the chair and tearing across the bookshop. Audrey called after me that she'd wait there with Houdini, but I was too focused to even shout back an "Okay!"

Ten minutes later, I jogged back into the nook with a slender, featureless black book in one hand and a fistful of pens in the other.

"I found the book," I said, a little out of breath from all the running around the bookshop. I was bound to have bruises on my shins soon from all the shelves I had run into and chair legs I had tripped over. But I had found the book I remembered from that class.

"What book?" Audrey asked.

"The definitive guide to magical code breaking," I said. But I couldn't wipe the grin from my face as I handed it to her.

"Tabitha," she said after a long moment's perusal. "This book is completely blank. Even the cover."

"It only *looks* blank," I said, and brandished the pens at her.

"We have to... what, color it in?" she asked.

"These are spy pens," I told her. "Once we find the pen that matches the book, it will unlock. Then we can read the whole thing."

"The pens unlock codes?" Audrey said. "Why don't we just try to find the one that matches the accounting book?"

"That's a good question, but I promise you it doesn't work that way," I said. I realized I was still grinning and forced my face back to match her own serious, almost worried expression. "We need to unlock the book, then use the book to figure out what code Agatha used to write that page in her book. The pens might work, or they might not. Given Agatha's skills in mixing things like tea and herbs, I have a feeling she crafted her own ink. But the book will help us figure that out. And maybe the pens *will* help, which is why I brought them all here rather than unlocking the book myself and bringing just that."

I might have gotten my face to conform to the gravity of the moment, but I knew my words were still rushing out in an excited jumble. Faster than Audrey could respond to, anyway. I reminded myself to practice patience as she looked at the black book, then the pile of pens, then the open page of the accounting book.

"I thought ritual magic was complicated," she sighed.

"This isn't going to be that bad, I promise," I assured her. I was gushing again. I couldn't help it. But this time she gave me a smile that was both encouraged and encouraging. Like we were forming a confidence-enhancing loop with each other.

I picked up the pens one by one and just tried scribbling over the featureless black cover of the book. The fourth pen brought out patches of dark red. For a horrifying moment, I thought I'd somehow made the little book bleed, and I recoiled, pulling the pen away.

But the pen had done its work. As we watched, the patches of dark red thickened then drew together to form letters. Soon we could read *The Definitive Guide to Magical Code Breaking* splashed across the cover.

"That's its name? I thought you were just being descriptive," Audrey said.

I shot her a quick grin, then opened the book. The interior was all there now, black ink on a cream stock paper that felt as new and mass-produced as any prosaic book. I scanned the table of contents, then started jumping around the book, skimming the most promising chapters for clues.

Audrey watched this for about half a minute, but I was flipping through pages too quickly for her to follow. I'm sure it was more than a little dull, watching me basically devour a book at the highest setting of my "skimming for the actual good bits for research" mode. But she didn't complain. She just picked up the pens I had pushed out of my way and tried them one after another on the accounting book.

They didn't work. Like I had figured they wouldn't.

But by the time she had tried the last one, I was sure I had what we needed.

"I think I know what Agatha did," I said, flipping back and forth between two different chapters, sort of reading half a sentence from each before switching back again. "It's complicated, but it fits her, I think."

"What is it?" Audrey asked, setting the last pen aside to give me her full attention.

"She used two kinds of magical inks," I said. "One to remain always visible, and one to remain always hidden. All you have to do is reverse the spells on the inks. Then the visible will hide and the hidden will emerge."

"All you have to do?" she repeated. She sounded vaguely alarmed.

"Sure," I said with more confidence than I felt. But that was too much like a lie for me to keep it up. "Well, I'm 90% sure. Maybe 85."

"All *you* have to do?" she repeated with more emphasis.

"Well, obviously by 'you' I mean '*you*'," I said. "You have to do it. I can't do spells."

"I can't do spells either," she said.

"No, that's not true," I said, and she shot me a warning look. "Sorry. Obviously, I haven't walked a mile in your shoes. It's just, it sounded like your trouble with magic wasn't magic itself."

"What's my trouble with magic?" she asked.

So much danger in that tone. If I said the wrong thing now, it would be like dropping a bomb on the fragile beginnings of what felt like a very important friendship.

"Look, you said that you studied ritual magic because you thought if you just memorized every word and gesture, there'd be no way you could mess things up, right?"

"That's what I said," she conceded. But that tone was still there.

"Well, I'm here to tell you exactly what to say and do so you don't have to research it yourself. All you have to do is *do* it. Which I can't," I finished, deflated. I could feel my cheeks flaming with shame, a specific shame I had so enjoyed *not* feeling since I'd come to the Square.

But this was different. This wasn't some class assignment I knew I was going to fail spectacularly at. This was actually important.

But if I tried it, I knew I would still fail. Spectacularly.

Audrey sucked in a long breath, then let it out in an even longer sigh. Then she took the code-breaking book from me, being careful not to lose the two places I was holding open with my fingers. I sat quietly as she scanned first one section, then the other.

"It says it requires more focused intensity than normal spells," she said, her voice carefully neutral.

"They always say that," I said dismissively. She gave me a stern look, like a teacher who didn't appreciate snide answers in her class-room. "They do!" I insisted. "But in this case, maybe it's a little true. You can't break one spell then the other, I mean. You have to do both at once. But we've got this. I promise."

She scanned both sections again. I was in agony, waiting quietly, but there was no way I was going to try to pressure her to decide faster. Because I knew what her pressured response would be for sure.

"I suppose it doesn't hurt to try," she said at last.

"It's going to work!" I promised her. "I'm going to write it all out and we'll go over it together before you try it for real." Then a sudden thought struck me, and I fought down a wave of panic that all my plans were about to go down in flames. "You have a wand, right?"

"Of course I have a wand," she said with half a grin. "I *did* graduate from ritual magic, you know."

"Of course you did!" I agreed.

Then that half grin became a three-quarters grin. "Cs get degrees."

"And they also get wands," I added.

That finally got a grin for real. For a second. Then she was serious again. "I left my wand in my bag back in Agatha's apartment."

"Okay. I can start writing this out while you go get it," I said. But I had a whole stack of pens that probably weren't suitable for this purpose and no paper at all, so I'd have to run for supplies before I could start.

"Actually," Audrey said slowly, then stopped.

"What is it?" I asked.

"I know you said this isn't like ritual magic at all, but it's going to be the first spell I'm attempting since graduation," she said. Her cheeks were pinkening again, but she plowed on. "I think I need to take a night first to meditate, sleep properly, then do a dawn energy-gathering ritual. Just to be sure."

"Of course," I said. "Actually, that's good for me, too. I want to double check some of what this book says against a few other texts."

"You think it's wrong?" she asked, suddenly worried.

"No, I think I can make a few adjustments to the spell that will make it better, that's all," I said. "I like to draw from multiple sources when I can."

You know, in all that magic I've done that never works out.

But Audrey gave me a brisk nod, like we were peers at the top of our field in complete agreement.

"So, meet back here when you're ready?" I said.

"Yes, meet back here," she agreed. "Good night."

"Good night!" I said.

She started to leave the nook, but she turned back at the last minute to look at me again. "Be sure you get some sleep, too. I know I'll be doing all the spellwork, but don't burn yourself out like I have a feeling you're about to."

"Of course," I said. But my look of shocked surprise didn't fool her.

"I know we just met, but I've known too many research fiends like you in the higher level ritual magic courses. Make sure you eat dinner, sleep for more than four hours, and eat breakfast before we meet again," she said. She even pointed a commanding finger at me.

"I will!" I swore.

After she disappeared from sight, I turned to see Houdini sitting up on his chair again, blinking at me sleepily. Then he said, "I don't know why she believes you when you're obviously lying."

"Hush up!" I hissed at him. "I totally meant what I said."

"Oh, sure, you *meant* it," he said. "Like that's going to matter in the morning when you're tired and starving."

"You sleep enough for both of us," I told him. "I'm going to find a couple of books before I start copying out the spell."

And that was how I found out that Houdini's mind-talking had a range limit, and I could get out of it pretty quickly when I was walking fast.

THIRTEEN

Despite having no magical abilities, I always loved homework. Digging into old texts to compare dozens of methods to arrive at the same result and collating them into one master method was probably my favorite way to burn an evening and half of a night.

I had missed homework. I hadn't expected that.

I really hoped when my uncles came home, that I got to stay in the Square. In the prosaic world, there would be no opportunity to do this kind of work. And even unpaid as it was, I wanted to keep doing it. It was even better than homework, really. I wasn't working to earn a grade, after all.

I was working to solve a murder.

But just like when I went deep into the weeds with homework, I totally lost track of time. I had dozens of books piled up on the table around me—what had originally felt far too big for my personal use was turning out to be too small—I would come across a reference to another text I just *knew* we had somewhere in the bookshop. And then I'd have to track it down.

It was well past midnight but still hours from dawn when I laid out my four best attempts at the spell and crafted my final, most perfect version.

That was also when I started to spark.

I had stopped noticing the static electricity that shocked me every time I ran through the bookshop and then touched something. How I could spark off of books and wood shelves, I didn't even ponder for a second. I was too used to it.

The cloud of staticky hair standing on-end was another thing I was too used to for me to pay much attention to it now.

But when the pen I was writing with started shooting sparks off the parchment, I *did* notice that.

I was in a very flammable space, after all. One I had already nearly set on fire once. I didn't want to risk it a second time. Especially not when my uncle Carlo was somewhere deep in the Carpathian Mountains at that moment.

Still, I couldn't bring myself to stop. I slowed down and focused, writing every letter carefully with a slickly over-inked pen nib. It didn't spark again, but the ink had a burning smell to it as it dried.

Once that was done and I set the pen aside, I pushed away from the table, then stumbled back out of the chair. I was still sparking, I could feel it. I was still a real fire hazard.

Especially when I made the mistake of trying to touch my hair. It was crackling, reaching out towards my fingertips in a way that really didn't feel like it was going to end well.

I adjusted my glasses instead of touching my hair, and that seemed to help a little bit.

Then I ran up the stairs, all the way out of the bookshop and through my uncles' apartment to my attic room. I didn't take more than my shoes off before I jumped into the shower. An electric smell filled the room as the water plastered my hair down over my head.

I stayed under the water for a long time after that smell had faded, just to be sure. Then I stripped off my wet clothes, toweled off, then quickly got into my warmest pajamas. It wasn't a cold night, and it hadn't been a cold shower, but I still felt all shivery.

I had one last thought, that perhaps this shivery feeling was from missing dinner, which I had promised Audrey I wouldn't do. But the idea of getting food at that hour really didn't appeal. I'd have to stay awake to eat it, for one.

I threw an extra blanket over my bed and snuggled down inside of it. I was out of it even before my toes got warm.

I want to say I slept like a rock, but I woke up at one point between collapsing in the bed and the beginning of dawn. I sensed a presence in the open doorway to my attic room, but not one that frightened me at all. Which sounds weird, because when it first loomed there, it felt absolutely enormous. Like it was too big to fit through the door.

But then I heard nails on the floorboard and realized it was just Houdini. I had left him alone in the bookshop. I guessed he had woken up and found me gone, and I felt a little bad about that. As much as I could, anyway, when I was more asleep than awake.

He came into the room but stopped just inside the doorway like he was listening, or more than listening, like he was sensing the world around him with more senses than I could even imagine. Once he decided it was safe enough, he moved to stand beside my bed, but he hesitated again before jumping lightly up to land at the foot of the bed.

He hesitated a third time, head cocked as he *perceived*, although just what he was hoping or fearing to detect, I had no idea. Finally he turned himself around three times, then flopped hard against the backs of my knees, tucking his nose under his own leg and falling into as deep a sleep as I soon found myself returning to.

The first light of dawn woke me a few hours later to find Houdini still there, pressed up against the backs of my knees. When I shifted my weight, he woke up at once, standing straight and tall and ready to go.

It took me a little longer to get moving myself. I found a package of instant coffee shoved far into the back of my uncles' pantry and made a double-strength cup of that plus the last heel of bread in the breadbox, and that was my breakfast.

"Do I need to get you kibble or something?" I asked Houdini.

Houdini made an indignant huffing noise. But that didn't really answer my question.

"We can go to Agatha's later and pick up anything you'd rather have over here. It's up to you," I said.

"I am completely fine," he said at last. "You, on the other hand, are going to be late to meet Audrey for your very important spell."

"Right," I said, shoving the last of the dry bread in my mouth, then picking up the coffee to take with me down all those flights of stairs.

Audrey was already in the nook when we arrived, studying the parchment I had left out to dry the night before. The ink was too heavy, particularly at the end, but it had sat in the low-humidity bookshop air long enough to dry without smearing, so all the letters were still clearly legible.

"This is a lot of books," Audrey said to me. Then she took a sip from a take-away cup with the Loose Leaves Teashop logo on the side. The fragrant smell of bergamot and some variety of smoky tea reached my nostrils, so much more appetizing than my coffee crystals. Clearly, she had been up earlier than me. She was neatly dressed, her hair clean and brushed smooth down her back. She had meditated, I knew that without asking just by her air of serenity, and I suspected she had eaten as well. More than a hunk of dry bread, for sure. And she had mixed her own tea in her grandaunt's shop.

All before meeting me at dawn.

"You're a morning person," I said, I didn't think out loud, but then she looked up at me with a quirk of her eyebrow.

"You're a night person," she said, and gestured at all the books and loose stacks of parchment scrawled over with earlier attempts at the spell as well as gads and gads of notes.

"Yeah," I admitted. "You looked it over. What do you think?"

"It's in Latin, so I can pronounce all the words," she said. Then she flushed and added, "not all ritual magic is, you know. People think it is, but it isn't. It's usually in far deader languages. Languages without such clear-cut grammar and pronunciation rules. One mistake, and if it just fails to do anything, that's your best-case scenario."

I already knew that about the languages, because I had a working knowledge of most of them. But I decided not to mention it just then. I needed her confidence in her own ritual magic skills to be high.

"Do my notations for the gestures make sense?" I asked. I took another gulp of coffee, grimaced, then put my eager listening face back on.

"Sure, that all looks easy enough," she said, looking down at the parchment again. "You're a little vague on the wand work."

"If it's a gesture I've seen, I can describe it. But if it's something that happens through the bond between wielder and wand, I can only guess at that," I admitted. "Educated guesses from lots of reading, but guesses."

"That makes sense," she said, still examining the parchment closely. She took another sip of her tea, and that citrus and smoke aroma hit me again. I was definitely going to have to ask her to let me try her blend sometime.

"It's not a difficult spell, I don't think," I said slowly. She tipped the parchment down to give me her full attention. "The only trouble is, we only get one go at it. Any failure here is almost guaranteed to destroy the book. It will ruin the ink or mar the pages, or maybe even set the whole thing on fire."

Because I set things on fire a lot. Not that I said that part out loud.

"I guess I can't mess it up too badly," she said. "Speak these words, do this gesture, then move on to the next."

"Right," I said, but she could hear my hesitation and stopped half-doing the gestures in a practicing sort of way to give me all her attention again. "What I mean is, there is a flow. The ink is dry now, but its inherent character is and always will be fluid. So the spell reflects that. It ebbs and flows, like waves on a beach."

"Okay," Audrey said, but I could tell she wasn't quite getting what I was saying.

"You'll feel it when the spell starts," I promised her. Not that I had ever felt it in my life. But I knew most magic users did. "The gestures are where you flow in more power, and the words are when you ebb off the power but exert more control."

"Oh," Audrey said, but with an uptick. Like what she had really meant to say was *eureka*. She read through the entire spell one more time, then set the parchment down on the table. "Yes, I can see how that's there, like a subtext for everything on the page. I never would've noticed that."

"It's easier to notice from an outsider's perspective, I think," I said shyly.

"You mean all spells are like this?"

"With their own rhythms based on the elements in play? I've always thought so," I said.

"Wow," Audrey said. "I suddenly want to go back to all my old textbooks and see what I missed when I was actually taking the classes. None of my teachers ever explained it like this. It was all just repetition. Like they thought I would get it if I just tried it enough times. But I never did."

"I think so many people grasp it intuitively that no one has put much thought into how to teach it to the ones who don't," I said. "But the proof is in the pudding, right? We should try the spell."

"We should definitely try the spell," Audrey said.

But now she was the one who couldn't stop grinning.

We moved all the books aside—I could re-shelve them all later—then put all the useless scraps of parchment notes and drafts into the kindling box next to the fireplace. Soon all that was left on the table was Agatha's accounts book, open to the coded page.

"Should I get a stand for the parchment?" I asked. "Or I could just hold it for you..."

"No, I have it all right here," Audrey said, tapping her temple smartly. "I didn't fail for lack of trying, you know. I'm very good at memorizing spells."

"You didn't fail," I reminded her.

"Cs get degrees," she finished for me.

Then she lifted her wand like a conductor signaling the orchestra to begin.

Her voice as she spoke the words of the spell was stronger and deeper than her usual speaking voice. No hint of a lack of confidence there. And her pronunciation was crisp and clear, but at the same time she found the rhythm and rhyme in the syllables. She found the flow.

I had never gone anywhere near a ritual magic class. My special permission to study theory would've held no water with that crowd. But I had seen it done on occasion. It's a very showy form of magic, inclined to be dramatic and over-the-top, even when the wizards in question aren't wearing their most awe-inspiring wardrobes.

But Audrey delivered what a critic would surely call an understated performance. It was absolutely perfect, but no more than it needed to be. She felt no need to show off.

I was so engrossed watching her work I almost didn't notice the sparks I was shedding onto the carpet. Not sparks of static electricity this time. No, this time I was conjuring actual sparks of fire.

I stomped out the few that had dropped onto the carpet around me, then turned and fled the nook. I had to get away from anything flammable. In a normal bookshop, that would be tricky. But in a magical bookshop, fire extinguishers were not the first line of defense. Especially not when some of the artifacts themselves were the likely sources of fire.

Every level of the shop had a fireproof room, and I ran to the one on the fourth level. It was halfway back, built into the stone wall that divided the bookshop from the rest of the building on the teashop side. It looked like a space about the size of an elevator shaft or storage closet, completely empty with nothing on the stone walls, or on the stone floor below or stone ceiling above.

I was raining sparks. I had never done this before.

I closed my eyes and focused on my breathing and not on my growing panic. My heart rate finally slowed to match my controlled breaths. But still I didn't open my eyes.

"Well, that was interesting," I heard Houdini say. I unclenched my hands, then looked down at my feet. A few of the sparks had left smoky halos on the stone floor, but they were long expired, and no more were falling.

I adjusted my glasses sharply, then looked up at Houdini standing in the doorway. He had that one paw up, touching the star on his chest as he regarded me intently.

"I have it under control," I told him.

He said nothing.

"I do," I insisted, holding out my hands to him, as if that proved anything. "I stopped sparking."

"Indeed," he said dryly. Then he blinked at me slowly before saying, "Audrey has finished the spell. When you are ready, she would like you to join her in basking in your mutual success."

"Right," I said brightly, adjusting my glasses one last time for luck. Then the two of us went back to the nook.

If Audrey wondered why I had run out in the middle of her spell, she didn't ask or even give me a questioning look. No, she was entirely consumed with paging through a much larger book that I only belatedly realized was a decoded accounts book.

"It got bigger," I said nonsensically. Surely she had already noticed that.

"It's not an accounts book at all," Audrey gushed in enthusiasm. "It only looked like one. There are all sorts of things in here. It's part diary, part listing of her most secret recipes, part botanical sketchbook of plants I've *never* seen before. It's going to take me years to go through it all!"

"Years," I said tiredly and slumped into the chair next to her at the table. I needed sleep. And a proper breakfast. Then more sleep. I put my head down on my folded arms.

"Well, years to go through all of it, but what we were looking for isn't going to be quite so time consuming," she said smugly. I heard the rustle of paper as she shoved something towards me and I lifted my head enough to look at a neatly written list of names.

"What's this?" I asked, sitting up to look at the names more properly. Most were clearly prosaic. Prosaic and not familiar. But two I recognized at once.

"Agatha had this list of names pinned inside the front cover of the book. Like she tucked it right inside her coding spell. Isn't that clever?" She was practically bouncing in her seat, her enthusiasm level was so high.

"But what is it?" I asked.

"I don't know!" Agatha said. "But it has to be a clue, right? She filled this book years ago, but this list is more recent. And she tucked it inside for safekeeping. It must mean something."

"Customers, maybe?" I said. "This name here, Barnardo Daley, is definitely a customer. He's a regular. I've met him many times. But why would your grandaunt keep a secret list of customers?"

"Maybe she was selling something illegal on the side?" Audrey guessed. But she didn't sound like she believed it either. "Well, we can certainly go around and talk to all these people. Maybe that will help."

"The only other person on this list I know is this one, Cleopatra Manx," I said, putting my thumb under that name. "She runs the Inanna Salon & Spa, and I don't think I've said more than five words to her, ever. But the rest of these names are all prosaics. It doesn't make any sense."

"Maybe it will when we start talking to people," Audrey insisted. "We can start with the one you know. Barnardo Daley."

"All right," I gave in.

But if I thought I was showing a lack of good grace, that was nothing compared to the vibe that Houdini was radiating from where he sat at the head of the table.

"You're going there? There, to *her* house?" he demanded.

Audrey frowned at him. "Barnardo is a woman?" she asked.

"No, but he has a cat named Miss Snooty Cat. That's who Houdini is objecting to," I explained to her. "And there's no reason you have to go, you know. Feel free to stay here. Mi librería es tu librería," I said to him.

"Like I'd leave you to face her *alone*," Houdini said with such chill I was half surprised that his words didn't form into ice and fall out of the air to smash into pieces on the table.

Well, this was going to be a fun interview.

CHAPTER
FOURTEEN

I was startled when we stepped out into the Square to realize it was noon already, the sun blazing down hotly from the very top of the sky. How had I lost an entire morning?

And no wonder my stomach was grumbling so loudly.

"Ritual magic," Audrey said grumpily. I thought she was talking to me, but when I looked over at her, she was looking up at the sun with the same confusion as I was feeling.

"That wasn't ritual magic, though," I said. "It was just a spell."

"Sorry," she flushed. "I was drawing on my training more than I thought. It distorts the perception of the flow of time, among other things. Well, for instance, how much time do you think passed after you left the nook and before you came back again?"

I wracked my brain. "Maybe fifteen minutes? Tops?"

"And for me, it was more like two hours," she said with a smile.

"But that doesn't make sense," I complained. "Time was passing faster out here than inside the area of your spellwork." I pointed up at the sun like it proved my point. "I should've felt like it was hours while you felt like it was fifteen minutes. Right?" I finished lamely. I was very tired. Too tired for math around time paradoxes.

But Audrey just shrugged, her smile lingering still. "I said it distorts the *perception* of time, not the actual passage of time. And I didn't say it did that consistently. Clearly, you've never tried to plan a meetup with other postgraduate ritual magic students."

"Clearly," I agreed.

"Are we doing this or not doing this?" Houdini grumbled from down by our feet. "Because I certainly vote for not doing this."

"We're doing this," I said, and bent to pick him up. I thought he would struggle indignantly, but after a moment's hesitation, he just burrowed his head in under my chin and leaned his whole weight against my chest. Like he was starving for cuddles.

I stroked down the length of his spine, careful not to get too close to his ears. If he were a cat, he would've been purring.

"He's on the second level," I said. "Almost directly over the teashop."

"Interesting," Audrey said as she led the way to the nearest stairwell. "If he acquired the teashop, he would be living right over the store."

"Is that a motive, though?" I pondered. "He never showed any interest in Agatha's business. Besides what she provided for him as a customer, I mean."

We reached the door to his apartment, and Audrey knocked briskly. We could hear movement within almost at once. Then the door swung open and Barnardo Daley was standing there, Miss Snooty Cat in his arms. He was dressed as always, like a prosaic in business casual for his workday in some anonymous office somewhere. Only he was home at noon on... I think it was a Wednesday?

"Tabitha," he said. He looked like he wanted to reach out to give me a hug, but Miss Snooty Cat gave a warning growling sound. This was quickly echoed by an even louder growling sound from Houdini in my own arms.

"Barnardo, we're sorry to disturb you in the middle of the day, but it's about Agatha," I said. Then I gave Houdini a chastising squeeze and he let off with the growl before it could grow into a full-on barking frenzy.

"About Agatha?" Barnardo said, pressing a hand to his forehead as if he were trying to remember a forgotten appointment. Or like he felt a headache coming on. On second inspection, he was not quite as put together as usual. There was more than cat hair clinging to his cream sweater; now there were food stains too.

"Are you doing all right?" I asked him.

"Yes, fine," he said, but he continued to press at his own head.

"Do you need more of what Agatha used to sell you?" I asked him.

"I have a bit left still," he told me. Then, his voice even tighter, he added, "I've been rationing it."

"Mr. Daley, we haven't met, but I'm Audrey Mirken. Agatha's grandniece," Audrey said.

He finally lowered his hand from his forehead, then extended it to her politely. He was flinching away from the sunlight, though, I could tell. His eyes were blinking a lot, too. And we were well in the shade of the walkway above us.

"Maybe we should step inside?" I suggested.

"Yes, of course," Barnardo said with an apologetic smile for forgetting himself, then stepped back to let us into his living room.

The room was all cream and white, from the art on the walls to the furniture and carpeting, but the effect was the farthest thing from bright and cheery. With all the windows shaded, everything was in different degrees of shadow. The total effect was very muted. And while everything was not just tidy but clearly kept meticulously clean, there was a stale quality to the air. I didn't think Barnardo ever opened those windows.

But there was something more. Some sense of something missing. It was like the ghostly form left on a wall when a picture was taken down, only I couldn't tell just what was missing. I only felt the lack.

"I'm letting him in out of respect for Agatha, but I really must ask you to keep hold of him. This is Miss Snooty Cat's abode and I won't have him marking territory here," Barnardo said as he led us to a sectional sofa arranged around a low glass coffee table.

"Of course," I said, and gave Houdini another warning squeeze. He made a snorting noise, I guessed a response to the very idea he would "mark" his "territory," but he said nothing.

"I was just about to have tea and sandwiches myself. I always make too much, if either of you are hungry?" he said after the two of us had settled onto the cream-colored sofa.

To my great dismay, my stomach answered for me. Loudly.

But Barnardo just nodded as if I had used my most polite words to accept his invitation, then turned to Audrey. "And you?"

"That sounds lovely. Do you need any help?" she asked.

"No, I just need to bring it out here rather than eating alone in the kitchen. Really, it's nice to eat with others for a change. No trouble at all," he said. Then, carrying Miss Snooty Cat, he disappeared into his kitchen.

"He seems perfectly lovely," Audrey said, then leaned closer to whisper, "although I get the sense that cat is very well named."

Houdini huffed his agreement, but curled up on my lap as contentedly as any lapdog and promptly went to sleep.

Barnardo returned with a heavily-laden tray in his hands, Miss Snooty Cat strutting along behind him. He set it at the center of the coffee table, then poured out three cups of tea before handing each of us a little plate and napkin. The sandwiches were cut into perfect triangles and arranged by type on one of those three-tiered silver serving things you see in proper tea parlors.

There was no way he had just done this. Not unless he, too, was using ritual magic to change my perception of time. Did he really dress up his lunch like this every day?

Or did he harbor a secret desire to host high teas? To run a teashop of his own?

"These are cucumber and cream cheese on the top. The middle layer is tuna salad, my late father's recipe. And the bottom is roast beef and Swiss, my father's actual favorite, despite the fact he was forever preparing the tuna fish," Barnardo explained. Then he bustled back into the kitchen and returned with a plate of vegetable crudités and a bowl of fresh berries generously topped with hand-whipped cream.

"You must have been expecting company," Audrey fretted at the sight of all that food.

"I really wasn't," Barnardo said before he disappeared yet again. He returned with another three-tiered serving tray, this one laden with a variety of cookies. Only once it was arranged within easy reach of any of us did he settle back onto the couch and take a sip of his own tea.

"This isn't my grandaunt's blend," Audrey guessed as she sipped at hers. I sampled mine. It was a very good Earl Grey, but I suspected she was right even before Barnardo started blushing a deep shade of rose.

"No, I'm afraid this comes from the Abergavennys' corner store. In bags, even! Please don't tell her," he said. Then his cheeks went full crimson as he realized what he had just said. "I'm sorry. That was thoughtless of me. I had quite forgotten... Never mind. I'm sorry for your loss."

"We were all close to Agatha in our own ways," Audrey said. "It's all our loss, really. But I wanted to say, if you have something you need that's in her book, I can make up as much as you need. There's no need to ration it out."

"Oh, thank you!" he said with palpable relief. "I wasn't sure what was going to happen with her shop, or if anyone had those recipes at all. Frankly, I had no idea what I was going to do. Did I, Miss Snooty Cat?"

Miss Snooty Cat made a soft yowl of agreement, then set to work cleaning her ears. But she kept a constant watch on Houdini out of the corners of her eyes, I noticed.

"Are you planning to stay and run the shop?" Barnardo asked Audrey with almost painful eagerness.

"I hadn't decided yet," Audrey admitted. "And the will hasn't been read yet, so deciding would be premature. But I'm here for a little while longer. I'll find you in her books and mix up a batch of what you need this afternoon, I promise. Whatever happens with the teashop, I promise you'll have a copy of whatever recipe my grandaunt was giving you. You can find someone who can make it up for you, I'm sure."

"Thank you so much," he said, giving her knee an awkward little squeeze of thanks. Then, as if having that settled finally made it possible for his appetite to return, he turned his attention to the sandwiches with real gusto. "I, for one, vote for you to stay, young lady," he added before stuffing an entire triangle of tuna salad sandwich into his mouth.

"I hope so too," I put in, and Audrey busied herself filling a bowl with berries and cream, largely so that her long hair could fall forward and cover her own blush, I was sure.

"We wanted to ask you about something we found in Agatha's things," I said. "We're not sure what it means, but we're hoping you might know more."

"I don't know how I possibly could, but I'll help in any way I can," he said, flustered. I looked at Audrey, and she nodded, then dug the list of names out of her shoulder bag to hand it to him. He frowned as he scanned the names. "Oh, I see why you thought to ask me. My name is here. Sadly, I have no idea what it means. I'm so sorry."

"Nothing links you with these people that you can think of?" I prodded, as he handed the list back to Audrey.

"No, nothing at all. Most of those names I don't even recognize. They look prosaic, don't they?" he said.

"They do," I conceded. "All save you and Cleopatra Manx."

He wrinkled his nose disapprovingly at the mere mention of her name, but said nothing.

"Do you think this is a list of special customers?" Audrey asked.

"Oh, I don't see how that could be," Barnardo said, musing as he chewed on a carrot stick. "No, I have no idea what regulars she might have had in the prosaic world, but I would bet anything at all that Cleopatra Manx never set foot inside that teashop. No, she's a latte girl all the way."

"She goes to Titus Bloom's shop?" I asked.

"Not even," Barnardo said with a snort of a laugh. "No, she crosses the street every morning to go to that prosaic place across the street. Not just prosaic, it's that globally dominant chain that *everyone* goes to. How basic is that? Every morning she gets the largest latte with all the gloppy syrups and she nurses that thing in her salon all day long. Just for the look, right? It's got to be." Then he said to Miss Snooty Cat in a loud aside, "and she thinks she's so special. Turns her nose up at us, doesn't she, Miss Snooty Cat?"

Miss Snooty Cat might have been agreeing, or she might have been mimicking the same nose-up posture the Trio always maintained. It was really hard to tell which.

"I suppose we'd have to ask Cleopatra why her name is on this list, then," I said with a sigh. I wasn't looking forward to that conversation.

"Not today, I'm afraid," Barnardo said casually as he filled his plate with one of each kind of cookie. There were a lot of different kinds of cookies on that server.

"Why not today?" I asked. I was still pretty sure it was Wednesday. Nothing special happened on Wednesdays that I could think of.

"It's her day off," Barnardo said, as if that were common knowledge. "She'll be sunning herself somewhere warm all day."

"Like at Lake Harriet?" Audrey guessed.

"More like Mallorca," Barnardo said. "You'll have to catch her tomorrow. Be sure to admire her bronzed tan. She takes great pride in getting that the old-fashioned way. You know, by constantly teleporting across the globe. As if the rest of us could afford the portal fees for that. Every Wednesday."

"That's just as well," Audrey said as she and I both got up from what had turned out to be a really filling lunch. "I wanted to mix up that recipe for you, and I can already tell this is going to be an early night for me."

"For me too, I think," I agreed. I was bone-tired. But at least I wasn't sparking little fires anymore.

It's important to appreciate the small things.

"Please let me know if there's anything else I can help with," Barnardo said as he walked us back to the door. "Although I wouldn't worry so much about a list of names, you know. I'm sure once the will is read, the teashop will be yours."

"Oh," Audrey said, not sure how to respond to that.

"That's what you're worried about, isn't it? That she might have given it to someone else? You both have such serious energy, I just assumed it must be that."

Audrey and I exchanged a long look, and I knew we were in agreement. There was no need to let anyone else know that we suspected murder.

Not when we still had, seriously, no evidence. Just a hunch and a dog that no one but us knew could talk.

"Yes, I'm sure you're right," Audrey said at last, and gave him an appropriately tremulous smile.

Then the two of us were back out in the blazing sun. Sadly, no more illuminated than we had been before.

"But hey, the spell worked," I felt compelled to point out.

"The spell worked," Audrey agreed.

If only the book had spilled all of its secrets. But the decoded message was only slightly less opaque than the coded one had been.

What had Agatha been hiding? And from whom?

CHAPTER
FIFTEEN

I woke far too early the next morning to find Houdini standing on my chest, his nose so close to my face it was practically inside my mouth.

"You were making noises," he said accusingly, then moved off me to let me sit up. Judging by the gray quality of the light that barely filtered into my bedroom, it was not quite dawn yet.

"Sorry," I mumbled. "I think I was having a nightmare."

"What about?" he asked casually.

I rubbed at my head and tried to bring up any of it, but it was all gone from my mind now. Even though my heart rate was still up, and the sweat on my skin had not yet dried. Something had been disturbing me greatly, but it was gone now.

"I don't actually remember," I told him as I reached for my glasses. The room around me came into a better focus, including Houdini. As limited as a dog's facial expressions can be, I sensed a concern in him, now that I could see him clearly, that had been hidden in his casual tone of voice. "Did a woman come in here while I was sleeping?"

Not that I thought I'd had a mother dream. I usually remembered those.

I assumed.

"No, no one was here but the two of us," he said. He rested his chin on my knee and looked up at me with those sweet brown eyes. "I can detect astral and magical presences, even some elemental and spiritual ones. No one was here but the two of us."

"That's good to know," I said. "I guess it was just your run-of-the-mill nightmare then. But there's no going back to sleep for me now. You can nap some more if you want. I'm going to grab a shower and then get some food and coffee, I think."

"I'll stand guard," he said with deadly seriousness.

Then he curled up in the tangles of my bedding and went right back to sleep.

Somehow, I sensed this was not as incongruous as it looked. If he was right about his abilities to sense all manners of things, he could probably sense things in his sleep as well.

And he had been standing on my chest to wake me up, to pull me out of the nightmare. I was a little curious about what I might have been dreaming about, but a lot happy that I couldn't remember it at all. I don't have prophetic dreams or anything. Just random bits of things I've encountered throughout the day, morphing themselves into their most terrifying versions for my dreamscapes.

The random things you encounter in magic schools are nightmare fuel enough, but I think my dream brain likes to lay it on really thick.

I felt somewhat better after my shower, although my hair was still a problem. I only towel-dried it, not really being a blow-dryer person, but by the time I was dressed it was already dried to a crispy, staticky mass of disarray. I tried running a little hair oil through it, but my hair just soaked the oil up like water from a spilled sippy cup in the middle of Death Valley, ending in a state just as dry and unmanageable as it had been before I'd started.

And even though I'd unpacked my bags weeks ago and hung

everything neatly in the closet, all of it was severely wrinkled when I tried to find something to put on. The jeans were all right, but all the T-shirts looked like I'd let them air-dry while wadded up in a ball. Despite how warm I knew the day was going to be, I pulled a hoodie on to cover the least wrinkled of the T-shirts, then left in search of coffee and food.

I stumbled into the library about an hour later, oatmeal still warm in my belly and a second mug of barely tolerable instant coffee in my hand. It was just past dawn now, but I couldn't say I was surprised to see that Audrey was already there in my nook looking over the ledger.

"Couldn't sleep?" I guessed as I sat down across from her.

"I slept a little," she said, then glanced up from the ledger. I don't know what she was planning to say next, but it clearly fell right out of her mind when she got a good look at me. "What happened to you?"

"What do you mean?" I asked. "I promise it only *looks* like I slept in these clothes."

"It's not that. You look exhausted," she said, but then she shook her head. "No, not that. Or, at least, not just that. You looked exhausted and hyper fired up at the same time. Like it's the week before finals and no one can get you to stop pounding no-doze potions and take a break from studying to get a little proper rest."

"I slept," I said, a little defensively.

"She had a nightmare," Houdini announced as he trotted into the room, then disappeared under the table. He reappeared again, sitting at the chair at the head of the table. Sitting up straight, his chin just cleared the top of the table.

I should get him a book to sit on. But that wouldn't be comfortable when he took one of his many naps.

"Anything important?" Audrey asked.

That's one of the way we magical types are different from prosaic people. Not only do we legitimately want to hear about each other's dreams, we like to go over them thoroughly, examining every possible detail for clues of hidden meanings.

"I don't dream like that," I told her. "I dream like someone in the prosaic world. I just do it a lot, with great variety and imagination. It's exhausting."

"Even prosaics sometimes dream things that are important," she said. "It's an important tool of our subconscious to work on things while we're sleeping and find insights that our waking selves might miss."

"As much as that might be true, I'm afraid I really don't remember anything," I said. "Houdini woke me up, and all the images just evaporated from my mind. Good riddance."

"You woke her up?" Audrey said to Houdini.

"Indeed," Houdini said, pulling himself up a little taller. "She was in distress. I pulled her out of her dreamscape, and she was much calmer then."

"Pulled her out of her dreamscape?" Audrey repeated. "Are you just being poetic, or is this an actual power that you have? Do you literally dive dreams?"

"He can't do that," I said before he could answer. "That's a familiar skill, and he's not my familiar."

"It's not *just* a power of familiars," I heard Steph say from behind me. I turned in my chair to see him sweeping into my little nook. He was still dressed like Hamlet, as pale of skin and dark of hair as ever, but the jewel-toned cloak was gone. He took the chair opposite Houdini and gave the dog a long, steady once-over before turning his attention to me. "We had a date."

"Yeah, I'm sorry about that," I said.

"I came again the next day at lunchtime, but you weren't here then either," he said.

"I've been busy."

"You've been put in charge of this bookshop. How can you be busy and yet not here?" he asked.

"I'm sorry, but we've not been properly introduced," Audrey

butted in to say. She held out a hand towards Steph. "I'm Audrey Mirken. Agatha Mirken's grandniece. And I'm afraid I'm the one who's been keeping Tabitha all tied up. She's helping me figure out what happened to my grandaunt."

"Stephanos Underwood, but please call me Steph," he said, taking her hand and giving it a warm shake. "I've heard about Agatha, of course. My condolences."

"It's been so quiet in the bookshop, I didn't think it would matter much if I popped out for a bit," I said. His dark eyes moved back to mine, and I felt myself flushing. Two days was more than "a bit." Not that he said so. But I could feel him thinking it. "I should be here more, though. You're quite right."

"If you need help, I can arrange some for you," he said.

"Aren't you awfully busy working with the Wizard and all?" I asked.

"I am indeed," he said. "But I can summon a lesser elemental to assist you. Just something to watch the front desk while you're away."

"That would work fine for the magic side of things, but not so much for the prosaic side," I said.

"We were going to talk to Cleopatra today, but we can save that for lunchtime," Audrey said. "We can stay in the bookshop for customers in the morning and after lunch."

"I suppose that's the responsible thing to do," I agreed. Then sighed. "It's not like we had any other leads to follow up on in the meantime. Unless you found something in the ledger?"

"Not really," she said.

"Would you kindly ask that boy to stop staring at me," Houdini growled low in my mind. I looked over at the dog, standing on the chair now with his back bristling up.

I turned to Steph, but he just held up a hand to belay me. "I don't answer to 'boy', dog," he said with amusement in his tone.

As surprised as Audrey and I were to find another person who could hear Houdini, neither of us was as shocked as Houdini himself.

"You can hear him?" I said to Steph, while Houdini blubbered noises in the back of my mind. Apparently, it was possible to get tongue-tied even when using telepathy.

"Certainly," Steph said. "But why are you surprised? When I came in here, you said he wasn't your familiar. And yet you can hear him speak."

"I can too," Audrey put in.

"Do you know what's going on here?" I asked Steph. "It's his magic and not ours, right?"

"That much is definitely true," he said. "He chooses who can hear him."

"And I didn't choose *you*," Houdini growled, his back bristling still further.

"Well, that would be part of *my* magic, wouldn't it?" Steph said smoothly. He interlaced his fingers, then rested his chin where they crossed. He wasn't smiling at Houdini, but there was a humorous glint to his eye.

"What magic is that?" Houdini demanded. "What are you?"

"I'm the Wizard's apprentice," Steph said, as if that were all the answer he needed. "As to your first question, such things I keep to myself. But tell me, what are you?"

"I keep things to myself as well," Houdini grumbled, slumping lower into his chair.

"Fair enough," Steph said brightly. "I won't tell if you won't."

Houdini made more garbled complaining sounds in our minds as he turned around and around on the seat cushion. Then he flopped down out of sight. But I don't think any of us really believed he was napping.

Steph leaned across the table towards me. "About that book?"

"Oh, right! I'm so sorry for dropping the ball on that," I said. "To be honest, I don't even know if that book you were looking for is available anywhere. But I can go downstairs and check. I should turn the sign to 'open' anyway."

"I'll go with you," he said, pushing away from the table.

"I'll stay here, if that's all right," Audrey said. "We only skimmed this ledger before, I want to finish giving it a thorough look-through."

"Of course. I'll be back up to help in just a minute," I promised.

"No hurry," she said, then leaned over the ledger, back in the exact posture I had found her in before.

Steph followed silently behind me all the way down to the main floor, then through the rows of bookshelves to the front desk. Once more he followed me back behind the counter, watching over my shoulder as I opened up the magic tome and leafed through to the current page.

That spicy smell hadn't been the cloak.

And I was almost tasting butterscotch on my tongue again. But that might just have been a really vivid sense memory.

Because this time around, what I mostly felt was how warm he was standing so close beside me.

"It's interesting what you're doing with your hair," he said, snapping me out of my reverie like I'd been fired out by a huge slingshot.

"Excuse me?" I said.

"This isn't normal, you know," he said. He reached out a hand to touch my hair. Before I could pull away, an arc of blue spark short from my hair to the tips of his fingers. He hissed a little in minor pain and shook his hand, but he was grinning at me all the same.

"It's not normal for me either," I told him, trying desperately with both hands to flatten the staticky mess down again. Sparks were shooting everywhere, but not quite strong enough to be a fire hazard.

Yet.

"Is this part of how your magic manifests?" he asked.

"No," I said. It came out a lot more bitter than I had intended it. "Look, you said you know everything about everything."

"Did I say that?" he asked.

"So you must know that I don't have any magic skills at all," I went on as if he hadn't interrupted me.

141

"I don't know why you think that. Because *that*," and he gestured towards my hair again, but this time at a respectful distance, "is not normal."

"I'm not *making* it happen," I all but wailed. "It just does this. It's been too long since I've seen my mother. She can always set things right, but I can't exactly rely on her to turn up on any kind of schedule."

"That doesn't sound like a great plan, long term," he said with a frown.

"Well, also, my uncle made me these glasses," I said, and adjusted them on my nose. My hair shot off a few more sparks, then died down enough to rest softly around my ears. Some of the floating cloud effect had gone out of it, anyway.

"Interesting," Steph said.

"Listen, as someone who knows everything about everything—" I started to say.

"I never said that," he put in.

"Well, at the very least, you know something about Houdini," I said.

"Something," he conceded. Then maddeningly said no more.

"He's not a familiar. I don't think he was even Agatha's familiar," I said.

"No, nor I," he agreed.

"But he's not just a dog," I went on.

"No, definitely not. And yet he's not the problem either."

"Excuse me?"

Steph took a deep breath, then gave me an apologetic smile. "Forget it. Houdini will tell his secrets when he's ready. I'll say no more of what I suspect. Because honestly, I really don't know. But I will tell you that I sense he is no danger to you or Audrey. In fact, he feels quite protective of you both."

"That's something, I guess," I said, then turned my attention back to the tome. "There's a bookshop in Berlin that has what your

Wizard is looking for. Do you want me to have them send it here? It would arrive in the morning post through the portal."

"No, that's all right," he said, and when I looked up from the book, I saw that cloak just settling around him, as if I had just missed seeing it fly through the library to find him. "I can get there myself in no time. But you still owe me a lunch."

"I thought lunch was your treat," I said.

"It was, the first two times," he said. "A shame you never got to sample any of the delectables I prepared."

"I'm sorry," I said, and I really was. I had completely forgotten about him once Audrey had arrived.

But he held up a hand to belay me once again. "Don't be silly. Murder takes precedence, doesn't it?"

I almost gasped aloud. "You believe Agatha was murdered, too?"

"I know you do," he said. "That's good enough for me. I only wish I could spare the time to be of any help to you. But my master beckons, and I really much fetch that book. What we're investigating is important to everyone in the Square, or I swear I would be helping you solve this murder. Not that I think you need my help. That was nice work, decoding that book of Agatha's."

I felt my cheeks flushing, both at the compliment and at the sudden awareness that he really *did* seem to know everything. We had told no one about the book. No one knew but Audrey, Houdini and me.

We *will* have that lunch, though," he said as he gathered the folds of his cloak around him. "When your investigation is complete."

"That's a date," I promised.

Then he was gone, just winking out of thin air right in front of me.

Leaving me a clear view of the front door, open now as Liam was just stepping inside.

CHAPTER
SIXTEEN

At first, I was sure Liam hadn't noticed anything. The door had stuck on a fold in the old carpet and he had to look down to see the problem and flatten it out with his sneakered foot. I was sure he had been looking down pretty studiously until Steph had disappeared entirely.

But as he approached the front desk, there was a quizzical confusion on his face as he looked all around. Like someone who had just seen a cat dart off out of sight but was still trying to find it.

"Wasn't somebody just here when I came in?" he asked me.

"No," I lied blithely. I didn't really like how easy it was, but what was I going to do? Keeping the existence of magic, real magic, secret from the prosaic world was rule number one all over the magical community.

I had just never had to enforce it myself before.

"Are you here to shop, or...?" I trailed off. Then wished I hadn't. It made it sound a little like I was fishing for a date, which I absolutely wasn't. But no second half of that sentence came to mind, so I was stuck with that lame cliffhanger.

"No, I just wanted to see how you were doing," he said. Then he flushed a little. "I was going to bring you some hot food, but the last couple of times I've been by, the shop was closed."

"Yeah, sorry about that," I said. "I had some things to attend to."

"Because of the death of your friend?"

"Because of the death of my friend," I agreed.

We stood there in awkward silence for an eternal moment. The bookshop around us, if anything, amplified that silence. Heck, it amplified the awkwardness.

Liam wanted me to talk first, clearly. And after blowing him off, I owed him that. Only I didn't know what I could say.

Then a sudden flash of inspiration struck me.

He was a prosaic. And I had the need for a little prosaic knowledge at the moment.

"Look, I don't know much about philosophy majors and what skills they give you. But I'm hoping research might be one of them?" I said, then bit my lip anxiously as I waited for an answer.

"What kind of research?" he asked, not quite suspiciously, but close to it. Well, in all fairness, it was a weird question to throw at him out of nowhere.

"If I had a list of names, would you be able to go to a library or something and tell me all you can find out about them?" I asked.

"Why?" he asked. Definitely suspicious now.

"It's a bit of business my friend left behind after she died," I said. "But it's just a list of names. I'm not sure if she owed them money, or would want them to know she passed on because they were friends, or what."

"I suppose I can help with that," he said guardedly. "I mean, I *am* good with research. And I'm good with making connections other people don't see. But if I turn up something bad..."

Now it was his turn to trail off. Like me, I don't think he knew when he started just where he had planned to end that sentence, so it fell off a cliff.

But I bailed him out. "If you're feeling any conflict at all about what you turn up, you don't have to tell me anything. That's perfectly fair. But honestly, I have no reason to suspect anything bad is going to be turned up. I think they're probably just a list of people who were interested in buying her property. You know the teashop next door?"

"Do I?" he asked, squinting a little as he racked his memory.

"It's on the corner, between here and the comic shop," I said.

"Then I must've walked right past it a dozen times, but I can't say that I've ever noticed," he said with an apologetic look in his eyes.

"It hasn't been a successful business lately," I admitted. "Which is why I think she was keeping track of the offers. If there were offers. I don't know." I took a deep breath to clear my own frustration, then said, "Do you want to come up to the fourth floor with me and I'll give you the names?"

"Sure," he said, but not with an overwhelming amount of enthusiasm or anything. "It's not like I'm doing anything else at the moment."

"Still unemployed?" I asked sympathetically as we started up the stairs.

"Still unemployed," he agreed. "I have enough put away for another month's rent, but if I don't get a job soon, I won't get a paycheck in time for the next month's rent. I'd hate to ask my room-mates to carry me even for a week. I know their money is tight, too."

"Hopefully something will turn up," I said, then winced at how lame those words sounded.

But he just gave me a glum, "Yeah."

I could hear Audrey's voice as we approached the nook, but she fell silent at the sound of our footsteps approaching. I guessed she'd been talking to Houdini. It was a shame we couldn't answer him in the same telepathic way he talked to us.

My mind immediately jumped back to wondering what Steph wasn't telling me about Houdini. Would it do any good just to ask Houdini what his secret was?

Then Liam and I reached the nook, and Audrey had gotten to her feet, surprised that I had brought a visitor. Particularly one who was so clearly a prosaic. She was flustered, sweeping up the ledger and her handwritten notes and looking around a little desperately for where she could hide any of it. In the end, she dumped it all on the seat of her own chair, then leaned over it, hands grasping the wooden back of the chair so tightly her knuckles went white.

And yet, the ledger and her notes were possibly the least magical things around us at the moment. All the wall hangings had magical themes, the fireplaces on either side of the window seat had cauldrons on hooks. They were swung to the side, out of the way of any flames from the fires that weren't even lit at the moment. But anyone looking inside would see the residue on the bottom, bits of color that were just a little outside of normal experience. A magic-user would know at once that these cauldrons had been involved in potion-making. But I had no idea what a prosaic would think.

Clearly, it had been a mistake bringing Liam up to the fourth floor. The prosaics never got off the first floor. Not that that was any kind of rule my uncles had told me. It was just that they never wandered even to the bottom of the stairs. I wasn't sure any of them even noticed there were stairs.

Luckily for me, Liam had absolutely no interest in anything around us. Not in the rare materials books we had walked past, not in the little dog low-growling at him from the end of the table, not even in the materials that Audrey had just swept off the table.

No, his eyes never left Audrey. And I would swear he had been struck mid-step by the sight of her. His posture was really weirdly balanced. I kind of wanted to push on his shoulder to see if I could knock him over, or at least get him to stand up correctly.

For her part, Audrey was blushing furiously. She dropped her own gaze pretty quickly, fixating on the papers and books she had dumped into the seat of her chair, and repeatedly tucking her light blonde hair back behind her ears.

"He smells safe," Houdini announced to both of us, and promptly ducked out of sight, back to his nap.

"But who is he?" Audrey asked in a whisper. Then blushed even more deeply before saying in a clearer voice, "I mean, who's your friend, Tabitha?"

"This is Liam Kelly. He's a pro-... I mean, he's a local who can help us with that list of names. You know the one I mean?" I finished.

"Oh, right," Audrey said, and laughed nervously. She looked up again but made no move to find the list.

Liam finally blinked. "Sorry. I'm Liam," he said, and reached across the table to give Audrey his hand.

"Audrey Mirken," she said, giving his hand a quick squeeze.

"Audrey's grandaunt is the woman who died," I told him.

"I'm so sorry for your loss," he said.

"Oh. Thank you," Audrey said.

They both fell silent, but this was far from the awkward silence from before. No, the silence between them had a warm glow to it. I could almost see it. I could certainly feel it.

Or maybe what I felt was the acute sense of being a third wheel.

I cleared my throat, and they both jumped, then looked over at me. Nice to know I hadn't completely disappeared. "The list?" I prompted.

"Oh, right," Audrey said. She dug around the papers on the seat of her chair, then held out a scrap of parchment to Liam. He took it, a bemused look on his face as he touched the material. I doubted he handled much parchment in the prosaic world. But he didn't remark on it, just studied the names.

"Do you know any of them?" I asked hopefully. The more information we could have sooner, the better.

"No, but like I said, I moved in about the same time you did," he said. Then he tucked the list away in the back pocket of his jeans. "The library opens in less than an hour. I'll head over there now and grab a computer as soon as they open. Property sales are public record, but just inquiring about buying a property isn't really. So no promises."

"Anything you can tell us about them could be very helpful," Audrey said.

"I'll do my best," he said solemnly. Then added, "so, are you the heir? Is that teashop yours now?"

"We're still working on that, but probably yes," she said.

"You can help me convince her to stay," I said. I should feel terrible, being blatantly manipulative like that. But I didn't.

"You should stay. It's really a lovely location. The right person could do a lot with it," he said. So sincerely that if I hadn't heard what he'd said not ten minutes before, I'd never have been able to tell that he couldn't recall ever even walking past the place.

"Well, I'll be staying for a few days, anyway. To... deal with some stuff... with my grandaunt Agatha... her estate," Audrey stammered. She kept shooting looks at me every time she stumbled for her next word. But I just widened my eyes and shrugged my shoulders. Whatever she was trying to nudge me about, I wasn't getting it.

"Are we saying the word 'murder' out loud?" Houdini said from under the table. Or from the back of my mind, whichever. "That's what she's trying to suss out from you. That nightmare really did a number on your head today."

"I'm fine," I said. Liam turned to give me a curious look, and I realized I had not only spoken a complete non sequitur, I had almost snapped it out. "I mean, you said the library would be opening soon. Shall I walk you to the door?"

"Oh. Yes. Of course," Liam said.

But only because he was too polite to say out loud that he'd rather Audrey did it.

I took him by the arm and guided him back towards the stairs. But he seemed less distracted this time, more inclined to look around. I had to keep his focus off the magic all around us before he started asking questions.

"Audrey and I have sort of an appointment at lunchtime, and I don't know how long it will take," I said. "If the bookshop is closed, can you go to the teashop and wait for us there? It's not open for business, but if you knock we'll let you in."

There was magic there, too, but it was all out of sight. It would be safer to meet there.

"Sure. The teashop," he said, nodding.

"The Loose Leaves Teashop," I clarified. "Thanks so much for helping us out. We have so much to dig through already, if you can tell us what these names mean, we'd appreciate it so much."

"Let's see what I can find out first," he said. "I've done tons of research papers in my day, but this is more like private investigator stuff. It might not be in my wheelhouse."

"I'm sure you'll do great," I told him as we reached the bottom of the stairs. I opened the front door for him and he gave me a smile of farewell before heading down the sidewalk. The day outside was already hot, and even poking my head out the door was enough to start me sweating in my hoodie. I pulled the door shut, locked it, and turned the sign over to 'Closed' with a sigh.

This was really not what my uncles had hired me to do, but I was pretty sure they would understand if they knew the details.

Hopefully, talking to Cleopatra Manx wouldn't take long. And would lead to some useful bit of information.

I headed back upstairs to my nook.

CHAPTER
SEVENTEEN

I had never been inside the Inanna Salon & Spa in the short time I had been living in the Square. I had barely even walked past it. The closest I had come was when Titus and his wife had brought me inside the Bitter Brew Coffeeshop next door while Volumnia dealt with Agatha's body that tragic night.

Even if I hadn't been too distraught to care about my surroundings at the time, it had been the middle of the night. Not even the corner shop had still been open. The Inanna Salon & Spa would've been dark and shuttered.

So as Audrey and I stepped inside that mid June morning, pausing just inside the doors to appreciate the frigid blast of air conditioning so refreshing after the heat outside, we were both seeing the place for the first time.

It had everything a prosaic hair salon would have. Three chairs sat before mirrors with assorted combs, brushes, clippers and scissors arranged in organizers close at hand. Hairdryers, flatirons, and curling irons were docked in heat-resistant slots inside open drawers, all plugged in and ready to go. There were two chairs with water basins at the base of them for the spa pedicure experience, and two tables with opposing chairs under intense light for manicures. A pair of overhead dryers stood over comfy-looking leather chairs, currently unoccupied. And the back wall featured an expansive array of products for hair, skin, nails and I suspected more.

I was well aware that the world of beauty products contained more things than were dreamt of in my philosophy.

Although, so far as I could tell, there was nothing magical on offer. Everything was bright, beautiful, and sparkly. But for all that, it was also quite prosaic.

Even the clientele. They had clearly all come through the other door. I recognized no one I knew from the Square. Which was a little unusual. But two women were currently getting their hair styled in two of the three chairs, and four more were waiting in the little seating area closest to the door to the prosaic world.

I recognized Cleopatra Manx at once. She was standing behind a desk, sipping from an oversized cup of coffee from the chain across the street. Probably something frothy, although not being a clear plastic cup, I guessed it wasn't iced. She looked cooly gorgeous, like her own walk through the Square had left her untouched by sweat. Neither was she bothered now by the constant blast of air conditioning that was so cold I was starting to shiver already inside my hoodie, and I had just been out in the heat. But she, in her sleeveless sheath dress, seemed completely unbothered.

Her two protégées were also underdressed for the inside temperature, but also seemed not to mind. I looked from one blown-out blonde hairstyle to the other, took in the sapphire blue sundress and the emerald green one, then the shoes that were sensibly flat and yet so stylishly adorned they gave the illusion of being heels, and finally decided that Cressida Cade was the one closer to us in the green dress. That made it Delilah Dare in the blue.

Although if I looked again, I might change my mind. They were both clearly copying Cleopatra's look, but Cleopatra was almost divinely put together. She was the Platonic ideal they both aspired to. Which made them more interchangeable with each other, while not quite reaching the goal they were both striving for.

That's when I changed my mind about the magic in that salon. It was clearly there. It was just all in the hands of Cleopatra and her two employees. The tools they used were all perfectly prosaic, and the clients suspected nothing supernatural was going on. And yet I could see even with my lack of real magical ability that the way Cressida could make her client's hair flip under just so was less about her skill with the flatiron and more about the magic in her own hands.

"Can I help you?" Cleopatra asked us when she finally noticed us standing there. There was a slight sneer to her voice, like the mean girl voice inside of her was saying we were clearly both beyond help. "We're all booked up, I'm afraid, not just for today but clear into next month. But if you wanted to schedule something?" She trailed off, then took another sip from her coffee.

"We wanted to talk to you about Agatha Mirken and the Loose Leaves Teashop, if you had a moment," I said.

She frowned, but in a careful sort of way. Like she wanted to convey her dislike of the question, but she also didn't want to wrinkle her face to do it. "What on Earth would I have to say about that?" she asked.

"Just a few questions, please," Audrey said. "I'm Audrey Mirken, Agatha's grandniece."

"So you're asking me a boon? In the name of the recently departed?" Cleopatra asked. Like it was some formal gesture she would be obliged to make. But it was certainly not one I had ever heard of before.

"Please," was all Audrey said.

Cleopatra sighed dramatically. Then she raised her immaculately manicured hands and clapped them together. She had two thin gold bangles on each wrist and they tinkled together, a sound that carried throughout the room even after the sound from the clapping of her hands had faded away.

And then everything fell silent. I couldn't hear the chatter of the clients, or the soft roar of Delilah's hairdryer, or the bubbling of the water in the basins of the pedicure chairs. Only the blast from the air conditioner was still audible.

But when I looked towards the prosaic door, I could see the women waiting in the chairs still moving their mouths as if speaking to each other. And Delilah's blow-dryer was still moving around the hair on her client's head. And none of them seemed the least distressed. Apparently they hadn't been struck suddenly deaf, as I seemed to have been.

But the air conditioner roared on. I had that to hold on to.

"Clever spell," Audrey said in little more than a whisper.

"A handy one," Cleopatra allowed. "But there's no need to whisper. They can't hear us, and they won't really notice us unless one of you does something really drastic like start tossing fireballs."

"But we can hear you," Cressida said. I glanced over at her and was initially unsure if I had really heard her. She certainly seemed to be engrossed in styling her client's hair, and even seemed to be saying something to her that I couldn't hear. But then she smiled at me and gave me a wink, and I knew I hadn't imagined it.

"Now, rumor has it the two of you think Agatha's death was a murder," Cleopatra said, folding her arms as she glowered down at us. Her fingers arranged themselves just so along her toned and tanned biceps, the rosy color of her nail polish complementing the honey shade of her arms perfectly. It was almost distracting.

Or the soft clink as the change in position set her bangles sliding down her arms was doing more magic on me. I blinked and forced my mind to focus.

"We don't know what's going on, to be honest," I said. "But we're trying to sort some things out."

"My grandaunt had a list of names in a book in her teashop," Audrey said. "Yours was one of them."

"How very interesting," Cleopatra said, in a way that really meant the exact opposite. Then she said, "Look, how can I possibly help you find an explanation for that? Without knowing the other names or what the list was even for?"

"We don't know what the list was for either," I said. "And most of the list was names of people in the prosaic world. Which is why it's such a mystery to us."

"The only other person from the Square whose name was on the list was Barnardo," Audrey put in.

"Barnardo?" Cleopatra said, as if she had never heard that string of syllables put together before in her life. Then she wrinkled her nose, again just enough to convey her disdain without quite risking a permanent crease to her face. "Barnardo Daley? The scruffy man with the cat?"

"The same," I said. "Do the two of you have anything in common that you can think about?"

"As if!" she sniffed.

"Yes, he said much the same," Audrey said drily, and I fought back a snicker at the look Cleopatra shot her way. But Audrey just consulted the book in her hands, ignoring Cleopatra's death glare. "I'm sorry to be blunt, but I don't get the impression my grandaunt liked you very much."

"The feeling was quite mutual," Cleopatra said. "But so what? That doesn't mean I pushed her off a balcony, or whatever it is the two of you are really thinking. For all you know, you uncovered Agatha's hit list. You found a motive for her to kill me, not the other way around."

"We don't think it was a hit list," I said. "For one thing, Agatha *liked* Barnardo."

"Which is why we think this might be a list of names of people who were interested in buying the teashop," Audrey said.

I bit my tongue to keep from saying out loud that that didn't make any sense either. We already knew Barnardo had no interest in buying the shop.

It was just possible it was a list of people Agatha hoped she could talk into taking over her shop for her, maybe. But the plethora of prosaic names made even that theory a little untenable.

"Why would I be interested in that... place?" Cleopatra asked. I sensed she had belatedly remembered she was dealing with a grieving person and dialed back the word she really wanted to use to describe the Loose Leaves Teashop.

"It's a corner location," Audrey said. "With the bookshop sitting on one corner, the corner shop taking the other, and the Wizard's tower sitting on the corner at the end of the alley, it's the best location in the Square for attracting prosaic customers."

"First of all, as you can see, I have no trouble bringing in prosaic customers," Cleopatra said with a sweeping gesture towards her clientele.

I had to admit she was right about that.

"Second of all, the only desirable corner on the Square from the prosaic perspective is the one the bookshop sits on. It's on both of the two main roads outside this place. But your uncles aren't even using it properly. They have their only entrance halfway down the block of the lesser of the two streets. And don't think I haven't brought that up with them," she said to me.

"I'm pretty sure my uncles already have all the prosaic clientele they want to handle," I said.

"Yes, that's what they told me," she said. Then rolled her eyes but said no more.

"But the teashop—" Audrey started to say.

But Cleopatra cut her off. "It may be on a corner, but it's not a *good* corner. One side is the lesser main road, and the other is that dirty little alley. And next door to a comic book shop? You really think that's a draw for me? No, I promise you, I've never had any interest in your grandaunt's property. May she rest in peace," she belatedly added, then took another sip of her coffee.

"I didn't see you outside in the Square the night Agatha fell," I said. "Nearly everyone was there, but not you. Any of you."

"That's because we were together at a conference out of town," Cleopatra said blithely.

"A conference?" I said skeptically.

"It's true," Cressida put in earnestly. "We were in Vegas for a hair coloring seminar, and we stayed the night. You know, because it's Vegas."

"Do you want receipts?" Cleopatra asked. She threw that question down like it was a challenge she was daring me to accept.

But I just said as casually as I could, "No, I don't think that will be necessary. Of course we believe you. We'll get out of your hair. If you'll pardon the pun."

She didn't answer me, just clapped her hands to return us all to the same soundscape, then promptly ignored both of us. She ignored us so completely I was half-worried I had stopped existing and just hadn't realized it yet.

But Audrey caught my arm and dragged me back out into the heat of the midday sun. Which, after the cold air conditioning, was rather nice. For about half a minute.

I peeled off the hoodie, and Audrey pretended not to notice what a wrinkled mess my T-shirt was. "Come on," I said as I tied my hoodie's sleeves around my waist. "Let's go to the teashop."

We walked silently together along the tiled patio, past the bookshop to the teashop in the far corner. Luckily, our path was mostly in the shade.

"So you really don't think we should've asked to see her receipts?" Audrey asked. "You really believed her alibi?"

"I don't know about that," I admitted. "She strikes me as totally someone who doesn't feel it's really lying if she's decided I have no right to know what she was up to. You know?"

"I felt the same," Audrey said. "So why did you say there was no need?"

I sighed, but had to admit, "Because I do believe her when she says she didn't want Agatha's shopfront. She was definitely being honest there."

"Maybe a little too honest," Audrey said.

"We're finding nothing but dead ends in our little investigation," I said. "If Liam turns up nothing, I don't know what else we can do. It just doesn't seem like anyone had any reason to push Agatha off her veranda. And without a motive, I don't know how we've got a murder."

"And yet, Houdini doesn't feel to me like he's lying," she said.

And I had to admit, I felt the same. But without any evidence, who was going to take the word of a talking dog?

Or worse, who was going to take the word of two witches barely worthy of the name when they claimed a dog no one else can hear told them it was murder? Because I was sure Steph meant what he said about keeping Houdini's secrets.

And yet, I knew in my gut this *was* murder. So how could I let it go?

I couldn't. That was how. I just couldn't.

CHAPTER

EIGHTEEN

We went back to my nook in the bookshop, mostly so that I could turn the sign back to "open" and try to at least pretend to do the job I was there to do. But once again there were no customers from the magical side at all, and only a few random shoppers from the prosaic side who didn't need any help finding what they wanted when I went downstairs at the sound of the bell over the door.

Finally, at five o'clock, I turned the sign back to "closed," and Audrey and I agreed to go back to the teashop to make one last search for clues.

"Are you coming with us, Houdini?" I asked as we gathered our things and tidied up books and papers we had once more scattered all over the massive table.

"No," Houdini said without lifting his head from his curled position. He sounded so sad, it was like a stab to my heart.

"We'll probably be finding something for dinner afterwards. Can we bring you something?" I offered.

"No," he said, in the same tone as before. "I know where you put my kibble in your kitchen. I require nothing further."

Then he tucked his head further under his paw, and Audrey nudged me in the arm, silently urging me to take the hint.

I did. But I didn't like it.

"He's grieving," Audrey said to me as soon as we were outside in the still hot afternoon.

"I'm not sure that being alone is the best way for him to deal with that," I said.

"Tabitha, clearly, coming to the teashop where he spent all his days with Agatha is just too hard for him," she said.

I had to admit that was likely true. But I promised myself we'd make short work of our search and bring takeout back to the apartment over the bookshop. Houdini wouldn't be alone for more than an hour, tops. Not with the mood he was in.

Audrey unlocked the doors, and we slipped inside. At some point when she'd been there without me, she had closed up all the shutters on both sides of the teashop, and shut everything down. It was dark, and the air was still and hot without the air conditioning running.

At least it was still early enough in the summer that it wasn't yet oppressively humid, and the smell of all the various teas that lingered in the air gave the shop a dry sort of smell.

"Office first, I suppose?" I said.

Audrey chewed at her lip. "That is where we're most likely to find clues, but honestly, don't you think we were pretty thorough the first time around?"

"Yes, but..." I said, then just lifted my hands in a shrug.

"Right," she agreed. "Do you want to search there? I'm going to check the front area. Maybe she's tucked something in one of those tea canisters."

"Have you counted all those tea canisters?" I asked.

"I guess I'm about to!" she said with forced cheer.

I looked around the office, trying to guess what we might have missed before. But in the end I decided to just be—like Audrey had said—thorough. I started to the left of the door and went through everything. I searched through every drawer and folder, every ceramic objet d'art crammed on the shelves in case they had accessibly hollow interiors, even under the faded carpet on the floor and Houdini's little dog bed.

But in the end I had nothing. I made one last pass through the magazines and books—all with a tea focus, either just the beverage or the full English meal version—turning through all the pages and examining the spines and covers for hiding places. But still, there was nothing.

I went back out to the front room and found Audrey up on a step stool, putting canisters back on the topmost shelf.

"One hundred and twelve, in case you were wondering," she told me. "Nothing inside of any of them save for tea, though. Nothing taped to the bottom or to any of the shelves."

"I suppose you already checked the register," I said, but bumped the drawer open without waiting for an answer. There was nothing inside. Which was hardly surprising; in all the time I had known Agatha, I had never once seen her use it. When paid, she simply tucked the money away in the pocket of her apron. No one had ever needed change.

"There's a back storage room," Audrey said. "I've been through it before when I was pulling things out of that fridge and bringing them up to the apartment before I shut the power off. But I suppose we should give it another look to be sure."

I just nodded.

The back storage room felt even more abandoned than the other two rooms had. I guessed Agatha had stopped using it long before her untimely death, except for perhaps the fridge, which was positioned close to the doorway to the rest of the shop for easy access. The storage shelves were bare save for dust so thick it was drifting into ridges in places. A few corrugated boxes had been broken down and stacked on the topmost shelf, but from a glance at the shipping labels, those had been from deliveries made more than a year ago.

"This dust isn't great for me," Audrey said after sneezing three times.

"The Houdini tea isn't helping?" I asked.

"Oh, it's helping," she said as she dug through her pockets for some tissue. "Believe me, without it, my head would be exploding goo by now. It's just a lot."

"I don't think we're going to find anything else back here, anyway," I said. "Let's go out to the dining area and sit down for a minute. Did you want to brew a fresh cup of that tea?"

"No, I'll be okay," she said, but was quicker than I at getting out the storeroom door.

We sat down at one of the cute little tables, and I fidgeted with the fake flower that sat forlornly in its little vase in the center of the table, lost in thought. Audrey gazed out a gap between one of the shutters and the window frame, although with the angle of the sun through the glass, there was nothing to be seen through it at this hour.

"I believe Houdini," I said at last. "That's all I keep coming back to. We have no clues, only a persistent feeling. That, and Houdini's word."

"Feelings could be wrong," Audrey said glumly. "And if Houdini won't talk to anyone but the two of us, there is nothing we can do about what he's said. Anyway, he doesn't have proof either, does he? Just a hunch."

"He was with her every day and every night. And yet he didn't see what happened, and he doesn't know who might've done it," I said, as much to myself as to her. "You're right. It is just a feeling for him, too. So where does that leave us?"

Audrey looked at the teashop around us. "I guess it leaves me figuring out what to do with this place. They'll be reading her will soon. If she's left this all to me, I should know what I want to do next with it, I think."

"I had a thought about the names," I said.

"Tell me," Audrey said when I didn't go on.

"Well, I totally think she left this place to you. That feels obvious to me," I said. "But she might have worried that you wouldn't want it. I mean, you might not want to stay here and run it. I think that's what the names were for. And why so many of them were prosaic. Very few wizards want to deal with prosaic customers. The few shops around this Square that do are pretty unique in that way."

"I've been to other shops in other places that serve both sides," Audrey said.

"But so many of them all together in one place?" I asked her.

"No, you're right," she said after a moment's thought. "So the only people she thought might be interested in the property were Barnardo and Cleopatra? Does that make sense?"

"Barnardo recently lost his father," I said, speaking slowly as I thought it through out loud. "He might be looking to make a change. I think Agatha had a small hope that he might want to run her business after she was gone."

"But Cleopatra? Even if she wanted to open a second salon, she wouldn't do it so close to the first," Audrey said.

Then I found myself grinning, as inappropriate as that was.

"What?" Audrey asked, fighting a grin herself even though she had no idea what I was thinking.

"I have a terrible thought, but the more I think about it, the more I think it's true. It's just what Agatha would do," I said.

"What?" Audrey asked again.

"She would suggest Cleopatra as a buyer just to goad Barnardo. He might not want to be bothered running a teashop, but he'd do it in a heartbeat just to get something that Cleopatra wanted," I said. "Or, you know, something he thought she was going to want. I don't know if there's a back story between them or what, but his hatred of her is pretty palpable."

"Yeah, I sensed that," Audrey said. "But all the prosaic names?"

"I guess we won't know until we hear back from Liam, but if they all turn out to be property agents or people looking to start or expand their own businesses, we'll have our answer."

"That could be it," Audrey said. But then she sighed. "But that really doesn't help us solve what happened to her, then. It's all one big red herring."

"Eliminating false leads is part of the process," I said. As if I knew anything about investigating murders.

"We don't have anything like a *true* lead," she reminded me.

"No, I think we're at a dead end with our murder investigation," I said.

But Audrey caught the word I had stressed and said, "You think there's another investigation?"

"Agatha was sure she had been cursed," I said. "Someone was interfering with her ability to craft magical brews. Maybe we can find clues to that."

"Interesting," Audrey said, looking around again. But then she slumped back in her chair. "But how? Where would we even start? Surely Agatha could never figure it out herself, and she was always clever."

"I was trying to find a way to help her, before she died," I said. "I was searching the bookshop in my free moments for spells Agatha hadn't tried yet. I found a very old one, a spell to detect poisons."

"Wouldn't she have tried that?" Audrey asked.

"She was using magical drops at one point," I said. "It was before I came to town, but she told me about it when I offered her the spell I found. Every cup she brewed, she dropped three drops of this elixir in before she served it. It was supposed to glow in the presence of magic or curses. But it never showed a thing."

"So how is the spell you found any different?" Audrey asked.

"It works over a wide range," I said. "Like, the entire shop. We don't have to test cup by cup. Once the spell is cast, anything in its vicinity will glow as green as a Mr. Yuck sticker. But Agatha wasn't remotely interested, and, of course, I couldn't try it on my own. But I have it all written up, like the other spell you did for me. We can work together again."

"I would love to perform another of your spells," she said with a smile. "I don't even care if it doesn't help with our crime, although I hope it does. I just like the feel of working your magic."

I smiled back, but inside, my heart ached a little. I wished I knew what it felt like, to work my own magic.

I quickly ran up to the bookshop and found the parchment with the spell on it. Houdini had left the nook, I noticed in passing as I dug a green glass bottle out of a cabinet by one of the fireplaces. I brought the bottle and the parchment both back down to the teashop.

"It's an easier spell than the decrypting one," I told her as I set the bottle on the teashop counter. That was pretty centrally located in the space, covering the office and storeroom as well as the cabinets of tea nearest the dining area.

Audrey read over the spell, her lips moving ever so slightly as she subvocalized the words. "It has such a lovely rhythm. And it flows with the gestures so well. You really should've tried ritual magic."

"Believe me, that would've been a disaster," I said. But for once, the thought didn't strike me like a stab of pain. For once, I was happy enough where I was not to mourn where I hadn't gotten to go. It was rather a nice feeling.

"Okay, I'm going to try this," Audrey said, taking out her wand.

"Just focus the energy into the bottle," I told her as I backed away to give her room.

"Right," she said, then set to work.

I loved the sound of her voice when she worked magic. It was rich and sonorous, and so much more confident than her usual speaking voice. I swear she grew a couple of inches taller, but perhaps that was just how she raised her arms, floating up onto her tiptoes, then settling back down again.

When she was done building the power, she tapped her wand against the open mouth of the bottle. It blasted out a bright green color that filled the room in a blast of patterns of green light, like looking through an all-shades-of-green kaleidoscope.

"Is it working?" Audrey asked as the light danced around us in swirling tiled patterns.

"We have to look around for anything that's glowing back," I said. "The spell will last for a few minutes, but not long."

We both raced behind the counter then started taking canisters down one after another, peeking inside each before setting it aside to reach for the next. Then we split up, me taking the office again while she went back to the storeroom. But there wasn't much in the office to *be* poisoned, so I finished up first and ran to help Audrey with her room.

She saw me come in and gave me a quick shake of her head that she hadn't found anything yet. But she was still searching, at the moment attempting to pull open a drawer that was built into the side of the rickety table that stood beside the refrigerator. I hadn't noticed that drawer before, and I gathered Audrey hadn't either because the way she was pulling on it, leaning back with all her weight, I guessed it hadn't been opened in many years.

"This curse was a recent thing," I said. "And Agatha wasn't exactly strong enough to pull that open with all the trouble it's giving you."

"It's the last place to check," Audrey said from between gritting teeth.

I heard a sound like cracking glass coming from behind me, and I knew the spell was about to end. The bottle could only contain the magic for so long before it would shatter.

Then the drawer burst open all at once, sending Audrey tumbling back onto her butt in the middle of the room. The drawer came with her, following an arc as her hand flew up, then landing in her lap with a slap that sent a cloud of thick dust into the air all around Audrey's face.

Now she was coughing, wheezing and sneezing all at once, so violently I could tell she was having trouble drawing breath. I pulled her to her feet, and she dashed past me to get around the counter. The bottle gave another ominous crack, but remained intact enough for the spell to continue its dancing kaleidoscopic patterns all around us.

I looked at the drawer left lying on the floor, but there was nothing there. Nothing but dust. And as bad as that was for Audrey, it was just ordinary dust. No hint of the spell's warning green color.

I made my way back out to the front of the shop. Audrey was digging through the bag she had left at the table where we had been sitting before, searching frantically for something even as she continued to wheezingly fight for each breath.

I didn't know what I could do to help her. I felt even more useless than usual. But I hurried to get to her side all the same.

I was just slipping through the open counter when two things happened at once.

The bottle beside me shattered into a spray of glass, the spell too much for the prosaic material.

And I saw the inhaler that Audrey finally had in her hand glow that warning shade of green, even as she shook it and brought it up to her lips.

CHAPTER
NINETEEN

I dashed across the dining area to the table by the window and tore the inhaler from Audrey's grasp just in time. She had already pressed down on the trigger, sending a vaporous cloud of what should have been medicine across her cheek rather than into her mouth. I saw that mist flash green, but less intensely than the inhaler itself had before. The spell was fading all around us.

Audrey pulled away from me and attempted to get the inhaler into her mouth again, but I snatched it from her hand and tossed it violently away. It clattered against the far wall, then fell to the tiled floor.

Audrey bent with her hands on her knees, still fighting for breath. She couldn't say anything to me, and when she looked up at me, her red and streaming eyes were too miserably symptomatic to convey any concrete emotion.

"It was poison, Audrey," I said even as I put an arm around her and guided her out the door to the open patio on the Square. "Your inhaler was poison."

But she couldn't answer me. I got her settled on a chair, but there was nothing more I could do but sit down across from her and wait for fresh air to aid her.

Yep. Still feeling pretty useless.

But her wheezes were slowing, and she was getting more and deeper breaths between. Far sooner than I thought she'd be able to, she choked out the word, "Poison?"

"Not the dust, your inhaler," I said.

"Why?" she gritted out.

"I think someone might be trying to kill you too," I said. "The murder investigation is back on. Only now we have to get this figured out right away. Before someone can take another shot at you."

"Who knew?" she asked, each word laboriously delivered.

"That's the question, isn't it?" I mused. "Who here would know you used an inhaler? You've only been here a few days, and I've never seen you use it. I suppose someone might have seen it in your bag. But you've not left that anywhere unattended, have you?"

She shook her head vehemently.

"Do you have more with you?" I asked. She was clearly still not breathing properly, even if the most dangerous moment had passed.

She shook her head again. She looked truly miserable.

"Bartholomew Bullen runs the Potions & Magical Sundries shop on the other side of the Square," I said. "He also can fill prosaic prescriptions through some arcane bureaucratic process I don't even want to know too much about. We should go there now and see if he can help you."

But she was shaking her head again.

"Audrey—" I started to say.

"I go," she said firmly. "You stay. Wait for Liam."

"All right. I suppose that's sensible," I said. But I didn't like it.

"I'm fine," she said. If she could've said both the words together on one breath, I might even have believed her. But I made no move to follow as she pushed up from the chair then made her slow away around the Square.

I really hoped Bartholomew Bullen could help her. I'd only met him twice, and only very briefly, but he seemed like a caring fellow. If he couldn't help her, I thought the odds were good he'd stay with her until he found someone who could.

I went back into the teashop and into the back storeroom to fetch a broom and dustpan to clean up all the broken glass. I was just coming back out around the counter when I heard a tentative knock on the prosaic door. I peeked through the gap between the shutters and the window frame and saw a flash of sunlight on blond hair.

Liam.

I unlocked the door and opened it to let him in.

"Oh, good. I was worried you wouldn't be here," he said as he slipped inside. "It looks completely abandoned from the outside. Like, long abandoned."

"It's only been closed for a few days," I assured him. I closed and locked the door, then turned to see him scanning the teashop for any sign of Audrey.

"Audrey had to run an errand, but she'll be back in a minute," I told him, and he flushed beet red.

"I'm that obvious, am I?" he asked, not quite looking at me.

"A bit," I admitted.

"Sorry," he said. But he seemed to find the one word inadequate and with a pained look, said all in a rush, "I mean, I got the sense when I offered to bring you lunch that you already had something going on. I mean, you *said* it wasn't a date, whatever you were... Ugh. This is so awkward."

"It shouldn't be," I assured him.

"So you are seeing someone," he said with barely contained relief.

"Well, not really, but it's still fine," I said. "I mean, you and I were friendly enough, and I hope we can still *be* friends. But that moment when you met Audrey? That was something else."

The grin that spread across his face was clearly not one that he could suppress. "You're being unspeakably cool about this," he said.

"It's not awkward," I assured him again.

But it was a little bit awkward.

Then Liam remembered why he was there in the first place. "Oh! I have something for you," he said, setting his backpack on one of the tables and fishing in the main compartment until he came up with the list I had given him, plus a hefty stack of paper that looked like computer printouts.

"So you found something," I said, hardly daring to hope that it would turn out to be something useful.

"It took longer than I thought because I fell down so many rabbit holes," he said.

"With the names?"

"No, not with the names. They are mostly property agents with a few local businesses that are on public record as looking to expand to new locations. That's all pretty normal," he said as he handed me the papers.

So that was a theory confirmed, anyway.

"So, who was the rabbit hole?" I asked as I scanned the pages.

"Not who, what," he said. Then he added with a great air of mystery, "Or rather, *where*."

"Explain," I said, because the pages were telling me nothing.

"This place," he said, pointing at the ground under his feet. "Not just this teashop, but this whole block. Do you have any idea what a mystery this whole place is?"

"No," I said, but my stomach spun itself into a knot that quickly yanked itself tight. Sailors in a knot-tying competition would be jealous of how fast my stomach could achieve that.

"This entire block simply doesn't exist in any property records I can find," he said. His face glowed with excitement over his discovery. Luckily, he was so caught up in it that he didn't notice I wasn't mirroring his excitement. At all.

"But these property agents were interested in it?" I asked.

"Not even!" he said, even more enthused than before. "I called a few of them. None of them had ever even heard of this place. They were as intrigued as I was when we tried on our separate computers to pin down the address. It exists in a general form in all sorts of databases. There are street numbers and connections to utilities, for instance. But when you try to make a more specific search, like by name of any of the shops on this block, it disappears again. The. Whole. Block."

I summoned a weak smile, because he was starting to notice I wasn't riding the excitement train with him.

But my stomach spun itself in one more knot just to be sure it was secure, then yanked down even tighter.

"But these businesses exist," I said. "The Weal & Woe Bookshop. Loose Leaves. The Inanna Salon & Spa."

"They do, obviously. I've been inside them, they obviously exist in the physical world," Liam said. "But in the world of paperwork and bureaucracy? They're all ghosts. That shouldn't even be possible."

I tried for another smile, but I couldn't get it going this time.

I felt so sick. I would wish Audrey were back, but I wasn't even sure what she could do to help me. There was no way to explain this, and I deeply regretted inviting Liam to go digging into what, I was finding out way too late, was a place where the secret of our magical existence was so easy to uncover.

"Do you know what this means?" Liam asked, his eyes bright.

"No, what does it mean?" I asked, although I was afraid of the answer.

"I don't know either!" he said. "But I'm not going to stop until I find out. How can this place not exist? I mean, the exterior of this building is downright Sullivanesque."

"I don't know what that means," I admitted.

"Sullivan was the architect known as the father of skyscrapers and the father of modernism. But that was in the 1880s to 1920s. This building must be one of the oldest still standing in Minneapolis. I mean, I bet when it was built, St. Anthony had only just become part of Minneapolis proper. Maybe that's part of the glitch. I don't know!"

I had never heard anyone sound so excited about not knowing something.

But that only meant he was about to do a lot of digging. And I didn't know how I was going to dissuade him.

"I have to start searching the old archives. Those weren't at the library; I'd have to contact the Minnesota Historical Society for a little guidance, and probably the city itself to get permission to access older records."

"I really don't need you to do that," I said weakly.

"No, of course not. Those names turned up nothing. But there might be a book in this if I find something really interesting. Like a secret history of Minneapolis. I could totally write that. It's not like I have anything better to do. And look! I bought a new journal on the way here to start keeping my notes in."

He pulled a leather-bound journal out of his backpack, the kind that ties shut to protect the pages. It was as thick as an old-school phonebook.

And he opened it up to show me the first dozen or so pages already filled with his writing.

My only hope at that point was to somehow get Audrey to put him off. He just might listen to her.

But Audrey struck me as someone who wouldn't play with someone else's feelings like that. She clearly knew he was crushing on her, after all. And whether she felt the same or not, she wouldn't try to use his feelings for leverage against him.

I mean, I wouldn't, if I were in her place.

But what choice did I have? Distracting him with a pretty girl seemed like the only thing I *could* do. And I wasn't even sure if that would work.

"Liam—" I started to say, but got no further before the doors behind me crashed open and Steph came sprinting in. He skidded to a stop and pulled out his wand.

Great. This secret-keeping was getting harder by the second.

"Tabitha?" Liam asked, looking from me to Steph—dressed all in black, his hair floating around his head in a way no amount of product could achieve without magic, and brandishing a black wand of twisted, knotty wood—then back again. I couldn't blame Liam for feeling on edge. Steph's posture was very aggressive. But I could see Liam was still holding tight to the hopes of there being a rational explanation for all this.

If only I could give him one.

"The comic shop next door—" I started to say, but Steph cut me off.

"This is the guy, right?" he asked me. "The guy setting off all the alarms?"

"Alarms?" Liam repeated, looking back over his shoulder at the door to the prosaic world. "I knocked. She let me in. What alarms?"

"Alarms?" I said as well. I had no more clue than Liam did what Steph was talking about.

Steph just blew out a frustrated breath, then turned his full attention to Liam. "What are you doing here, prosaic?"

"Prosaic?" Liam said, still looking between the two of us. "I was just helping Tabitha with a thing... Say, didn't I see you this morning? Like for half a second in the bookshop. I thought I had imagined it, and there was this whole thing with a cloak... Anyway, that was you, wasn't it?"

Steph didn't answer. He just raised his wand up towards the ceiling and whispered a word I didn't quite catch. His wand flashed like a strobe light three times, blindingly bright.

When I could see again, I saw Liam blinking uncertainly. Then he looked down at the journal still in his hands.

"I'll take that, I think," Steph said, slipping his wand away then holding out his hands.

"Right," Liam said, handing it over without a moment's hesitation.

"And the rest of it?" Steph prompted.

"The papers are Tabitha's," he said, and in fact, I was still holding them. Then he looked inside his backpack. "Nothing there but the remains of my lunch."

"Nothing in any of the little pockets?" Steph pressed.

"No. Not at all," Liam agreed.

"Very well. You may go," Steph said, and even made a begone-with-thee little wave as if to shoo Liam towards the door.

"Right. Let me know if you need me to look into anything else, okay, Tabitha?" he said to me. But he sounded so dazed, I wasn't sure if he would even remember coming into the teashop at all in another five minutes.

"Sure," I said, but I was feeling more than a little stunned at the moment myself. Liam unlocked the door to let himself out, and I wandered over to lock it again behind him.

Then I turned to Steph. "What just happened?"

"Mind wipe," he said as he paged through the journal.

"How very sci-fi of you," I said drily.

"There are rules, Tabitha," he said sternly, then shut the book and tossed it up into the air. It reached the apex of its flight, then flashed out of existence before it could fall back down again.

"He remembered you from this morning," I said. A little bit child-ishly, but Steph did look ever so slightly guilty at my words.

"Yes, I lacked judgment in that moment," he admitted. But then he fixed me with a stern gaze. "The magics that hide this place are always vulnerable. Always. As powerful as they are, it only takes one too many prosaics noticing that we're here to bring it all crashing down. I know you know this."

"I just wanted to know more about the list of names. I never asked him to look into this place," I said. But I knew I didn't have a leg to stand on, really. I had put us all at risk. "I'm sorry," I said with real contrition.

"You don't have to apologize to me," he said, finally softening. "Just, don't do that again. I had to leave the Wizard alone in the middle of a delicate experiment to deal with this before the protections entirely unravelled. If you think I was just harsh with you, that's nothing compared to the tongue-lashing I have coming for not catching the problem sooner."

"And for vanishing from the bookshop in front of a prosaic?" I couldn't help adding.

But his eyes crinkled ever so slightly in a smile, and I knew he knew I was just teasing.

"I'm hoping he doesn't know about that," he admitted.

"He won't hear it from me," I promised.

He gave me a nod of thanks, then looked carefully around the interior of the teashop. "No normal people in sight," he said, then vanished without so much as a goodbye.

I set to work sweeping up the glass. That was one mistake I could clean up after myself.

TWENTY

It was more than an hour before Audrey came back into the teashop, but when she did, she looked much better. She still was a little sniffly, but she wasn't fighting for each breath.

And she didn't even seem to mind that Houdini was right with her, close at her heels as they passed through the doors together.

"You missed Liam," I said.

"Oh," she said. That little syllable was holding a lot more emotional weight than it normally did, but she said no more, just went into Agatha's office to look at her big book.

I looked down at Houdini. "How are you doing?"

"I shall be quite fine," he said stiffly. But he was trembling in that way that rat terrier chihuahuas do. I wanted to pick him up and snuggle him tight, but I didn't think he'd appreciate that.

And anyway, he had said he "shall" be fine. He wasn't there yet. But confronting this space was part of that path for him.

"I'm always here if you need me," I told him.

"Thank you," he said, still overly formal. And still trembling.

I left him on his own to talk to Audrey.

"The list of prosaic names were all property managers and business owners who might be looking to move or expand to a second location," I said from the office doorway. Houdini said nothing, just curled up in his little dog bed and went to sleep.

"So your theory was correct," she said as she turned the pages of the book.

"Well, that part of it, anyway. But that leaves us with yet another dead end," I said.

"Did you want to quit?" She actually looked up from whatever she was searching the book for to meet my eyes when she asked that question.

"Not at all," I said emphatically. "Someone tried to kill you, Audrey. Someone who knew about your health history, and had access to your inhaler and maybe the teashop, too."

"I was thinking the same thing," she said. Then she looked back at the book again with a frown. "This book could use an index, just to start."

"Are you looking for something in particular?" I asked, trying not to sound impatient. If she needed a different tea to deal with her allergies, any of my ideas for the next step in our investigation would have to wait.

Not that I had any ideas. But the impatience was always there, just under the surface.

"I am, actually," she said. "Agatha had a special tea. A very special tea. I had forgotten all about it until Bartholomew Bullen's medicinal vapors kicked in. I don't know what he used, but once the smell penetrated my sinuses, not only did my lung passages open up and let me breathe again, I think it cleared up my head as well. I mean, my mind came out of a fog. And suddenly there it was, like I had left it lying out on my mental front table so I wouldn't miss it on my way out the door. Metaphorically speaking," she quickly added.

"I get you," I said. "But I don't know what tea you're talking about. But, then again, Agatha never talked about her magical teas with me at all. Since she couldn't mix them anymore, I guess she preferred not to think of them. What does it do?"

"It should open up the mind of the drinker," she said as she scanned two more facing pages before turning to the next. "I mean, we've been poking around quite a bit. It's possible we've seen what we need to know, we just didn't realize what it meant when we saw it. This tea, if brewed correctly, will help us make connections we've been missing."

"That sounds like a very handy sort of tea," I said.

"Well, if you drink it too often, you will go insane," Audrey said off-handedly. "Agatha never gave out the recipe, and she was very judicious about brewing it herself. You had to tell her why you needed it, and she would decide if it was worth the risk."

"How often is too often?" I asked.

"Maybe twice in your lifetime might be too much," she admitted.

"Okay, that sounds like an extraordinarily dangerous sort of tea," I said. "Do you really think we've come to that point? Maybe we should work the case a bit more."

"Someone tried to kill me, Tabitha," she said. Her voice was steady and even, but her words still sent a shiver up my spine.

"Fair enough," I mumbled. Although I was half-hoping the recipe wasn't in that book at all. "Are you sure it's in there?" I asked her. "Maybe it's in the coded ledger book. If she wanted to keep it safe."

"I looked there first," Audrey said, then stopped scanning pages to look more closely at the bottom of the lefthand page before her. "I think this is it. It's faded, and she's written something else over the top of it, but I think this is it."

I stepped up to look over her shoulder. There were indeed the faint traces of a recipe written behind a more recently added recipe for a mint and coriander tea. I was momentarily distracted by trying to imagine those two flavors mixing. Would it be delicious or vile? Or maybe just a "meh?"

"Can you read it?" Audrey asked me anxiously, and I focused my attention on the ghost letters.

"I think so," I said. "But look, it's more than mixing tea leaves. There is a spell component to this."

"Of course there is," she said. "But if you write this up for me in your special way, I think I can pull it off."

"Are you sure?" I asked. "You said there was a possibility of insanity if we got it *right*. Is this worth the risk?"

Audrey chewed at her lip for a moment. "Why don't you write it out for me, and then we'll see how you feel about it."

"All right," I agreed, and took the book off the stand to bring it to Agatha's desk. I found a sheet of parchment and a pen and wrote out letter by letter everything I could discern. But there were a lot of letters that were too faded, or too covered-over by the new writing for me to be sure of, so when I was done I had basically a half-solved game of hangman in long form.

"Right," I said, handing the book back to Audrey and taking out another sheet of parchment. Audrey moved behind me to put the book back on its stand, and after that, I lost awareness of her entirely. My whole mind was focused on the letters in front of me as, word by word, I reconstructed the recipe and the spell. It was written in a long-lost offshoot of Gaelic somewhat related to Manx, but not quite the same.

Luckily, I had taken several semesters in the various dead languages used in old magical tomes. I was rusty, but when the rhymes revealed themselves, I grew more confident.

"Is that it?" Audrey asked, in barely more than a whisper, as I pushed away the first sheet of parchment and looked over my work.

"Not quite," I said. "I mean, this is what Agatha had in her book. I'm sure of it."

"But?"

"But I think I can tweak a few things," I said. I could feel the hot blush on my cheeks, but when I looked up at Audrey, nothing on her face showed any sign of her thinking I had overstepped myself. "I've seen you work. I think I know how to make this flow in a way that would better suit you."

"I trust you implicitly," she said. "But why don't you write out the ingredients for me, and I can gather what we'll need while you rewrite the spell?"

"Absolutely," I said, and turned the first parchment over to write out the various teas, herbs and spices that would be needed. Nothing there was too unusual, but even if it had been, I doubted anything was further than a walk to Bartholomew Bullen's shop away.

The sun was low in the sky by the time I had finished, and the tea itself had to be left alone to steep for an hour before we even attempted the magic. Audrey mixed everything up and put it in one of Agatha's cast-iron teapots, added hot water from the electric kettle, then wrapped the pot in a tea towel. Then the two of us headed over to the pub for a quick meal of fish and chips before going back to the teashop.

It was twilight when Audrey started my spell, the only light from the tea candles I had lit around the edges of the countertop since the power was still off.

Again, I was thoroughly enchanted hearing Audrey speak the words I had labored over. Enchanted, but still a bit jealous.

Once she was done, her hands were glowing whitish-blue. I whipped the tea towel out of the way so she could place them on either side of the pot. She went through the incantation one final time in that sonorous voice of hers.

Then she poured out two cups of the tea.

"We're both drinking?" I asked.

"Didn't you want to?" she asked worriedly.

I wanted to. But I was pretty sure it wouldn't do anything helpful to me. I had too much experience in not having magic work out for me.

But I also had half a thought that one of us should stay away from it just in case something went wrong. But what would I do if something magically went wrong with Audrey? I couldn't dispel magic or anything. I would only be able to watch, and maybe call for help.

"Houdini," I called into the office.

"I will watch over you," he promised without even needing to hear me ask it.

"It's probably safe, I'm sure," I said to Audrey as we stood together with the cast-iron cups resting on the palms of our hands. "But, just in case."

"Right," she said, looking down at the cup in her hands. "Well, bottoms up?"

"Bottoms up," I agreed.

We both drained our cups. It didn't taste like tea so much as a potent brand of mineral water. Very metallic, almost electric. But there was no lingering after-taste.

There was also no effect. I looked at Audrey, and she looked at me, but after the clock had ticked away fifteen minutes, we both had to admit we knew nothing more than we had before drinking the tea.

"Maybe it would help to go over everything we know again?" I suggested lamely.

"You want to go back up to the nook in the bookshop?" she asked.

"What else can we do?"

She looked down at the bottom of her empty teacup. Then she picked up one of the candles, bringing it closer to shed light inside the dark cast-iron cup.

"Right, the tea leaves," I said, and looked into my own cup. Not that I thought I could really scry anything. But I could maybe discern a pattern that Audrey would be able to interpret.

But there was nothing in either of our cups. The tea had gone down smoothly, leaves and all.

"All right. Let me wash up, and then we can go up to the nook and look at the ledger," Audrey said, holding out her hand. I handed her my cup, and she took it and hers as well as the pot over to the sink in the back room. I looked around, planning to tidy up any canisters left out from the recipe preparation, but Audrey was too neat for me. She had put everything away before we'd even gone out for dinner.

"We're missing something," I mused as she washed the china cups one by one and set them in the drainer to drip-dry. "Something important. Don't you feel it too?"

"From the tea?" she asked, a little too eagerly.

"No, I've been feeling it since before we made the tea," I said. "We have two books that almost seem to be hiding clues, and yet she had left them both just... out to be found."

"It wasn't easy to decode the ledger," Audrey said. "You wrote a beautiful spell, but from a ritual magic standpoint, it wasn't exactly easy to perform. It took a lot out of me."

"I know," I said. And yet I couldn't help feeling, maybe we had broken that code a little *too* easily. Maybe two barely competent witches shouldn't have been able to pull it off at all.

"She couldn't really have meant to sell this place to a prosaic," Audrey said as she dried her hands on a towel.

"It would mean closing this space off from the Square, like the comic shop is," I said.

"Was that list of names meant to persuade Bernardo, like you said Cleopatra's name was?"

"I really don't know," I admitted.

"Because once the book was decoded, that page was right there. Like it was waiting for me," she said.

"Is this a tea insight?" I asked. Because I still didn't feel any different.

She rolled her eyes up and to the left as she checked in with her feelings. Then she shook her head. "I don't think so. Just a random thought, I guess."

We blew out all the candles and went out into the still-hot night air. I watched as Audrey locked the doors and put the key away in her pocket.

Houdini was there with us, but still strangely quiet. He sniffed the smell of fried fish on the air—coming from the pub, which was far more crowded now than it had been when Audrey and I had eaten there—but said nothing.

We should've started walking at that point, but Audrey just stood there facing the locked door as if lost in thought.

"What is it?" I asked.

"I don't know," she said, sounding far away, as if speaking to me from out of a dream. "I feel like I want to talk to Titus Bloom. But I don't know why. Do you feel that way, too?"

I closed my eyes and waited for an impulse to strike me. But in the end I just had to shake my head at her. "If you think you should, then you probably should," I said. "Did you want me to come with you?"

Audrey was blushing again. "I don't even feel like this is part of investigating the murder, you know? I think it might just be something I have to do personally. Maybe we were supposed to focus on the problem we wanted to connect the dots about before we drank the tea?"

"Nothing in the recipe said that," I said.

"But that's what you were thinking about, wasn't it?" she asked. "Weren't you?"

"I was kind of thinking about a lot of things," she admitted. "I might have been thinking more about what is going to happen next than what happened before. Titus might be able to help me figure out what's next for the teashop. Whether I stay or go, I mean. I don't know the first thing about running a business, but he does."

"Maybe," I said slowly, but Houdini was growling low in his throat, and had been since we'd started talking outside the door.

"What is it?" Audrey asked him.

"I hate that name," he grumbled. "I hate that man."

"Do you think he killed Agatha?" I asked him.

He just carried on with the low warning growl.

"I think you might be right about why you're compelled to talk to him," I said to Audrey. It was weird, Houdini wasn't growling out loud so there was no need to talk over the sound. And yet it was so loud in my mind and Audrey's that we kind of felt like we had to. "But just in case, Houdini and I should definitely come with you."

"Of course," she said. "Is the coffeeshop still open at this hour?"

"We're about to find out," I said, and led the way past the book-shop to the far side of the Square.

CHAPTER
TWENTY-ONE

We had just passed the Square door into the bookshop, not quite in sight of the coffeeshop through the trees that grew closer to the tiled walkway on this side of the Square, when a sudden movement in the shadows caught my eye. I grabbed Audrey's arm, using all my strength to drag her to a halt.

She really wanted to get to the Bitter Brew Coffeeshop.

But I didn't need Houdini's sudden outburst of barks and howls to know something wasn't right.

Then Audrey yanked her arm free of my grasp. I was about to lunge and grab her again when I realized that she wasn't trying to keep walking. She felt something wrong around us too. She pulled out her wand, but didn't seem to know what to do with it once she had it in her hand. So we both just stood there, trying to stare into the shadows around us.

They were far inkier a shade of black than they should be, given that there was still a little light left in the twilit sky to the west of us.

Then there was another flicker of motion, right in front of us, even bigger than before. I bit back a scream, even as Houdini's barks morphed into full howling yells of a volume no rooster could hope to match.

"Relax, it's just me," Steph said. I still couldn't see him. But then it was like he was emerging from some vertical pool of the darkest ink. It clung to him goopily as he stepped towards the three of us. That wasn't just a trick of the light, either. He had to turn and give his cloak a hard shake to break free from the last of the inky goo.

The necessity of that gesture seemed to annoy him. But then he took a deep calming breath before approaching us.

"Houdini, stop," I hissed at the dog, who broke off mid bark but ducked behind me to press his trembling body against the backs of my calves.

"You sense it too," Steph said to him, but Houdini didn't answer.

"Sense what?" I asked. "You just scared the life out of us."

"No, I'm here for a reason, and Houdini feels it too," he said. He lifted his chin as if scenting the air. "This is the weirdest night I can ever remember passing in the Square." Then he looked directly at me. "I guess I'm including our afternoon adventure in there."

"What afternoon adventure?" Audrey asked.

"Liam," I said with a sigh. Then I looked at Steph. "Liam, right?"

"Yes, your friend with all the questions," Steph said. "But I dealt with that. This is a different problem."

"You mean the thing where the shadows are inky pools?" I asked.

"No, that's just a side effect," he said even as he started searching the area for I knew not what.

"Side effect of what?" I asked, but he didn't answer.

"What does he mean he 'dealt with that'?" Audrey demanded of me in a shrill whisper. Steph was peering into the shadows all around us. I got the sense that he was examining them with more than his mere human eyesight. He was certainly ignoring the two of us at the moment.

"I didn't tell you the whole story before," I admitted. "Liam came in with the list of names."

"Property agents and business owners," Audrey said with a nod.

"Right. Only, there's no record of any property on the Square in the official systems he was searching," I said. "He was going to do some more digging. I was trying to dissuade him, but—"

"But you were never going to succeed," Steph interjected smoothly.

So he wasn't *completely* ignoring us. Even as he still moved from patch of shadow to patch of shadow in some sort of hunt I didn't understand.

"You didn't exactly let me finish trying," I said.

"What did you do?" Audrey demanded, moving to stand directly in front of Steph. He looked up at her with a blink.

"Just a mind wipe. That's the standard protocol for that sort of breach of our primary rule."

"You wiped his *mind*?" Audrey said accusingly.

"It *is* standard protocol," I admitted.

"You could've let me talk to him," she said.

"That was what I was *trying* to do," I said.

"I didn't overstep my responsibility," Steph said. "I have a duty, and I fulfilled it. But I did it in my usual manner."

"Which means?" Audrey asked, crossing her arms as she kept her glare fixed on him.

I was just glad it wasn't me. She could go toe-to-toe with a basilisk when her dander was up, apparently.

"Which means I wiped the bits of his memory that needed to be wiped with, shall we say, surgical precision," he told us both. Then he scoffed. "Any surgeon in the prosaic world would die to have my level of precision, but I trust you understand the metaphor."

"So you only affected the parts of his mind about the Square?" Audrey asked. "The parts that violated the rule for secrecy?"

"Only those," Steph said. "They were easy enough to remove, they had only existed for a matter of minutes, barely more than an hour all told."

"So he's not going to be like a vegetable or anything?" I asked.

"No," Steph said, with a hint of laughter in his voice. Like my question was a little over the top.

Maybe it was. But I could tell Audrey was still upset, and I didn't know what she needed to hear to feel better about things.

But apparently Steph did, because in a warmer voice than he had been using before, he said to her, "He still remembers meeting you. There was no need to touch that."

She flushed, but nodded.

"Not that bringing him up to the most magical parts of the bookshop was a *good* idea," Steph said to me.

"And vanishing in front of his eyes?" I shot back.

"I think we already agreed that was my mistake," he said blithely as he resumed his search.

"What are you looking for here, anyway?" I asked.

"There was a disturbance in the magical energies," he said vaguely.

"Like how you sensed Liam asking too many questions about the Square?" I asked.

"No, this is very different. Although just as rare. Just as attracting of my and the Wizard's attention," he said with a frown. "But I can't figure out where it's coming from exactly."

"Shouldn't you be able to?" Audrey asked with a concerned frown.

"Yes, I should," he admitted without embarrassment. "Someone is cloaking their actions. But they slipped up. They started cloaking just a little too late."

"Or they did it on purpose," I found myself saying.

"Why?" Steph asked, and his dark eyes locked with mine.

"I don't know. Just thinking out loud," I said.

He considered this, then gave a nod before turning away from me to look up the side of the bookshop. Seven stories on the inside, not quite so many on the outside, but still a lot of brick and stone.

"Do you think it's inside the bookshop?" I asked.

"It might be," he said, his voice low as if afraid he'd be overheard. "Do you mind if I search it?"

"No, I don't mind," I said as I started digging out the key. "The door is just over there. We only have to backtrack a little."

"Tabitha," Audrey whispered with some urgency.

"Oh, right," I said, looking at the key in my hand. "We were in the middle of a thing. Say, you don't think this magic you're sensing is coming from the coffeeshop, do you?"

"The Bitter Brew? Definitely not," he said. "Is that where you're both heading?"

"It *was*," I said in a slow drawl.

"I can go without you if you needed to deal with this other thing," Audrey said, but I could tell that she was just being polite. She didn't really want to go alone.

"We can all stick together and do both," I said.

"I'm afraid my mission is a bit high priority," Steph said. "The magic I'm sensing is masked from me now, but I still have a sense of where I felt it before. I have to find it before that sense fades."

"And I have to do what I'm going to do before the tea fades," Audrey said.

"Okay, so no pressure, then," I grumbled, mostly to myself. Then I looked down at Houdini, still pressed tight behind my calves. "Do you have a vote?"

"Neither option appeals," Houdini said. "But I'll go where you go."

"Fine. We're going with Audrey," I said. To Audrey's palpable relief.

I walked over to Steph to give him the key. Not that I thought he needed it. He could teleport inside anytime he wanted to, and there wasn't a thing I could do to stop him. My uncle Carlo, maybe, had ways to truly lock the bookshop down. But I had none.

"I prefer to do things the polite way," Steph said, as if reading my mind again. He held out his hand, and I put the key gently on his palm. He closed his fingers over it.

195

"Are you sure it's safe to go in there alone?" I asked.

"No," he said briskly. "But duty calls."

"I could..." I started to say. But I had nothing more to follow it with.

I couldn't. I couldn't do magic. I couldn't protect him or watch his back. I couldn't help at all.

But then he was touching my hair again, his fingertips triggering sparks that lit up the shadows around us.

"Stop that," I said, stepping out of his reach.

But he just gave me a ponderous look. "It's not part of what I'm sensing, but it is a very interesting sort of mystery," he mused.

"What is?" I asked.

He laughed to himself, then said, "Well, you."

Then he was gone, lost in the shadows between where we stood on the tiled walkway and the door to the bookshop not twenty feet away from us.

"Tabitha," Audrey said imploringly.

"Coffeeshop. Let's go," I said.

And we continued on our way.

CHAPTER
TWENTY-TWO

I guess I could've predicted what would happen next, if I'd given it a moment's thought.

Or maybe not. I had stopped thinking of Houdini as being just a dog once he'd started talking to me. I wasn't sure *what* he was, and if pinned down, I still couldn't tell you what I was even imagining he was when I thought of him inside of my own mind. He sounded like a wizard, not a puppy. He was clearly something more than a mere rat terrier chihuahua.

So, even though I'd just had to stop him barking at Steph when he'd appeared from the shadows, I had forgotten that barking was just what his doggy self did. And as far as I could tell, Houdini *liked* Steph. Or at least he didn't mind him.

But I wasn't thinking any of that through when Audrey and I went inside the half-lit coffeeshop.

Not until Houdini caught sight of Titus sorting through some papers behind his counter. Not until the barking began.

Titus was saying something to me and Audrey, but I had no way of hearing just what it was.

"Would you stop that?" I hissed at Houdini. "I know you don't like the guy, but you agreed to come here."

Houdini didn't answer me, at least not in words inside of my mind. But his barking did transition over to the baying and howls that were, quite frankly, far too loud for the bouncing acoustics inside the coffeeshop.

"Please, put him outside!" Titus bellowed over the noise. I could see him struggling to remain polite, and could appreciate that was pretty tricky to do when the noise level necessitated shouting.

"Houdini, quit it!" I said to the little dog practically bouncing up and down on his four ramrod-stiff legs. Like some kind of Japanese toy. Clearly, he had no intention of letting up.

"Tabitha," Audrey said pleadingly.

"Right," I grumbled, and picked up Houdini.

"Put me down right this instant," he commanded inside my head.

"No, sir," I said as I carried his struggling body back out the door. "We have to talk to Titus, and you agreed to come."

"I never agreed. I never agreed!"

"Fine, but you followed us," I said. I put him down on the grass just beyond the tiled walkway. "You can go help Steph if you like."

Houdini snorted. Inside my mind. It was a weird sensation. But his disdain was clear.

"Or go back to the teashop. Or up to my bedroom. Or the nook. Basically, your options are limitless here. You just can't come back inside that shop," I said. He turned his face away from me, nose up in the air, almost violently ignoring me. "I, on the other hand, do need to go back into that coffeeshop. So, what are you going to do?"

Houdini said nothing for a small eternity. Then he huffed. "Fine. I'll wait here. But I hate that man. I hate him!"

"Yes, you've said before," I said. I rubbed tiredly at my forehead. I was getting a headache. Probably from the tea. No magical insights for me. Just a smidge of pain.

"Just because I can't say why I hate him doesn't mean I'm being irrational," Houdini said petulantly.

I sighed. "Look, we won't be long, and you can watch us through the windows the whole time."

Houdini made an inarticulate sound inside my mind. It was irritating, and at some point we'd have to have a conversation about not using telepathy to blast my brain with non-word noises.

But this was not the time for that.

"Five minutes, tops," I said to him. Then I went back inside the coffeeshop.

Audrey and Titus had already started talking, and I was thrust into the middle of their conversation.

"Yes, I *was* interested in buying your grandaunt's shop. But *she* was never interested in selling to *me*," he was saying to Audrey as he stacked up his papers and tucked them inside a ledger book of his own. His cover was green where Agatha's had been red but otherwise they were identical. They must shop at the same prosaic stationery store.

"So you just dropped the offer?" Audrey asked.

"I never formally made one," he said. Then he sighed. "She was very clear about her wishes, and I respected those wishes. Not that I ever knew why she felt the way she did. She never bothered to explain. But she didn't have to, did she? She had no legal obligation to tell me why she wouldn't entertain any offers from me."

"What about a moral obligation?" I asked. "Or a social one? To keep peace and be neighborly within the Square?"

"Wouldn't that have been nice?" he said wistfully. Then he shook his head. "But no. That wasn't her way."

"You were the one who called me when she died," Audrey said.

"That's correct," he said.

"You knew how to contact me? Just you?" she asked.

He frowned at her question. "Well, I didn't know directly how to find you. But I knew how to find out. Any of us on the Square could've done that. I guess I just thought of it first."

"Your wife did," I found myself putting in.

"What's that?" he asked, sort of automatically, like he wasn't really listening to me. Then a thoughtful look crossed his face. "Yes, you're right. It was her idea. I remember now. We were right there at that table by the window when that came up. I'm surprised you remember. You were pretty upset."

Audrey gave me a look of deep sympathy, and I gave her hand a squeeze. But I made my eyes as blank of emotion as I could before saying to Titus, "I remember lots of things."

"Am I being accused of something?" Titus asked, looking from me to Audrey, then back again.

"Tell him I don't trust him," Houdini said in my mind. Clearly looking in through the closed glass doors wasn't blocking him from hearing or at least knowing what we were saying.

But I ignored him.

"Who here knows that Audrey has respiratory issues?" I asked. "Who knows that she uses an inhaler?"

"How could I answer that question? I didn't know those things about her myself," he said. "And what does that have to do with anything?"

I looked at Audrey, and she gave me a little nod. "Someone tried to kill her. Using her inhaler. They poisoned it. And we think it was whoever killed Agatha."

"Yes, that makes sense," he agreed, nodding as he thought it through. Then a look of alarm flooded across his face. "Wait, you think it was *me*?"

"We only have your word that you took Agatha's refusal to hear your offers as calmly as you claim," I said.

"You can ask my wife," he said, sweeping his hands up towards the ceiling. I guessed this meant they lived directly upstairs. Between the coffeeshop below and Agatha's apartment above.

How very convenient.

"And how would we know she wasn't lying to protect you?" Audrey asked.

"The authorities have ways. But apparently this isn't an authority matter," he said, realizing it was just two young women asking him all the uncomfortable questions. "They concluded the cause of death was an accidental fall, the last I heard."

"We don't think so," I said.

"Because of what happened with the inhaler?" Titus guessed.

"That, and other things," I said, shooting a glance at Houdini. He was sitting right outside the door now, close enough to the glass that he could press his nose to it if he wanted to.

"This is ridiculous," Titus said under his breath. "Look, why don't we call the authorities now? Let them sort it out. If they need my alibi, I can give it to them. But I don't see how anything I can say is going to be any comfort to either of you. I don't know how to make you believe that I mourn Agatha Mirken's death as much as anyone on the Square. Her teashop is an institution, here. She was one of the original cornerstones of our community. She's been here since the beginning. She was here when St. Anthony Falls collapsed, for crying out loud."

"No way," I said disbelievingly. "That was like a century ago. Wasn't it?" I shot a quick look at Audrey.

"It was like in the 1880s?" she guessed.

"1869," Titus told us. "Look it up."

"But that would mean Agatha was..." I trailed off, defeated by the math.

"No one knows how old Agatha was when she died," Titus said. "Older even then Volumnia, maybe. Maybe." He shook his head mournfully. "Like I said, no one knows. A wizard doesn't live to such an advanced age without being very guarded about their personal information."

"But only wizards of great power can live to be so old," I said. "Agatha, in the end, couldn't even mix tea."

"What?" Titus gasped. He seemed genuinely shocked at this piece of information.

"Wasn't that common knowledge?" I asked. "I knew, and I was new."

"I didn't know," Audrey reminded me.

"Barnardo knew," I countered.

"Perhaps it was just the two of you. She trusted the both of you. I can promise you it wasn't remotely common knowledge. The gossip mill in the Square is healthier than most. I would've heard if anyone even had a suspicion," he said.

"She kept it secret," Audrey said. "He's right. She told you and Barnardo because she trusted you both."

"The minute she met me?" I demanded.

Audrey and Titus said as one, "That sounds like Agatha."

In a normal conversation, this chorusing would've led to laughter or cries of, "Jinx!"

But this was far from a normal conversation.

After a long silence, Titus said, "I don't know what happened with your inhaler, Audrey. I'm sorry. But as to Agatha's death, I was at home in bed at the moment she fell. I was one of the first down to the scene, and I was the one who summoned Volumnia. You saw me there in my pajamas. I let you into my shop. Don't you remember?"

"I remember," I said. "But that's not an alibi. You could've pushed her over the railing in your pajamas, then ran down three flights of stairs rather than just two to get to where I found you when I arrived. It's not an alibi."

"But I was with my wife the whole time," Titus said. "I know you're both skeptical, but the authorities would take her at her word. Can you do any less?"

"We should talk to her," Audrey said. I couldn't tell if she was still following the compunctions from the magical tea or not, but she was very firm in her tone.

"Fine. We'll talk to her," I sighed. "Is she here?"

"No, she's just upstairs," he said. Then he turned to the cabinet that ran the length of the wall behind the counter and moved a knickknack on a shelf from one position to another. I leaned in closer and saw it was a snow globe, the snow still swirling in the liquid after being moved, the scene within a winter-scape of the spoon and cherry sculpture from the Sculpture Gardens.

"She'll be down momentarily," he said.

Audrey and I nodded, then settled into chairs around one of the tables. Titus sat down with us, clearly agitated by the entire situation.

"Have you thought about what you'll be doing with the place at all?" he asked Audrey. If it was an attempt to break the awkward silence, it was a failed one. The question hung over all of us, and when Audrey didn't respond, the silence became more awkward than ever.

It was a bit of a relief when Titus's wife Nell approached the door on the Square side.

But that relief was short-lived.

TWENTY-THREE

As aggressive as Houdini's dislike towards Titus had always been, it paled in comparison to his reaction to Nell. Not only was he barking and howling and baying for all his little ten-pound body was worth, he was making little lunging attacks at her. He wasn't quite trying to bite her, but he looked like he really wanted to.

I guessed the way his hair was standing straight up all along his spine meant his hackles were up. I had heard that expression a thousand times without really thinking about what that looked like. It made Houdini look like some kind of furry dinosaur. A very tiny furry dinosaur, to be sure, but it was unnerving all the same.

Nell made eye contact with us through the window, raising her hands in frustration. Clearly, Houdini had no intention of letting her inside the coffeeshop.

"I'll get him," I said, and left Audrey alone with Titus to push back out into the warm afternoon. Houdini was still barking with all his might, bracing his legs as he put his whole body into the effort.

And he definitely didn't appreciate me scooping him up and

holding him close to my chest. He struggled in my grip, but at least he stopped making noise.

"That dog is a menace!" Nell said. She said it like she was half-joking, but the laugh she punctuated it with sounded forced.

"He's grieving," I said, stroking his back until his hackles went down again.

"Yes, I suppose he is," she said. The words were noncommittal to sympathetic, but I couldn't get a read on her tone at all. She quickly ducked inside the coffeeshop.

I looked down at Houdini. He had stopped struggling against me and was even leaning into me as I held him. His hair was all flat again, but I kept stroking his back all the same.

"What was that all about?" I asked him.

"I'm very unhappy," he said sulkily.

"Of course you are," I said. "But why take it out on Nell?"

"She's worse than Titus," he said.

"What did she do?" I asked.

"I have no idea. I've never met her before in my life. But she's done something. I can just smell it on her," he said, in a growling tone even inside my mind.

"What does that mean?" I asked. "Is that a magic you can do, or just a dog thing, or what?"

"I don't know," he said, even more sulkily than before. "Can you put me down now? I'll behave."

"Will you?" I said skeptically, but set him down on the patio tile. "Do you have any reason to suspect the Blooms, Houdini?"

"I didn't see what happened," he said. "I didn't sense anything happening. I was so blind. What use was I? None. None at all. Agatha is gone because I failed to protect her."

"Audrey is the one in danger now," I said, looking at my new friend through the coffeeshop windows. She was looking towards Titus as he spoke, so I couldn't see her face. But from the back of her head, she looked all right.

"I know," Houdini said glumly. "I'm going to fail again, aren't I?"

"If you do, you won't do it alone. I'll have failed as well," I said. Audrey turned and looked up to speak to Nell, tucking a strand of hair behind her ear as she did so. She didn't look upset or frightened or anything. But was the tea still in her system? Was it still doing whatever it did? Would being able to make connections that were unseen before drinking the tea lend her any kind of danger sense?

I felt no different myself. Nothing was joining together in my mind. Everything was still a jumble of dead ends and a lack of clues.

"How are we ever going to solve this with no clues?" I said to Houdini. He was sniffing around the tiles where Agatha had fallen. All the blood had been magically whisked away, and any cracks that might have formed in the tiles had been repaired. For all I could see, it was like nothing had ever happened.

"We have to, though," Houdini said to me. "We have to. For Agatha."

"Okay," I sighed. "I'm going back in there. Is there anything you can think of that we should ask?"

"No," he said, still sniffing. "It's not like she can tell you why she smells wrong. People can never smell themselves."

I said nothing more to him, but I wasn't sure he was entirely right about that. Well, on the surface, he was. I couldn't just ask Nell why she smelled like she'd been up to no good. Especially considering I couldn't smell her myself, not like Houdini could.

But I could hold that impression in my mind while I watched her face for reactions to our questions.

I really wished someone with better magical skills was going to be the one asking the questions. There were spells that helped discern truth from fiction, but I didn't have the time to pull one together for Audrey.

Not in time to save her life if the murderer tried again, anyway.

I went back inside the coffeeshop.

"Nell was just remembering the time I was here before, as a child," Audrey told me as I slid back into my seat at the table.

"Oh, yes?" I said.

"I barely remember it myself, but I guess I made more of an impression on Nell," Audrey said, ducking her head shyly.

"She was a very mature little girl, definitely Agatha's blood relative. I'm not surprised she went into ritual magic," Nell said. Audrey tucked her hair behind her ear again, embarrassed at the compliment. But a degree in ritual magic *is* impressive, even if she only barely achieved it.

"She's more than ready to take up Agatha's mantle, if she wants it," I said, and gave Audrey's arm a squeeze.

"It's just a teashop," Audrey said.

"So you're planning to open Loose Leaves back up again?" Nell asked.

I looked at her closely as she asked the question. Her tone was casual, and nothing about her face contradicted that. But she did notice me studying her and gave me a quick questioning look before turning her attention back to Audrey.

"I haven't decided yet," Audrey admitted.

"If you decide to stay, we'll all support you any way we can, of course," Titus said. "We're a close community here in the Square. We have our little differences—every community does—but when it matters, we pull together for each other."

"We don't actually know if Audrey inherited the property," I put in. "The will hasn't been read yet. But I guess we're all assuming she will."

"Yes, that makes the most sense," Titus said. "But if you decide it's not for you, know that we've long been interested in acquiring that property. We'll make you a good offer. If that's the road you choose to take."

"Why would you want it?" I asked as casually as I could. "I mean, it's on the less populated of the two roads. Isn't it a step down?"

"Getting a little further away from that chain coffeeshop would be good for us," Titus said. "The teashop is just out of sight of their signage. With a little low-key magic, that would be all we needed to build our business back up again."

"Low-key magic? On prosaic people?" I asked. That was a legal gray area in the magical community.

"I've discussed my proposals with the authorities already on that score," Titus told me. "The level I'm approved to use isn't moving the needle when we're this close to that shop. But around the corner? I really think it might be enough."

"That chain store must be run by wizards," Nell put in sourly. "Nothing else explains their success."

"Well, there *are* other explanations," Titus said, then cleared his throat loudly, as if this were an old argument between the two of them. One that he had accidentally stepped into and desperately wanted to step back out of it again in a hurry. "Anyway, Audrey, it's just something to keep in mind."

"Well, like I said, I haven't decided yet," Audrey said.

Then something passed across her face, a sudden flash of insight, I thought. She ducked her head again, tucking that strand of hair behind her ear more slowly this time as she glanced over at me out of the corner of her eye.

I gave her the smallest of shrugs. Whatever she was thinking, I didn't have a clue. But I tipped my head towards the Blooms, encouraging her to follow up on it.

"Of course, if I sold you the shop, I would still keep Agatha's books. Those should stay in the family," she said.

"Oh, that wouldn't be an issue," Titus said with a little laugh. "I mean, we're still brewing coffee here. Not tea."

He laughed again, softly. But next to him, his wife's face had suddenly gone cold and still. She saw me studying her again and quickly put it back into a semblance of warm concern for Audrey, but too late. I had seen it. There was something dark lurking behind her eyes. Something not quite right. Maybe even not quite human.

And Houdini had smelled it.

"Not that the books are worth all that much," I said. Audrey shot me a quick, shocked look, but I pressed on. "The ledger is in some indecipherable code, and all the good recipes in her big red book were faded and written over with prosaic recipes."

"Oh, that's a shame," Titus said. But he didn't sound like he quite understood why I was pointing this out. He definitely had no interest in those books.

"Perhaps in the end, when that curse kept her from brewing any of her teas, even the prosaic ones, she thought destroying her own work would help somehow." I gave a careless shrug. "I mean, what's the use of a mint cardamom tea?"

"That does sound..." Titus began, but words failed him.

But Nell was giving me an icy stare. Not like she was trying to figure me out. I don't think she was confused by what I was doing.

No, she knew exactly what I was implying. And her look felt like a threat. Like a very clear, very strongly meant threat.

"Nell, where were you that night? When Agatha fell?" I asked.

Titus gave me a startled look. "Well, obviously, she was with me. We were together in our apartment just over the shop. You saw us both when you came out. We just discussed this."

"We're discussing it again, now that Nell is here," I said. "You both *looked* like you'd just gotten out of bed. Pajamas and slippers and robes, the whole ensemble. But that's a pretty easy costume to put on."

"Just what are you accusing us of?" Titus demanded.

"Not both of you," I said. "Just your wife."

Nell's glare had turned, if anything, icier than before. At my words, Titus turned to look at her, and recoiled a little when he saw her.

"Nell?" he said.

"You should probably just give me the books," Nell said coldly. "That would be best."

"Nell? What are you talking about?" Titus asked, but she ignored him.

"This isn't about the shop at all, is it?" Audrey guessed. "What are you really looking for?"

"Apparently something you haven't found yet, or you wouldn't need to ask," Nell said disdainfully. "You don't deserve access to such power, neither of you. A lack-magic and a failed ritual magician? What could you even do with it?"

The word "lack-magic" burned. I had heard it a lot in my school-days. But in that moment, it felt like the lesser of the two insults. "Audrey didn't fail ritual magic," I said.

"Near enough," Nell scoffed. "Agatha sat on her true source of power for far too long, waiting for a worthy heir. No one knows how ancient she truly was, only that she was older than time when she moved here a century ago. Do you know what sort of power that takes? More than can be contained within the body of a wizard, I promise you."

"Nell, what are you talking about?" Titus asked. His eyes were wide and desperate. He was still hoping that there was some rational explanation for his wife's strange new demeanor.

But from the way she was subtly expanding as she towered over the three of us at the little table, I doubted there was one. I could see her swelling up like a pufferfish, only more slowly, each breath expanding her form ever so slightly. It wasn't pleasant to look at.

"Quiet, you," she snapped at her husband, and Titus quickly dropped his eyes back to his hands on the tabletop. Apparently he didn't like looking at her ever darkening face any more than I did.

"You didn't want the teashop," I said. "Or the books. You were looking for something else."

Audrey shot me a confused look, but I didn't meet her eyes. I had no idea what the thing would be either. We had searched the apartment as well as the teashop, and all we had found were the two books and lots and lots of tea.

But I felt more strongly than ever that we must have missed *something*.

"Agatha had some source of power that kept her alive?" I ventured. I couldn't quite look at Nell, and even I could feel the magic in that. Some sort of supernatural repulsion, a magical command to look away. I could just focus on her hands gripping the edge of the table.

And my stomach knotted up tight. She was towering over us, I knew that for a fact.

But she was still sitting at the table. She hadn't stood up.

Yet.

"Her control was slipping, I could feel it," Nell said with evil glee. "The moment was ripe to take it from her."

"So you cursed her? You're the reason she couldn't make tea anymore?"

"What nonsense!" Nell spat. "When I was ready to attack her, I attacked her. And splatted her on the ground. Whatever problems she had with her *tea*," she said, weighing that last word with the heaviest of disdain, "were of her own making."

"But you *did* kill her," I said. It was taking real effort to keep my voice from trembling. The command in my mind not to look at her was pressing down on me, smothering my brain.

I had never been so frightened in my life. This situation was spinning wildly out of control.

But I still didn't understand what was going on.

"You killed her, you admitted that. But you still didn't find what you were looking for?" I said. I just managed to edge a little disdain of my own into that question.

Which was a mistake. The air around me was suddenly uncomfortably hot and close, and I broke out in a sweat as Nell just bellowed in frustrated rage.

"I will have it! You will give it to me!" she shrieked. "Alive or dead, it makes no difference to me."

"Nell!" Titus protested, but his wife didn't spare him so much as a glance. She pushed back from the table and stood up, and it was just as awful as I feared when she did.

She loomed over all of us, but she also seemed to expand, like a ship's sails filling with the wind. And I swear the dimensions of the little coffeeshop expanded too, to make room for her. But just for her.

For the three of us still cowering low at the table, there was very little space at all. And even less air.

I had no idea what she was. A very powerful wizard, perhaps. The ones who did too much of the wrong sorts of magic became something less than human, or so the cautionary tales always said. Or maybe she was something else that had been merely disguising itself as human. For who knew how long.

Titus stumbled away from her, falling to the floor. There was no way the shock on his face was faked.

"Nell?" he said in a quiet, plaintive voice. But she just kept filling the space and filling the space. I steeled my courage and looked Nell straight in the face.

Mistake. It had morphed into something too terrible to be looked directly at. My mind screamed, then my voice followed.

Then she began to speak, words I didn't recognize. But I knew it was magic, old magic. Powerful magic.

And all I could do was hold tight onto Audrey, and she held tight onto me. And we waited for the blast of power that was surely about to hit us.

TWENTY-FOUR

I could hear Houdini baying urgently outside the coffeeshop doors, but he sounded impossibly far away. The oppressive quality to the air was like an ever-increasing weight on my back, part of the magic Nell was building.

It was going to crush the air right out of my lungs before too long.

I could hear Audrey mumbling something in her deep spell-casting voice, and for a moment I thought we'd be okay. She was still holding onto me with one arm, but she was brandishing her wand in the other. Her voice grew stronger even as the oppression pressed down on us with ever greater force, and I really thought it was going to be okay. Audrey had this.

But then she stumbled over a word, her tongue twisting over a train wreck of consonants all in a row. She recovered quickly, but she had to start her spell again from the beginning.

And I could tell her confidence had taken a huge blow. Her voice wasn't as full this time, and her incantation had lost its driving rhythm.

All of that was going to affect the magic. Whatever spell she was casting, it might not fizzle out all together if she made it all the way to the end this time, but it was definitely going to be far less potent than it would've been the first time around.

And then she tripped over the same word again.

Nell laughed. I still couldn't bear to look at her as she filled the entire back half of the coffeeshop, but that laugh sent fresh shivers of dread down my spine. The few glimpses of her body I could catch out of the periphery of my vision were just of a massive inky black glob bursting out of the tattered remains of her neat gray cardigan and sensible slacks.

Was she really trying to kill us? All three of us? Even her husband Titus? Or was the oppressive spell just to force us to submit to her wishes?

I didn't much feel like submitting.

Sure, I had no spells I could throw back at her.

But there was always the table.

I let go of Audrey even as she restarted her spell for a third time, and I used both hands to flip the flimsy coffeeshop table, sending it crashing into the blob that had recently been Nell Bloom.

I don't think it hurt her much. But it did stop her laughing, at least for the moment.

I turned and ran to the door, but no matter how I pushed or pulled, I couldn't budge it. I could see Houdini through the glass, but I could no longer hear his barking. I could see he was still doing it, with all his might, barking and barking and barking. But the sound no longer penetrated the glass doors and walls.

And I had a sinking feeling it wasn't just his barking I couldn't hear. Surely he was trying to talk to me in my mind. Something was blocking that as well.

Something was blocking everything.

Whatever Nell was, she had more magic at her fingertips than anyone I had ever met. And she flung it about so casually, as if it cost her nothing.

I leaned close to the glass and shouted, even though I knew extra volume wouldn't be any help at all, "Houdini! Get help! Get help!"

For a moment, he just kept barking. Then he seemed to understand, if not my words, at least the situation. He turned and bolted away, his black fur quickly vanishing into the darkening night.

But that still left me inside the coffeeshop with Nell and her crushing power. Audrey had moved to the far corner of the coffeeshop, but the door to the prosaic world was just as sealed as the one to the Square. She stopped trying to force it open and turned to try her spell again. But she kept the arm not brandishing her wand flung across her eyes. Whatever Nell was, Audrey couldn't bear to look at her, either.

Nor could Titus. He just sat where he had fallen after getting up from the table. He looked paralyzed with shock and fear, gaping at nothing with a thousand-yard stare.

Never in my life had I wished I could do magic more than I did in that moment. I wanted to save my friend. I wanted to save myself. I even wanted to save Titus. Whatever was going on, he hadn't asked for any of it. It was possible that every time Houdini had barked at him in warning and alarm, it had only been residual Nell smell he was reacting to. I'd have to ask him about it later.

If I ever got the chance.

I looked down at my hands curled into tight fists, useless as they were. Throwing a table at her hadn't done more than give her pause. What could I hope for if I tried to punch her?

Then she started laughing again, a condescending laugh. Like she knew every thought in my head, knew just how powerless I felt, and was absolutely delighted to be the cause of that.

I grabbed the nearest chair and hurled it towards her end of the coffeeshop. Then another. And another. Adrenaline was rushing through my body, and in that moment, I felt like I could keep throwing chairs forever.

Then I ran out of chairs, so I flipped another table. Only this time, I felt a jolt of electricity as I touched it. It was like all the static I had been building up for weeks and weeks surged out of my body and into the table. Only it didn't just spark an arc of light between me and the metal. It lingered. The table crackled and glowed.

But it all happened in an instant. I just felt this rush of electricity move through me, then the table was sailing through the air as if someone with ten times my strength had hurled it this time.

It hit the Nell thing, and not only did she stop laughing, she gave a cry of surprised pain.

I looked up at her, not meaning to, but it was just a reflex. She had finished her transition to inky black glob, her bottom half ten times its normal size and spreading out over the tiles like goo, her top half about five times its normal size but still vaguely human in shape. The table had struck her full in the face, leaving an actual dent in her form. She shook it off, and her face molded itself back into shape. Then she pinned me with eyes that were kaleidoscopes of rage and pure crazy.

And she started to ooze closer to me.

"Tabitha!" Audrey shouted.

I didn't answer her. I just looked down at my own hands. They were crackling with electric power. This was worse than when I had watched Audrey do her spell. I was sparking like mad. If I wasn't careful, I was going to burn the whole Square down.

But more than that, I was afraid if I tried to touch another table, it would happen again. That rush of electricity had hurt. And there was more of it now, just waiting to be discharged.

And I was really afraid if I did it again, this would just keep compounding. Whatever was going on, I was definitely not in control of it.

I could take down Nell. I was pretty sure that was true. But at what cost?

That spark had hurt. And I was sparking so much more intensely now.

What if I couldn't even choose not to do it again now? What if it was going to happen no matter what? What if I was about to explode?

I really felt like I was about to explode.

"Tabitha!" Audrey shouted again, real panic in her voice. I didn't look up. I could feel the weight of Nell's magic pressing down on me. I knew I was running out of time. But I forced my brain to find something it could do and focus on it. I had to focus on something besides the power that was surging through me. But what?

Then I had it.

"What does it mean?" I shouted at Audrey. Then I attempted to say the word she kept stumbling over.

"What?" she stammered, but then said, "Power. Like, ethereal power."

I ran her words through my memory again. It was hard to concentrate. I was all too aware of Nell oozing ever closer. I could feel her breath now. It wasn't pleasant.

Plus the power inside of me was starting to hurt. Even without touching a table. My skin was on fire.

But finally the perfect word jumped to the front of my mind. "Use 'eldritch' instead."

"But that's not elder tongue. That's just English!" she objected.

"It's older English. Look, just try it!" I said. I had backed as far into the corner of the shop as I could. Sparks were falling from my fists, sizzling as they hit the tiled floor.

I needed my mother. It was maybe a strange thought to have in that moment. Or maybe it was perfectly natural. Didn't lots of people call for the mothers when death was near?

But most people had experience with having their mother come when she was called. My own experience was quite the opposite. Wherever in the world my mother was, she was too far away to help me now. Even if she could hear me. Even if she wanted to rescue me.

Audrey said the spell again, but I could hear the doubt in her voice the entire time. She started punching the rhythm of the spell, and the rhyme was already there for her, but she couldn't bring her confidence to it to glue it all together. When it finally left her spell, a bolt of—yes, eldritch—power struck Nell right in the temple.

But it sank into the goo with a fizzle.

Nell shook out her inky hair, then pulled her oozing form tighter beneath her, rising up even higher above me.

Then I heard another voice saying Audrey's spell. A man's voice. I couldn't see around Nell's expanding form, but Houdini must've brought help. Whoever it was, they repeated Audrey's incantation word for word, speaking with all the confidence that Audrey had lacked.

And the bolt that struck Nell square in the back of the head exploded black goo all over me, hard enough to send my glasses flying. I instinctively covered my face with my hands, trying to keep it out of my eyes. Trying to keep it out of my mouth.

Then the oppressive pressure was gone, so suddenly I felt myself falling to my knees as if it had been the only thing holding me upright. I dropped my hands to suck in breath after breath of cool, freely moving air.

And looked down at Nell sprawled across the tiles in front of me. She was her old self again, a rather unexceptional-looking middle-aged woman in the tattered remains of a gray cardigan and sensible slacks. She didn't look like a witch at the moment, let alone a creature of unspeakable power.

Standing over us both was Titus. He had a wand in his hand and was breathing hard as if he, too, couldn't get enough of the suddenly plentiful oxygen.

Audrey stumbled across the ruin of the coffeeshop to stand beside him. I stayed where I was on the floor with my back to the wall. I didn't trust myself to stand up just yet.

The electric power inside of me was still building. I could see sparks of electricity and fire both snapping randomly out from my hands. And I couldn't make it stop. I focused and focused, but I couldn't make it stop.

Then the door burst open in a blast of magic, and Houdini was suddenly all over me. He kept jumping and jumping, trying to lick my face and nip at my nose all at once. I couldn't push him away. I tried to catch hold of him to calm him down, but he just squirmed out of my grasp, only to start jumping at my face all over again.

"Get him away!" I begged, but it was too late. All the power was reaching a critical level. It *had* to come out now. I couldn't hold it back.

Then hands closed around my wrists and I found Steph crouching down nose to nose with me. "Let it out," he said to me, his voice low and calm. A controlled sort of calm, the kind meant to make *me* calm. But I was too far gone to settle down now. "Let it out, Tabitha," he said, a bit more firmly. "Don't try to direct it into anything. Don't focus on holding it back. Just let it all out. Spread it out far and wide. But let it go."

It was the most unnatural of commands, and the hardest thing to do. To lose control? I didn't want to.

But his hands on my wrists gave me a reassuring squeeze, and really I couldn't hold onto it all any longer.

There was a blast of energy all around us. Luckily, the fight had pretty much destroyed the coffeeshop already, so I did no more damage.

But more than that, I felt like Steph had done something too. He had absorbed the worst of it with a barely perceptible grunt of pain.

And then it was gone, and I felt more normal than I had in months.

Then Houdini was jumping all over me again.

"He was worried about you," Steph said as he stood up. He took in the broken furniture, the pools of black ooze everywhere, and Nell laying on the floor. "What happened?"

"Is she...?" Titus asked in a whisper, but couldn't get the last word out. It didn't matter. We were all wondering the same thing. Was she dead?

"It was a stunning spell," Audrey said in a wisp of a voice, like she had fried her vocal cords trying that spell over and over again. "We used it for dueling when I was studying ritual magic. It's sort of a nothing spell, really, but it was all I could think of."

"It certainly did the job," Steph said, dropping to one knee beside Nell. He pressed his fingertips to her temple and got a faraway look in his eyes for a moment. Then he looked up at Titus and gave him a nod. "She's out, but not gone. You put a lot of intent behind that spell. I didn't know you had it in you."

"That makes two of us," Titus said, looking down at the wand in his hand. Then he tossed it aside as if the sight of it sickened him. "I couldn't let her hurt Tabitha and Audrey."

"No," Steph said, but he sounded distracted, deep in thought.

Houdini, winded, finally collapsed into my arms. "Are you okay, little buddy?" I asked him.

"I will never leave your side again," he said inside my mind. "Never."

"That might be a little extreme, but I understand the feeling," I said to him. Audrey glanced at Titus, but he seemed too caught up in his own head space to wonder why I was having a conversation only half of which he could hear.

Steph walked a few paces away then returned with my glasses. Still intact, if a bit greasy as the last of the goo dripped off them. He polished them up with the inside of his cloak then settled them back on my nose.

"Thanks," I said, and adjusted them ever so slightly.

"I have to bring Nell to the Wizard," Steph said at last. "He'll know what to do."

"I didn't know," Titus said earnestly. "I didn't know what she was or what she had done or any of it. I would swear she was there with me all night long when Agatha was murdered, but I was asleep. Nell could've gone and been back before I woke up, couldn't she have?" He gave a humorless chuckle. "I don't know what she could've done. Anything. Everything. I don't know."

Steph raised a questioning eyebrow at me.

"We haven't pieced it all together yet, but the short version is that Nell killed Agatha, then tried to kill Audrey," I said. "All over some sort of object of power? We don't know what she was looking for. She said we would know if we had found it ourselves."

"I'm so sorry you were in danger," Titus said to the two of us. "I don't know how to make it up to you."

"It wasn't you," Audrey assured him, putting her hand on his arm. "We know it wasn't you."

He nodded each time she spoke. But then he buried his face in his hands and turned away from his wife and all of us.

"I'll bring her to the Wizard," Steph said again. He looked over at Titus, who had taken several steps away from us, then leaned close to whisper to me. "He hit her pretty hard. She might not come out of this on her own. But the Wizard can bring her back."

"And then what?" I asked. The idea of her being awake again, being able to turn back into that unspeakable form, bothered me a lot.

"Do none of you recognize what was just happening?" he asked, looking from me to Audrey to the back of Titus some feet away from us.

Audrey and I looked at each other, but both shook our heads.

"She made a deal with something from the under realms," Steph said. "From the shape she was assuming, I think it was from the oceanic region of the under realms, but the Wizard will know for sure."

"Evil?" Audrey asked.

"Meh?" Steph said, making a noncommittal gesture with his hand. "It wanted the power, and was willing to do anything to acquire it. It used Nell to achieve its own aims. But it wasn't what I'd call *pure* evil. Just very driven."

That sounded like hair-splitting to me. I didn't need something to be pure evil to be something I wanted very far away from my home and my loved ones. But we could quibble about definitions later.

"Is it still inside her?" I asked.

"No, it's gone. That's why she looks human again," Steph said. "But it could come back, potentially. But don't worry, the Wizard and I can prevent that while we have her in our custody."

"Then what?" I asked.

"Then she gets turned over to the authorities," he said.

"We can't prove what she did," I said helplessly. "Unless there's some sort of contract between her and this under realms being in her possession somewhere, we have no evidence of anything."

"You don't need evidence," he said. "She's done more than you know, and *that* I can prove."

Then he rested his hand on Nell's forehead and winked them both out of existence before I could even ask what he had meant.

CHAPTER

TWENTY-FIVE

S adly, the wheels of bureaucracy move no faster in the magical world than they do in the prosaic one. I knew that Nell was still in the Tower with the Wizard and his apprentice Steph, and I knew the authorities had come and gone from that tower several times over the next few days. But that was all I knew. And Audrey and Titus had heard no more than I had.

But we all had little trouble finding work to do to pass the time. Titus had to close his coffeeshop for cleanup and repair after our battle. I had broken a lot of his furniture throwing it at his wife, but he promised me the bulk of the damage had been done by the black ooze. It had soaked into the tile floor and through it into the basement below, which served as his storeroom. Most of the interior had to be pulled out and built anew. Luckily, with magic, this wasn't too much of a problem. But magical contractors are a lot like prosaic ones when it comes to the difference between estimated timelines and the reality of such a complicated project. Audrey and I had seen little of him in the ensuing days.

For her part, Audrey kept herself busy in the teashop and Agatha's apartment, going through everything and sorting things she wanted to keep from things that could be donated to prosaic or magical charities to outright garbage. However long Agatha had lived, she had acquired more than her fair share of things that were no longer as usable as they had once been, both in her home and in her shop.

Of course, I knew that Audrey was also sorting through everything in the increasingly vain hope of discovering the power object that had led to her death. But so far, she had turned up nothing.

And me, I had a bookshop to run. After being closed more than open for several days, business was suddenly booming both on the magical side as well as the prosaic one. I was kept hopping from opening to close throughout the weekend and into the week that followed.

But I had seen no sign of Liam. I was worried that Steph's memory wipe had taken more from him than Steph had said it did, but there was no way for me to know for sure. Because I hadn't seen Steph either.

The rest of the Square gathered on Tuesday at midnight to witness Agatha's remains being interred in one of the nooks in Volumnia's walls, as per Agatha's wishes, although she had been cremated first. Her ashes were in a wooden box of oak that was plain of adornment, but clearly very old. When I asked Volumnia about it, she had told me that Agatha had given that box to her for just such a purpose when they'd both first arrived to establish the Square in the 19th century. But it had been old even then, and Volumnia didn't know the story behind it.

"It was probably from a tree from her home back in the Old World," she had said to me. "But I never asked."

I also asked her about the mark on the back of Agatha's neck, the one she had suspected was not merely dirt. She had given me a soul-searching stare at that. I think she had told me that the Wizard would speak to such things in due time, but honestly, I can't be sure. Those eyes still wigged me out, and that stare had been too much for too long. I had scurried away from the crypts just as soon as I politely could.

Now it was Thursday, and still there was no news. I turned the sign on the door to "closed", locked up, and headed to my nook on the fourth level.

Audrey was there, dressed in the same black skirt and sweater she had worn to the internment. She had been looking at the decrypted ledger book again when I approached the table, but shut the cover and pushed it away when she saw me.

"The reading of the will was today?" I guessed.

"Yes. The Loose Leaves Teashop is indeed mine," she said.

"Of course it is," I said, but I couldn't get a read on her feelings from her face. "What are you thinking?"

"Well, Titus approached me as I was leaving the advocate's office," she said.

"That's not even in the Square. That's in the hidden city downtown," I said. Stupidly. She had just been there. Of course she knew where it was.

But she caught my meaning. "He wasn't there to pressure me about anything," she said. "He just wanted to check in and see how I was doing. I think he was actually there to deal with something with the authorities. Their main offices are in the same structure under the city."

"So that's where Nell is now?" I asked.

"No, I think she's still in the Tower," Audrey said. "Anyway, he offered to buy the shop from me for whatever price I wanted to name, then offered to run it for me under my ownership if I wanted."

"Interesting," I said. Was he really feeling just that guilty?

"But I said no," she said with a rush of breath. Like she'd been holding it all this time and was finally letting it out now that she was with me. She gave me a tentative smile. "I want to stay. I want to run the teashop. I mean, it's not like I have bigger plans or anything."

"Who needs bigger plans? I think you're going to do great," I said.

Audrey shrugged, but I could tell by the way she fussed over tucking her hair behind her ear that she was touched by my confidence in her.

"There was one other thing, but it really pertains to you," she said, and turned to dig in the bag she had left on the seat of the chair beside her.

As if those had been some kind of magic words, Houdini suddenly sat up from where he had been napping under the head of the table again. He yawned and blinked, and slowly the ears that hung sleepily limp lifted up and deployed to full radar dish dimensions.

"It pertains to me?" he said in our minds.

"She was talking to me, I think," I told him.

"Actually, it's about both of you," she said, frowning as she had to dig deeper into her bag. "I put it right on top. I don't know how... Oh! Here it is."

"Both of us," Houdini said. "I knew I was in the will. I guess you are too."

"I don't know why," I said. "I barely knew her."

"She felt like she knew you well enough," Audrey said as she finally came up with what she was looking for. She handed me an unmarked sealed envelope.

"What is it?" I asked, looking around for a letter opener of some kind. A small sword the size of a butter knife suddenly became apparent to my eyes, resting in the middle of the table. I was certain it hadn't been there before, but I picked it up without another moment's thought and carefully slit the envelope open.

"You didn't inherit any kind of property," Audrey said even as I pulled out the single sheet of paper within and unfolded it. "You inherited a responsibility."

"What responsibility?" Houdini asked. He put his paws on the table and leaned in, as if he could see the words on the page in my hands from there.

As if he could read.

"Tabitha Greene has been named your guardian," Audrey told

him even as I scanned the letter that said the same thing, only using way more words.

"Guardian?" Houdini said, as if the meaning of the word escaped him.

"Until such time as you can guard yourself," I told him. "That's what the letter says. Only I don't understand it. Aren't you as big as you're ever going to get? So either you're a free agent now, or you never will be."

"I don't know about *that*," he said moodily.

"I'm sorry to admit I'm glad it's not me," Audrey said, and briefly touched her nose. "Allergies and all. There's no way I can sleep with him in the room with me."

"Yeah, the two of us manage that just fine," I said as I scanned the letter a second time. "It's just... I'm not sure if I'll be able to stay in the Square after my uncles get back. We haven't talked that far out."

"Yet," Audrey said. "And if they don't want to keep you, then you'll have to move in with me and help me with the teashop."

"Well, that brings us back to your allergies," I said.

"We'll work something out," she said, but the confidence in her tone rang a little bit false.

I looked down the table at Houdini. He was a little dog, easy to transport, easy to fit into any kind of living arrangement. But he was still a lifetime commitment. Maybe not *my* lifetime, but his. If I said yes to this guardianship, I would never be able to change my mind. Houdini and I would be together forever, wherever life took me.

"What do you think about all this?" I asked him. "You've been sleeping in my room, and you've been eating your kibble in my uncles' kitchen. But you're not my familiar, and you're not my pet. So what does this guardianship mean for us? And do you want me to say yes to it?"

Houdini sat back in the chair and pondered. "I am my own entity. I belong to no one," he said.

"Agreed," I said, but he wasn't done yet.

"I am not your familiar, and I am not your pet. But I am—or at least I'd like to be—your companion. If you will have me," he added as an afterthought.

"I'd love to have you, but I might not always be here in the Square. What happens then?"

Houdini half-closed his eyes this time, as if consulting something I couldn't see. Then he sat up even straighter in his chair.

"That's no problem. Unless I am called away by larger forces, I will always be with you," he said.

"Companions, then," I said, and he made a jerk of his chin that was almost a nod.

Then he curled back up on his chair and went back to sleep.

"When do your uncles get back?" Audrey asked.

"Not until the end of August," I said.

"Lots of time to make plans, then," she said. "And you can help me with the teashop."

"Absolutely," I said, and summoned up a smile that she returned with, I was sure, a bit more sincerity than I had managed.

But I could tell she was still worried, the same as I was. It was like we could feel the presence of Nell still in the Square, a constant nuisance in our minds. Like a bit of popcorn stuck between your teeth, it was small, but impossible to ignore.

If only Steph would pop into existence before me the way he'd popped out of it more than once before.

But until he did, all I could do was wait.

CHAPTER

TWENTY-SIX

Another week found Audrey and I once again together with Houdini, only this time we were in the teashop. I had closed the bookshop for the morning to help her finish the last preparations for her big reopening. We had already done the bulk of the work, repainting the walls and furniture and cleaning all the glass until everything was gleaming like new.

I had just barely had enough time to finish my reopening gift for Audrey. I had been using the breaks between customers in the bookshop to work on copying out every single recipe, hidden or not, from Agatha's big book to a new, even larger bound book. I had sorted it all by categories and then indexed everything by title, ingredients, and intended purposes in the back of the book. And everywhere I had left room for her to add more as her business grew.

It had been a lot of work, but as the pressure to finish had increased, the number of customers stopping into the shop had decreased. I ended up with just enough time to finish it before the reopening.

Almost like magic. Like happy little magic. Some remnants of my uncle Carlo's magic, or the magic of the bookshop itself, I wasn't sure. I was merely grateful.

Which was nothing compared to how many times Audrey thanked me after seeing what I had done.

"This is amazing!" she said for maybe the tenth time as she turned the pages of the index. "I don't know how to thank you enough!"

"I'll settle for a cup of that smoky, citrusy tea you're always drinking," I said.

"Of course," she said, and dashed behind the counter to start preparing it. "How do you take it? Sugar or milk?"

"Just black," I said.

"The same for me," a voice said from just behind my elbow. I could taste butterscotch on my tongue even before I turned to see Steph standing there. He looked pale, thin and very, very tired. I supposed I should've taken pity on him and not immediately seized his arms to demand answers.

But I wasn't quite capable of doing that.

"Please tell me you have news," I said as I grasped him tightly.

"Nell Bloom is gone from the Square," he said. "Never to return." Then he slumped into the nearest chair, as if delivering that message had taken all the reserves he had had left in him.

"Does Titus know?" Audrey asked from behind the counter.

"He does," Steph said. "The sheriff and her deputy are with him right now."

"Is he being detained?" I asked, appalled. I had been so sure that he had known nothing about Nell and what she was up to.

"No, no," Steph said quickly. "They just agreed that I should speak to the three of you, and they would handle Titus and then the rest of the Square."

"The three of us?" Audrey said.

"Me," Houdini put in and came out of Agatha's office, nails clicking softly on the tiled floor. "He means me."

"I do, indeed," Steph agreed.

"How much can you tell us about Nell and all that?" I asked.

"Everything I know," he said. "Not that that's a whole lot. Her deal with the under realms entity was a recent thing, so Titus isn't under any suspicion on that score. He didn't see the change in his wife over the last few months, and maybe he should have, but not noticing things isn't against wizard law or anything."

"He's punishing himself enough already on that score," Audrey said, then turned as the kettle behind her started to whistle.

"Perhaps," Steph said noncommittally.

"If this deal was a recent thing, what provoked it?" I asked. "Was it because Agatha wouldn't sell the teashop?"

"Partly," Steph said. "Nell Bloom was unhappy with her life, and feeling like a change of shop location would help the business was a part of that. But a very small part of it. And it wasn't the trigger that set her off."

"What was the trigger?" Audrey asked as she poured steaming water from the kettle into one of her largest teapots. The smell of citrus and smoky tea wafted over to me, momentarily distracting me.

But Steph, looking at Houdini as if waiting for the dog to answer that question, caught my attention.

Only Houdini didn't say anything. He just paced over to the front door to look out of it, as if praying for the interruption that customers would bring to our conversation.

"The presence of the great power suddenly inside the Square," Steph said at last. "She sensed it and wanted it for her own purposes. But she knew that Agatha had gotten to it first, and as old as she was, no witch would ever be able to get the drop on Agatha. So Nell had summoned an entity from the under realms and made a deal with it. A very foolish deal, but then all such deals are always very much ill-advised."

"Where we you and the Wizard when great power was suddenly up for grabs in the Square?" I asked.

"You're right to accuse us. We dropped the ball, so to speak."

"I wasn't accusing—" I started to say, but stopped at his raised hand. Well, not so much that as the pale weariness of the face behind that hand. I don't respond well to commands of silence, but I could see that the conversation was draining what little energy he had left. He clearly needed a good night's rest, then a big meal, and then another long rest after that. Wash, rinse, repeat.

"We were away, conferring with another Wizard at a location I can't disclose to you," he said. "We left wards, of course. But they transmitted no warning to us. I think the moment that this power was exposed, perceivable to all who cared to look for it, was very, very brief."

"But Agatha and Nell both felt it," I said.

"And Agatha got to it first," Steph said. "Then Nell made her bargain."

"Was she lying about cursing Agatha, then?" I asked.

"No, in fact, she was not," Steph said, and I could tell that hadn't been the answer he had expected. "That was Agatha herself. She over-extended her own magic to protect the source of power. To cloak it from others, or so the Wizard and I suspect. But of course, Nell could tell us nothing about any of that. She was very careful, after her bargain, not to cross paths with Agatha. Not until that last night, when they had passed each other on the staircase, Agatha going up and Nell going down. That's when she put her mark on the back of Agatha's neck. And Agatha—again, I assume because she had been burning out her magic—never felt it at all. But that mark is what the under realms entity used to... puppeteer Agatha over the railing of her veranda."

"And Houdini sensed nothing because nothing was actually there," I mused. "Nothing but Agatha."

"When he is older and his senses are more acute, that sort of spell will be easy for him to spot, I'm sure. But he's still a... puppy. No, he sensed nothing amiss."

"And the Wizard knew nothing about any of this?" Audrey asked as she brought the teapot and cups and saucers over to us on a large tray.

"We felt the moment she placed the mark," Steph said. "Well, we had been feeling ripples in the web of magic around us for quite some time. But they were always small movements, small and all-too-brief. In hindsight, that was Nell and her entity taking some action. But at the time, nothing I did revealed to me what I hunted for. It was like on that last night, she always cloaks just a second or two too late."

"And the Wizard? He couldn't find the problem either?" I asked. Something about how I had phrased that question triggered a flash in my mind, but I didn't know what it meant. It was so distracting I barely heard his answer.

"The Wizard never leaves his tower," Steph said. "But I doubt it would've mattered, anyway. These sorts of beings from the under realms excel at cloaking themselves and their magics."

I suddenly gasped aloud as the connection I had been reaching for finally hit me, and they both shot me startled looks. I could feel my cheeks flushing, but said, "This is the problem you kept talking about. When you kept telling me I *wasn't* the problem."

"Indeed," Steph said, watching as Audrey filled his cup with fragrant tea. He leaned forward to blow the steam from the surface but didn't attempt a sip just yet.

"But I still don't understand, what *is* the source of power?" I asked. "And if Agatha was so powerful already, why did she need it? I mean, why would she burn out her own magical powers to acquire it? It makes no sense."

"She didn't try to acquire it," Steph said. "She was trying to protect it."

"Protect it?" I repeated.

"Well, protect *him*," Steph amended. He took a careful sip of his tea.

And then he looked at Houdini.

"Houdini?" I said to the dog. His ears were flat against his head, his tail limp and shapeless. I had never seen him so despondent.

"Agatha gave me that name," he said. "So I would remember that

I always needed to hide. I needed to disappear. But also, if I were ever caught, that I alone had all the power I needed to break myself free again."

"Good name," Audrey said appreciatively.

"I've grown to like it," he conceded.

"Do you want to tell the story, or shall I?" Steph asked him.

"Do you know it?" Houdini asked him.

"Parts of it," Steph allowed. "But I am still hesitant to speak for you. I don't want to decide what secrets you still want to keep and what secrets you are ready to reveal."

"Then I shall tell it, although I promise you, any desire I had to keep secrets died with Agatha," he said, and grief was choking his mental voice once more.

"We can do this later, if you like," I told him.

"No, now is the time," he said, and hopped up on the fourth chair at our little table. He set his paws on the edge of the table and looked at each of us in turn. "I am called Houdini because Agatha gave me that name, but also because, so far as I know, I was never given any other. I know nothing of my family, nothing of my people, nothing of how I came to be here in this world."

"Maybe we can find out for you," I said.

"I would dearly love that, though I fear it will be a difficult undertaking," he said, and Steph nodded his solemn agreement. "You see, I am not of this realm. My people come from one of the outer realms. One of the most distant ones. Our plane seldom over-laps with this one, let alone what you call the prosaic world outside the walls of the Square. And yet it was in that very prosaic world where Agatha found me."

"Who are your people?" I asked.

But at the same time, Audrey asked, "How did she find you?" She gave me an apologetic look for talking over me, but pressed on. "Agatha never left the magical world. She let prosaics into her shop, but she never left magic-infused lands. Ever."

"And yet she did. To fetch me," Houdini said. His ears were

drooping more than ever, and I could feel his grief like a squeezing of my own heart. "She sensed me suddenly in this world so close to her. She went out into the rainstorm to the back of the alley where I had huddled more dead than alive. Someone had hurled my egg against that outer wall of the Tower and then left me there to die. No one else was there when Agatha found me, and none of her magics could reveal what events had transpired before I was suddenly in this world. It's all still a mystery."

"You might not have been a victim of violence," Steph put in. "The Tower is known to attract magical things. If you in egg form had gotten separated from your parents and your people while moving through the realms, it's possible you would be pulled there by that attraction. Or do you remember differently?"

"I remember nothing at all," Houdini said. "Not until long after the damage was done. Agatha burned out the last remains of her own mighty power to cloak me in this form. A little dog, not worth anyone's second look."

"There are more spells than mere visual illusions on you," Steph said.

"That is true," Houdini said. "Being small and powerless is merely the one that irks. But I know now why she did it. To protect me. My true form may be larger than this one, but by the standards of my people, I am still young and small and all but helpless. I would look more fearsome, but that in itself would put me in danger from those who considered me a threat."

"I don't think she was so worried about hunters, although that must have been in her mind too," Steph said.

"What did she fear?" Audrey asked.

"To make a being such as Houdini a familiar is almost unheard of, because his kind do not serve humans," Steph said. "Not when they're grown. But a newborn, apart from others of its kind, is very vulnerable indeed. They long for bonding, and without their parents are prone to bonding with anyone in their vicinity."

"Why does that sound so creepy?" I asked with a shiver.

"Because it is," Steph said darkly. "Only the most twisted of wizards would attempt to chain such a being to serve their own will. It's abominable."

"But Nell was trying to do that?" Audrey asked.

"No," I said, before Steph could answer. "No, Nell only felt power and thought that Agatha was hoarding it. She sensed the power moving and thought Agatha was drawing more from some vast source, and that source was what she was after."

"But she was doing the opposite," Audrey finished for me. "She herself was the vast source. And she was using it to protect a vulnerable little newborn."

"I never asked her to," Houdini said mournfully. "And I guess I see now why she was so harsh with me at times."

"She didn't want you to bond with her in that way," Steph said.

"She told me many, many times," Houdini said. "I wasn't her familiar. I wasn't her pet."

"I can see why you grieve for her so strongly," I said, and put my hand on his little furry shoulder. "You lost so much more than a friend when she was murdered. But I hope you don't feel like you're all alone now?"

"No, I do not," he said.

We fell into silence for a long moment, each of us lost in our own thoughts.

Then Steph spoke again, but the words he said were in no language I had ever studied. And I had studied a lot.

"Yes, I agree," Houdini said.

"Agree to what? What did you just say?" I asked, looking from Houdini to Steph and even to Audrey in case she had caught something I had missed.

"He was speaking Draconic," Houdini said, and sat up straighter on his chair until his little spine was ramrod straight. He thrust out his star-patterned chest and lifted his chin in an immense show of pride. "I understand it, from my time in the egg. I haven't forgotten it yet."

"Draconic?" I said, all in a rush. "But that would make you—"

"A dragon," Houdini said with a little nod of his head. "That is correct. But I don't remember my true form at all. I have no idea even what color dragon I am. I have no idea what would happen if I summoned my magical breath, because that is impossible to do in this form."

"That's going to make it harder to find your people," Steph said. "But not impossible."

"So you're stuck like this? Looking like a dog?" I asked.

"Agatha used all her power to make this happen," Houdini said. "And now she is dead and gone."

"The Wizard and I could attempt to reverse it," Steph said, but Houdini was already shaking his little rat terrier chihuahua head.

"No. I'm not ready to be exposed. I trust to Agatha's wisdom. Until the time is ripe, I shall remain as I am."

I didn't realize how heavily I had sighed until three pairs of eyes turned to me all at once. "Sorry," I said. "It's just, knowing all this, it doesn't make any sense that I should be Houdini's guardian. Like, at all."

Audrey looked glumly down at her own tea. I was pretty sure she agreed with me, but didn't want to say anything. It wasn't like she could volunteer to take my place.

But Steph was touching my hair again, just a gentle plucking of a single curl between thumb and index finger. I wasn't sparking today.

But the day was still young.

"I can't think of anyone more qualified," he said, yet again not explaining at all what he found so fascinating about my hair.

"What do you know that I don't?" I asked, almost obsessively brushing back my own hair. Then I adjusted my glasses.

"Probably nothing," he said with a shrug.

He might not know anything, but I could tell he was thinking some things. He had theories about me.

Maybe the Wizard too. I really didn't want that kind of attention.

I had been studied before, as a young witch student. I hadn't enjoyed it.

"So how am I qualified?" I pressed.

"Well, for one, you make more effective camouflage with a little dog than, say, the Wizard," he said. "The Wizard suddenly walking around with a rat-cha would draw a lot of attention. Someone would work out that there was something special about that dog."

"But I can't protect him from harm," I said. "I can only maybe help hide him."

Steph opened his mouth to speak, but Houdini beat him to it. "I won't hear of another guardian. I won't hear of it. I'm little and I'm sneaky. If anyone tries to give me to another witch or wizard to be looked after, I'll escape. I'm telling you now, I won't live with anyone but Tabitha."

"Well, that's settled then," Steph said. Smugly, as if whatever he had been about to say had been largely along the same lines, only Houdini expressed it better.

"Is it?" I squeaked.

"You have the whole Square backing you up," Audrey promised, putting her hand on mine.

I wanted to argue more, but at just that moment the door to the prosaic world rattled, then opened to let the first of Audrey's customers come in.

CHAPTER
TWENTY-SEVEN

er first customer was a familiar face to us. But whether
we were still familiar to him was an open question.

"Hello?" Liam said as he stuck his head inside the
shop. "The sign says open, but the shutters are still
down?"

"I'll get it," I said, jumping to my feet to deal with the shutters.
Audrey got up as well, heading behind the counter to greet him at
the register with a cheery smile.

But there was a nervous hesitance to her smile. She, like me,
hadn't seen Liam since Steph had erased his memory of the details
about the holes in the Square's official prosaic history.

And I couldn't tell as he strolled in if he were trying to play it
cooler than the last time he'd seen Audrey, or if he only seemed
cooler because he didn't remember her.

He stopped at one of the little tables to set his backpack down,
unzipping the main compartment to carefully slide a bag from the
comic shop containing his latest purchases inside. He shot a quick
glance at the menu on the wall behind the counter, newly painted in
Audrey's careful script.

Then he looked at me even as I wrestled to unjam the last of the shutters and thrust it open to let in the morning light. He gave me a smile, but again I couldn't be sure if it was friendly because he recognized me or friendly because, frankly, Liam seemed like the sort to be friendly with everyone the first time he met them.

He zipped the backpack shut again, then did a double take as his gaze swept past Steph and Houdini sitting together at their table. Steph was just taking another sip of tea, and Houdini was eyeing the plate of shortbread no one had touched yet.

I thought Liam was startled by the sight of a little dog sitting up with his paws on the table in an almost human posture. But it was Steph he studied, chewing at his lip, before asking, "Don't I know you?"

"I don't believe so," Steph said calmly.

"No, I think we've met," Liam said, snapping his fingers as if trying to magically summon up a memory. Then he snapped one last time, louder. "No, we *didn't* meet. You were in the bookshop the last time I was in there. I would swear you vanished into thin air just as I came in the door to see Tabitha."

Steph picked up one of the pieces of shortbread and examined it before crumbling off a corner to offer to Houdini. As the little dog licked hungrily at his fingers, he said, "Well, that doesn't sound possible, does it?"

"Usually, I'd say no, but in your outfit, you look like you could be a struggling magician," Liam said.

I choked down a laugh, more at the look on Steph's face than anything. But Liam had shifted his attention to Audrey. He was facing away from me now and towards her and the counter she stood behind. But I could see him take a deep breath and square his shoulders before he approached her.

"So you're running the shop now?" he asked. Not the best attempt at sounding casual I had ever heard, but not the worst either. "You've decided to stay?"

"I've decided to stay," she told him with a shy smile.

"Well, that is good news," he said.

Then they just stood there, grinning at each other.

"Maybe you should just grab him another cup and saucer, and he can join us at our table," I said, maybe a little too loudly. Then I scooped up Houdini, taking his chair. He started to protest, but when I sat down with him on my lap, he quickly decided that arrangement was acceptable.

"I told you he was fine," Steph said as he reached for more shortbread.

Houdini squawked in protest as I leaned forward to speak low and close to Steph's ear. "That magic you can do, wiping memories and teleporting at all and whatever it was you did for me back in the coffeeshop?"

I hoped he'd pick up my thread, but all he said was, "Yes?" Then he wiped a few crumbs off the front of his multicolored hoodie. A hoodie he definitely hadn't been wearing a second ago.

A hoodie that looked a lot like his magic cloak.

"Do you have all that power because you're the Wizard's apprentice?" I asked. "Or did you get that position because you were that powerful in the first place? I mean, you barely look older than I do."

"That's because I barely am older than you are," he said coolly.

"Answer my first question," I hissed at him. But he just gave me an enigmatic grin.

Then Audrey and Liam joined us, Liam with a cup and saucer of his own and Audrey with a plate full of cranberry scones.

"Sorry, I should've properly introduced myself before," Liam said, extending a hand towards Steph. "I'm Liam Kelly. I live a couple of blocks from here and met Tabitha and then Audrey in the bookshop."

"Steph Underwood," Steph said as he shook Liam's hand. "I also live near here and met Tabitha and Audrey in the bookshop."

"Small world," Liam said.

"Big bookshop," I put in.

"A very big bookshop," Liam agreed. "I keep meaning to explore it more, but every time I go in I never seem to get off the first floor.

Well, you brought me upstairs to meet Audrey that one time, but I barely remember even looking around. It's all a haze. Isn't that weird?"

"I've heard weirder," Steph said. "Books just have a way of making a person lose all sense of time and place around them. You don't even have to be reading them for it to happen, if you're one of the susceptible ones."

"That's totally me," Liam agreed, and looked over at Audrey.

"Me too," she agreed around a mouthful of scone, raising a hand to catch any wayward crumbs.

"I as well," Steph said.

"I'm here until the end of August," I said to Liam. "I'll make sure you get off the first floor again while I'm still in charge."

"Promise?" he asked eagerly.

I glanced over at Steph, but he just gave me a quick little nod. Somehow, that nod told me that so long as I was careful, there'd be no reason to mind wipe Liam again. There were a lot of places upstairs I'd have to be sure that he didn't wander into, but there were a lot more that he could browse to his heart's content, until his mind was thoroughly blown.

"Promise," I said.

We drank tea and ate scones for about an hour before other customers started popping up. And while the conversation we all shared was warm and lively, I don't remember a bit of it.

Because the same thought kept circling around and around in my head. For years, I had had no friends. None. But now I had four. It had only been a matter of days, but I knew I was bonded with every single one of them. Even Liam. But especially Houdini.

And I had finally found a place that felt like home.

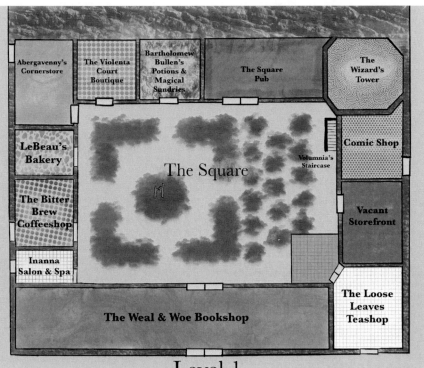

Abergavenny's Cornerstore

The Violenta Court Boutique

Bartholomew Bullen's Potions & Magical Sundries

The Square Pub

The Wizard's Tower

LeBeau's Bakery

The Square

Volumnia's Staircase

Comic Shop

The Bitter Brew Coffeeshop

Vacant Storefront

Inanna Salon & Spa

The Weal & Woe Bookshop

The Loose Leaves Teashop

Level 1

CHECK OUT BOOK TWO!

Tabitha Greene loves her new life. Working at her uncles' bookstore, hanging with her friends, cuddling with her dog Houdini. When he allows it.

Everything would be perfect. If only she could control her magic.

But her bad luck with spells plagues her, setting off random sparks and triggering too many accidents. Her friends support her in her attempts to get it all under control. But her other neighbors around the Square display much less patience with having an actual jinx around. Especially as they plan the biggest party of the year.

When Tabitha's bitterest nemesis turns up dead, no one thinks she did it. At least not intentionally. But not even Tabitha is sure she didn't cause it by mistake.

The only way to be sure? She and her friends have to get to the bottom of what really happened the night of the party. Even if it means that Tabitha's worst fears come true.

THE SALON & SPA SCANDAL, Book 2 in the Weal & Woe Bookshop Witch Mystery series. Available September 12, 2023 direct from RatatoskrPressBooks.com or October 17, 2023 in stores everywhere.

THE WITCHES THREE
COZY MYSTERIES

In case you missed it, check out Charm School, the first book in the complete Witches Three Cozy Mystery Series!

Amanda Clarke thinks of herself as perfectly ordinary in every way. Just a small-town girl who serves breakfast all day in a little diner nestled next to the highway, nothing but dairy farms for miles around. She fits in there.

But then an old woman she never met dies, and Amanda was named in her will. Now Amanda packs a bag and heads to the big city, to Miss Zenobia Weekes' Charm School for Exceptional Young Ladies. And it's not in just any neighborhood. No, she finds herself on Summit Avenue in St. Paul, a street lined with gorgeous old houses, the former homes of lumber barons, railroad millionaires, even the writer F. Scott Fitzgerald. Why, Amanda can practically hear the jazz music still playing across the decades.

Scratch that. The music really, literally, still plays in the backyard of the charm school. Because the house stretches across time itself. Without a witch to protect this tear in the fabric of the world, anything can spill over. Like music.

Or like murder.

Charm School, the first book in the complete Witches Three Cozy Mystery Series!

THE VIKING WITCH COZY MYSTERIES

In case you missed it, check out Body at the Crossroads, the first book in the Viking Witch Cozy Mystery Series!

When her mother dies after a long illness, Ingrid Torfa must sell the family home to cover the medical bills. Her career as a book illustrator not yet exactly launched, Ingrid faces two options: live in her battered old Volkswagen, or go back to her mother's small town in northern Minnesota.

The small town that still haunts her dreams more than a decade since she last visited it. Or rather, not the town but the grandmother.

All of the drawings she fills notebooks with witches and the trolls that do their bidding? Not as whimsical in her nightmares as she sketches them in the bright light of day.

If not for her beloved cat Mjolner, living in the Volkswagen just might tempt her.

But the cat wants four walls and a door, so north she goes. And finds trouble in the form of a dead body before she even finds her grandmother's little town. How much can a town of stoic fishermen possibly be hiding?

As Ingrid is about to find out, quite a lot.

Body at the Crossroads, the first book in the Viking Witch Cozy Mystery Series!

ALSO FROM RATATOSKR PRESS

The Ritchie and Fitz Sci-Fi Murder Mysteries starts with Murder on the Intergalactic Railway.

For Murdina Ritchie, acceptance at the Oymyakon Foreign Service Academy means one last chance at her dream of becoming a diplomat for the Union of Free Worlds. For Shackleton Fitz IV, it represents his last chance not to fail out of military service entirely.

Strange that fate should throw them together now, among the last group of students admitted after the start of the semester. They had once shared the strongest of friendships. But that all ended a long time ago.

But when an insufferable but politically important woman turns up murdered, the two agree to put their differences aside and work together to solve the case.

Because the murderer might strike again. But more importantly, solving a murder would just have to impress the dour colonel who clearly thinks neither of them belong at his academy.

ALSO FROM RATATOSKR PRESS

Murder on the Intergalactic Railway, the first book in the Ritchie and Fitz Sci-Fi Murder Mysteries, available everywhere books are sold.

FREE EBOOK!

Like exclusive, free content?

If you'd like to receive "A Collection of Witchy Prequels", a free collection of short story prequels to the Witches Three Cozy Mystery and Viking Witch Cozy Mystery series, as well as other free stories throughout the year, go to my website CateMartin.com to subscribe to my newsletter! This eBook is exclusively for newsletter subscribers and will never be sold in stores. Check it out!

ABOUT THE AUTHOR

Cate Martin has written stories which have appeared in the **Mystery, Crime and Mayhem** quarterly magazine as well as in the annual **Holiday Spectacular** Advent calendar of holiday stories. She is also the author of three witch mystery series: **The Witches Three Cozy Mysteries**, and **The Viking Witch Cozy Mysteries** and **The Weal & Woe Bookshop Witch Mysteries**. She currently lives in Minneapolis, Minnesota. You can learn more about her work at Cate-Martin.com.

Also by Cate Martin

The Witches Three Cozy Mystery Series

Charm School

Work Like a Charm

Third Time is a Charm

Old World Charm

Charm his Pants Off

Charm Offensive

The Witches Three Cozy Mysteries Books 1-3

The Witches Three Cozy Mysteries Books 4-6

The Viking Witch Cozy Mystery Series

Body at the Crossroads

Death Under the Bridge

Murder on the Lake

Killing in the Village Commons

Bloodshed in the Forest

Corpse in the Mead Hall

Slaying on the Lake Shore

Bones by the Forest Road

Sacrifice Behind the Falls

Body Under the Café

Assassination in the Glade (available January 16, 2024 direct from me or February 13, 2024 in stores everywhere)

The Viking Witch Cozy Mysteries Books 1-3

The Weal & Woe Bookshop Witch Mystery Series

The Teashop Terror

The Salon & Spa Scandal

The Bookseller Blunder

The Entrepreneur Enigma (Forthcoming)

The Novelty Shop Nightmare (Forthcoming)

The Courtyard Conundrum (Forthcoming)

Manufactured by Amazon.ca
Acheson, AB